ON ALL FRONTS

J.T. Laird has specialised in the study of war literature from Australia and Britain. His BA (Hons.) degree from the University of Sydney was followed by war service during 1941–46, from 1942 with the AIF in New Guinea and Indonesia. After the war, he lectured at the Royal Military College of Australia, completed an MA (Hons.) in 1959 and pursued postgraduate research at University College, London, in 1963. He retired from the University of New South Wales in 1985 as associate professor. Several of his numerous journal publications in Australia and abroad focus on Australian war literature; he is also the author of *Other Banners: An Anthology of Australian Literature of the First World War* (1971) and *The Shaping of "Tess of the d'Urbervilles"* (1975), and editor of *The Australian Experience of War: Illustrated Stories and Verse* (1988).

ON ALL FRONTS
Australian Stories of World War II

Edited by J.T. Laird

University of Queensland Press

First published 1989 by University of Queensland Press
Box 42, St Lucia, Queensland, Australia

Compilation, introduction and notes
© J.T. Laird 1989
The copyright in individual stories remains with the authors

Typeset by University of Queensland Press
Printed in Australia by The Book Printer, Melbourne

Distributed in the USA and Canada by
International Specialized Book Services, Inc.,
5602 N.E. Hassalo Street, Portland, Oregon 97213–3640

 Creative writing program assisted by
the Literature Board of the Australia
Council, the Federal Government's arts
funding and advisory body

Cataloguing in Publication Data

National Library of Australia

On all fronts : Australian stories of World War II.

Bibliography.
Includes index.

1. World War, 1939–1945 — Literary collections.
2. War stories, Australian. 3. Australian
literature — 20th century. I. Laird, John Tudor.

A820.80358

ISBN 0 7022 2160 0

Contents

Acknowledgments

It is a pleasure to thank Robin Gerster for allowing me to read his Monash University PhD thesis, now published as *Big-Noting: The Heroic Theme in Australian War Writing* (Melbourne: Melbourne University Press, 1988).

For permission to reproduce the material in this anthology, acknowledgment is made to Angus and Robertson Publishers for "Doing the Gentlemanly Thing" from *Come in Spinner* by Dymphna Cusack and Florence James (first published Heinemann, 1951) © Dymphna Cusack and Florence James; for "New Guinea" from *A Soldier's Miscellany* by Eric Irvin (1945); for "Emu Parade" from *Emu Parade* by T. Inglis Moore (1941); for "The Soldier in the Park" from *Forbears* by Elizabeth Riddell (1961) © Elizabeth Riddell 1961; for "The Trains" from *Collected Poems 1942–70* by Judith Wright (1971), © Judith Wright 1971; to the Australian War Memorial for "To Coolies and Prisoners of War" from *As You Were* by S.F. Arneil (1948); for "Reaping the Whirlwind" from *The Splendid Hour* by Kevin E. Collopy (1951); to Richard Beilby for "Retreat to Sphakia" from *Gunner* (Angus & Robertson, 1977); to Curtis Brown

(Aust.) Pty Ltd for "An Australian with the Maquis" from *The White Mouse* by Nancy Wake (Macmillan, 1985); to Courier Productions for "Down to Earth" from *Only Our Gloves On* by Pat Studdy-Clift (1981); to Peter Cowan for "Saturday Afternoon" from *Drift* (Reed and Harris, 1944); to John Farquharson for US rights to "Changi" from *The Naked Island* by Russell Braddon (first published T. Werner Laurie, 1952); and for "I Ran into the Gestapo . . . They've Got a Branch Here" and "No Way to Fight a Flaming War" from *The Climate of Courage* by Jon Cleary (Collins, 1954); to Georgian House for "On the Run in Greece" from *The Winds are Still* by John Hetherington (1947); to Lawson Glassop Estate for "Brawl On!" from *We Were the Rats* by Lawson Glassop (Angus & Robertson, 1944); to Harry Gordon for "The Desperate Months" from *The Embarrassing Australian* (Lansdowne Cheshire, 1962); to Michael Joseph for world rights (excluding US rights) for "Changi" from *The Naked Island* by Russell Braddon; to Macmillan New York for "Discipline Begins with the Instruments of Discipline" from *Young Man of Talent* by George Turner (Cassell, 1959); to Melbourne University Press for "Behind Japanese Lines" from *Fear Drive My Feet* by Peter Ryan (Melbourne University Press, 1959); to Octopus Publishing Group Australia for "Like Sisters of a Family" from *While History Passed* by Jessie Elizabeth Simons (William Heinemann 1954); to Ray Parkin for "Morale" from *Into the Smother* (Hogarth Press, 1963); to Penguin Books Australia Ltd for "Mission Accomplished" from *No Moon Tonight* by D.E. Charlwood (Angus & Robertson, 1956); and for "Beyond Bobdubi Ridge" from *The Last Blue Sea* by David Forrest (Heinemann, 1959); to Shakespeare Head Press for "The Barking Soldiers" and "Homecoming" from *The Veterans* by Eric Lambert and for "Victory at Tobruk" from *The Twenty Thousand Thieves* by Eric Lambert (Newmont, 1951); to the University of Queensland Press for "The Tomb of Lt John Learmonth AIF" from *Collected Verse* (1978) by John Manifold; and for "The Twilight War: The Fight in the Jungle" from *The War Despatches of Kenneth Slessor* edited by Clement Semmler (1987); to Val Vallis for "The Ballad of Changi Chimes", from *Songs of the East Coast* (Angus & Robertson, 1947).

Introduction

This anthology of Australian stories of the Second World War has been compiled with the general reader as well as the more sophisticated reader in mind. The term story is used to denote both factual and fictional kinds of narrative writing and embraces not only what are commonly called short stories and brief descriptive accounts but also newspaper dispatches and extracts from longer works such as novels and personal narratives.

In making my selection I have been guided by two criteria: first, that I should offer the reader a representative sampling of some of the best Australian literary writings about the Second World War, and, secondly, that I should choose for inclusion works and extracts that also serve either to illuminate significant elements in the Australian experience of the war of 1939–45 or to reflect some of the common concerns and preoccupations of the war writers. The stories are grouped into seven sections to constitute a wide-ranging yet coherent literary record, extending over life on leave, military life in general, the land war in the Middle East, jungle fighting, the war in Europe, the home front, and the prisoner of war experience.

Two rather jaundiced views of life on leave emerge from Peter Cowan's short story "Saturday Afternoon" and the passage from Eric Lambert's novel *The Veterans* called "Homecoming". Cowan's almost exclusive use of laconic dialogue skilfully creates an atmosphere of boredom and futility, as the two Australian servicemen perpetuate their weekly rest-day ritual of getting "full" at the neighbourhood hotel. Lambert's preoccupation is not with boredom but with moral seediness. "Homecoming" is an anatomy of the deterioration in moral standards in Sydney during the middle years of the war, a topic that also receives critical attention in two other well-known Australian war novels, *Come in Spinner* by Dymphna Cusack and Florence James and *Soldiers' Women* by Xavier Herbert. The animosity felt by Lambert's hero towards white American soldiers reflects the widespread friction that developed between Australian and American troops in Australian cities at that time.

Friction was not limited during the war to relations between allies, just as conflict was not limited to relations with the official enemy. As the stories in the second section of the anthology indicate, several writers were intent on demonstrating that life within the Australian armed forces was marked on occasions by discord — between individuals of the same rank, between individuals of different rank, between officers and the other ranks, and between members of the other ranks and the military police. In "Brawl On!", from Lawson Glassop's novel *We Were the Rats*, the educated private soldier Mick Reynolds finds himself forced to fight a camp brawl with the tough, uneducated private Eddie Wilson in order to prove his manhood and win Eddie's acceptance and respect. The incident accords with the comment of the critic David Walker that Australian novels of the Second

World War "all manage to relate the performance of the Australian soldier to an Australian tradition of physical prowess and manly bravado extending back through several generations".[1] In "Discipline Begins with the Instruments of Discipline", George Turner concentrates (as does Richard Beilby in the story "Retreat to Sphakia") on a violent personality clash between a sergeant and the lieutenant who is his platoon commander, which leads to tragedy at the end of Turner's novel, *Young Man of Talent*. "The Barking Soldiers", from Eric Lambert's novel *The Veterans*, describes with a certain amount of sardonic humour protests staged by Australian soldiers undergoing jungle training in North Queensland against what they regard as unjust treatment by their officers and the army at large.

Turner and Lambert are both critical of certain aspects of the Australian military system of authority and discipline; but the most bitter attack on the system occurs in the story "I Ran into the Gestapo . . . They've Got a Branch Here", taken from Jon Cleary's novel *The Climate of Courage*. Here the conflict reflects the deepseated hostility felt by many front-line soldiers during the war towards the military police, not so much the regimental provosts as the base provosts who were stationed far away from the sounds of battle. Significantly, the officer who secures the victim's release from brutal custody is a sympathetically portrayed character, a reminder that there are many favourable, as well as many unfavourable, portraits of officers in Australian literature of the Second World War, despite the anti-elitist, egalitarian social values inherent in the work of writers like Cleary, Lambert, Beilby and Hungerford.

The passage from Lambert's *The Twenty Thousand Thieves* entitled "Victory at Tobruk" is concerned largely with demonstrating the battle prowess of the AIF during the war in North Africa, the confident, laudatory tone, summed up in Captain Gilbertson's exclamation, "You fellers are the salt of the earth", echoing the heroic mood that distinguished most Australian prose writings about the original Anzacs published up to the middle of the nineteen-thirties. By contrast many of the stories about the unsuccessful Australian campaigns in the Middle East are sombre in mood, some of them expressing anger at what the poet John Manifold described as "muddle tall as treachery". John Hetherington's "On the Run in Greece", from the novel *The Winds are Still*, concentrates on the resourcefulness and determination displayed by a group of Australian and British servicemen left behind in enemy-occupied Greece in their efforts to escape to freedom and on the generous assistance they received from the Greek population; but Richard Beilby's "Retreat to Sphakia", from the novel *Gunner*, reflects the bitterness and disillusionment of men critical of both the political decision to send Australian troops to Greece in 1941 and the ineptness of the military planning of the resulting campaigns. A much more heroic account of the behaviour of some of the Australian troops during the retreat to Sphakia and in the months that followed, as a number of them eluded the German forces on Crete, is given in the extract "The Desperate Months", which is taken from Harry Gordon's biography of the Aboriginal soldier Reg Saunders, *The Embarrassing Australian*.

In most of the stories relating to the campaigns fought in the islands to the north of Australia the main enemy portrayed is no longer human: rather, it is the tropical environment in which the fighting takes place — the dense rain forests, the precipitous mountain ridges, the swamps and diseases of islands such as New Guinea and Bougainville. "The jungle has deadlier adversaries than the Japanese", Kenneth Slessor writes in his article "The Twilight War: The Fight in the Jungle". "At the end of the trail, the Japanese wait with knives and bullets. But the jungle enlists a thousand enemies before this last enemy of all. It is unending, unrelenting, unforgiving. It is maleficent. It is not made for man." The troops' detestation of jungle warfare thus emerges as a central theme in much of the literature, as is apparent in the fictional extracts "No Way to Fight a Flaming War", from Jon Cleary's *The Climate of Courage*, and "Beyond Bobdubi Ridge", from David Forrest's novel *The Last Blue Sea*. In both of these stories most of the Australian soldiers, whether AIF or militia, display a dogged courage against the enemy and mateship towards each other, but they fight without any of the illusions or ideals about the war that might once have sustained them and solely to ensure survival or to preserve self-respect. One of Cleary's AIF soldiers, rain-soaked and shivering with malaria, expresses the disgust that many soldiers felt with the nature of jungle warfare when he exclaims, "I keep thinking what a lovely war it was in the Middle East". In the non-fictional extract "Behind Japanese Lines", from Peter Ryan's personal narrative *Fear Drive My Feet*, it is the courage and determination of the two Australian soldiers and their native police-boys that remain uppermost in the reader's mind, although the book as a whole constitutes an almost unremitting testimony to the hostility of the New Guinea environment and ends with reflections on the folly of war.

D.E. Charlwood's "Mission Accomplished", from the personal narrative *No Moon Tonight*, is a sensitive account of the thoughts and sensations of an Australian airman during and after a night-bombing mission over Germany. Particularly revealing is his description of the airman's feeling of detachment from the death and destruction he causes in the enemy cities below. Another Australian who participated in the European theatre of operations was Nancy Wake, some of whose daring exploits as an agent of the London-based Special Operations Executive working with the French Resistance are described in "An Australian with the Maquis", from her autobiography *The White Mouse*.

Two very different perspectives of life on the Australian homefront are offered by the passages in Part 6. "Down to Earth", from Pat Studdy-Clift's personal narrative *Only Our Gloves On*, is a lively celebration of the contribution made by women to the Australian war effort, particularly by those who worked on the land at a time when most men were in the armed forces. The hardships and difficulties she was compelled to overcome as a sixteen-year-old girl returning from the city to help run the family property were not unlike those that faced many other young women who worked on farms all over the country during the war (as is apparent from Jean Scott's collection of short memoirs by ex-members of the Australian Women's Land Army, *Girls with Grit*). By contrast, "Doing the Gentlemanly Thing", from the novel *Come in Spinner* by Dymphna Cusack and Florence James, exposes the hedonism, selfishness and exploitation that flourished in some sections of Sydney's population during the war.

It is a stoical kind of courage that permeates the writings of Australians who have given us accounts of their experiences as prisoners of war in Japanese hands. Their lot was to endure suffering and hardship over a lengthy period of time, buoyed up by the hope that they would live long enough to gain freedom at the end of the war. That their suffering was at times less severe than at other times is pointed out by Russell Braddon in the passage from *The Naked Island* called "Changi . . . the

Phoney Captivity". Indeed, Braddon here directs the main force of his criticism not against the Japanese guards, who were seldom seen by the prisoners at Changi during the later part of 1942, but against the senior British and Australian army officers who ran the camp in what Braddon considered an excessively militaristic manner. Braddon complains of such matters as their insistence on maintaining "full military discipline" among the prisoners and preserving officers' privileges, especially those relating to the issue of clothing and food. Although similar complaints are to be found in other Australian POW writings — for example in the observation made by Ray Parkin, in the passage from *Into the Smother* called "Morale", concerning "officers vaunting privilege and neglecting responsibility" — it must be pointed out, in fairness to Australian officers who were prisoners of the Japanese, that many of their fellow prisoners have described relations between men and officers during their period of captivity as good and that some officers have strenuously defended the value of the discipline imposed by "the command" in helping to ensure the prisoners' survival.[2]

There is of course a large amount of space in POW books devoted to criticism of the Japanese and Korean guards. Their callousness is recorded in S.F. Arneil's self-contained descriptive account "To Coolies and Prisoners of War" and in the two extracts, Jessie Simons's "Like Sisters of a Family", from *While History Passed*, and Ray Parkin's "Morale". Such writings remain strong indictments of a nation's military behaviour at a particular time in history: they also emerge as powerful pacifist documents — indictments of the very nature of war itself — and, somewhat paradoxically, as moving tributes to the resilience and fortitude of the human spirit.

Notes

1. David Walker, "The Getting of Manhood", in *Australian Popular Culture*, ed. Peter Spearitt and David Walker (Sydney: Allen and Unwin, 1979), p.124.
2. See, for example, John Barrett, ed., *We Were There* (Ringwood: Viking, 1987), p.267; Hank Nelson, ed., *P.O.W., Prisoners of War* (Sydney: ABC Enterprises, 1985), pp.33–34; and J.H.T., "The Problems of Changi", *Journal of the Royal Military College of Australia 39* (1953): 32–36.

Part 1
On Leave

All day he slept, his mouth on pennyroyal,
His eyelids couched on clover,
His fingers twined around the stems of grass,
Doves near him, and the sun upon his shoulder.
The earth drowsed under him,
And the clouds slid over.
The boats on the bay rocked, the willows sighed.

How long ago was that?

That was in summer, some time before he died.

Elizabeth Riddell
"The Soldier in the Park"

PETER COWAN

Saturday Afternoon

THE rows of huts made a pattern like the sameness of the days. He stood on the step and watched
the figure garbed similarly to himself approach.

"Well," he said. "What's on?"

The other looked around and then threw his butt down,
crushing it with his foot.

"I wouldn't know."

"Well, let's get out of here, anyhow."

They walked towards the gate, showed their passes,
and went out. There were few people in the streets.

"Going to have a schooner?" the tall man said.

The other nodded. "Won't do us any harm."

They went into the hotel on the corner. It was early and

the bar did not hold many besides themselves. The bar-
maid at their part of the bar was elderly, her face too
much done up.

"The best, Les," the tall man said.

Les nodded, and they drank. He circled the bottom of
the schooner on the wet patch on the bar.

"Don't feel much like it, John," he said.

"A couple'll put you right," the tall man said. He
finished his drink.

"Yes, but I don't want to get into a session, and spend
the afternoon here. Hell, a man gets little enough time of
his own."

"You don't get much time to spend chasing schooners,
if that's what you mean. Don't waste it when you do."

Les finished the return drink. John ordered another.

"What I mean," Les said, "is that in these few hours
they give me of my own life I want to do something just
faintly intelligent."

"You shouldn't drink," John said, "if it takes you that
way."

"All I've got to decide is what to do."

"Your guess'll be as good as mine."

"Let's look at it," Les said. "In this reclaimed area of
scrub —"

"Break it down."

I can go to the races and do in my six bob a day, or I can
do it in swilling beer with you."

"Just a matter of whether you prefer two or four legg-
ed company."

Les laughed. "It's a shambles, John."

"I know that, my boy. But we've got to prevent
ourselves going mad at this tender age."

"I suppose I could go up to the public library and read.
But after a week like we spend I just can't. And if there

was a decent exhibition of pictures anywhere it'd be hidden so you couldn't find it."

"I think the whole situation calls for another drink," John said. "One you pay for. Now mind you, if there was some music I'd drag you along to that and try and make a bit less of a heathen of you. But that happens so seldom I can write the dates down and make a point of not missing it in the rush of knocking schooners over."

"You can listen to the radio, at least. In fact you can do that and drink. I can't think of anything that would appeal to you more."

"My boy, if you had ears instead of those queer looking things on your head you'd have heard that radio that's been going in here ever since we came in. And there's just a chance it'd give you the answer."

"Oh, hell," Les said. "It looks like another schooner."

"That's better."

"Mind you," Les said, "we could go to a welfare centre. I've never been to one."

"You and I couldn't," John said. "People trying hard to be good to you is a bit depressing. No, we'll stay here."

"Did you see that?" Les said. "What just looked in from the lounge door there. That could be good to you."

"You stick to the beer. I've got enough to worry about without having to protect you from females like that. You know, this beer's not bad."

"Must have forgotten to put the chemicals in."

"Well have another. This one's mine."

The bar was beginning to fill. The radio switched to a race broadcast. The men stood listening to the voice describing the horses at the barrier. There was only the one voice now in the bar.

"I suppose Harry's got this one in the bag," John said.

"He's got the good oil this afternoon."

"There's a man who's got the game right."

Les laughed. "Poor old Harry. He will pull some of these big ones off one of these days."

"It's a touching faith to live by," John said.

The hurried rush of words that swelled to the climax of the race was taken up by the voices in the bar as the commentary ceased.

"Hullo," John said. "Some of the boys."

The group of similarly garbed figures moved up to them. One of the newcomers bought a round. The bar was full of noise now. Les looked at the variety of coloured bottles and bright labels on the shelves behind the bar counter. Most of them were empty, just dummies. The barmaids were moving quickly, their smiles automatic, and the air was thick with smoke. He and John had bought rounds. The talk was turning to the week. It was being lived minutely again. He nudged John.

"Think I'll go out for a minute."

"That might be an idea," John said. "Back in a minute."

They went along the passage and round to the back. The latrine was dirty and stank.

"You know," Les said, "I don't mind a certain amount, but I'm bloody well not going to listen to shop. If I've got to do that all the week, well I've got to, but I'm not going to get to the stage where I start talking about it. If I get like that —"

"We'll have a few more drinks," John said. "But we won't have them here. Where'll we go?"

"Go in the lounge. I can't be bothered finding another blasted pub."

They went into the lounge. There were very few in there. Some sailors in one corner at a table with girls, a party of civilians. There were some women by themselves. They went up to the bar and bought drinks.

"May as well sit down," John said. "We can look as though we're used to luxury."

They sat down in two of the big leather chairs.

"This is much better," John said.

Les looked at the two girls at the table in the corner. One was a blonde, rather pretty in a showy way; the other dark, plain, with cosmetics used liberally, and rather well built. The dark one made no attempt to avoid his eyes.

He nudged John. "What d'you think of that?" he muttered.

"M'boy," John said in an unpleasantly loud voice. "They're bad enough singly, but when they hunt in packs — whacko." He finished his drink. "Give us your glass. I'll get another drink."

"I think I've had about enough."

"You need another to get you past that stage."

While he was getting the drinks Les smiled at the dark girl, who obviously expected him to complete the manoeuvre. He got up and went over. He wondered if he was as steady as John looked. The dark girl smiled at him. He asked if they would have a drink.

"Well, I don't mind," she said. "How about you, Elsie?"

Elsie smiled. "Thanks."

He went over to where John was picking up the two schooners.

"Hang on a minute," he said. "I'll get a couple more."

"What's going on?" John said.

"Well — have a couple of drinks with the girls. Might as well."

"Oh," John said. "Well, which one do I get?"

"Now break it down. Come on over."

"I'm coming," John said.

Les handed Elsie her drink and the other glass to the dark girl.

"That leaves you without a drink," John said.

"Like hell it does," Les said. He took one of the drinks from John. The girls laughed. They pulled the easy chairs up. Les sat near the dark girl. John looked at the blonde.

"I think I'm paired off with you," he said. "These things are settled in a nicely mechanistic fashion for me. Mind you, it's much simpler."

"Yeah?" Elsie said. She laughed.

"You know, when I was a small boy," John said, "I found —"

"Don't let him tell the story of his life," Les said. "I've heard it before."

"I usually do," John said. "It's very convenient."

"Don't take any notice of him," Les said to the dark girl. "He drinks like a fish, quite apart from the fact that he's got hollow legs, blast him. What's your name? I know Elsie's."

"Joan," the dark girl said.

John was looking fixedly at the bottom of his schooner. Elsie fidgeted and took a packet of cigarettes from her hand bag.

"Thanks," John said. He took one.

Les fished his own out. "Here have one of mine."

"Got one, thanks," John said.

"I'm not talking to you." Joan took one and they smoked. John sighed and got up.

"Glasses," he said. "We'd better have some more to drink."

"I'll have a gin and squash," Elsie said.

"What about you, Joan?" Les said.

"All right."

"Good," John said. "And I suppose you'll have a double-header King George?"

He went across to the bar.

"He's funny, isn't he?" Joan said.

"Very funny," Les said.

John came back with the gin squashes and two schooners.

"I think I'll have another of Elsie's cigarettes," he said. "She has a brand I've no means of procuring."

"Never saw these before the war," he said, lighting the cigarette, and exhaling contentedly.

"I don't think they're as good as Blank's," Elsie said.

"Oh Elsie, they're miles better," Joan exclaimed.

"I don't think so," Elsie said. "Blanks never worry my throat a bit, I think they're much better."

"As long as they don't worry the head, that's the main thing," John said. "Very interesting subject, this, you know. I've heard it discussed for three and a half hours once. I clocked it."

"Someone ought to clock you," Les said. He got up. "I think a few more would be in order."

He brought the drinks back. Joan looked at the watch on her wrist.

"What's the time?" Les said.

"About ten past four," Joan said.

"It can't be."

"Have a look." She held her arm towards him. He held her wrist to look.

"Satisfied?"

"No," he said.

She smiled. He pulled her arm gently. She let herself be pulled over to sit on the wide arm of his chair. She crossed her bare legs, the skirt showing the flesh above her knee. The under leg was quite liberally displayed.

Les put his hand on her knee. John blew smoke contentedly. Elsie took out another cigarette. John held his own out for her to light it from. She held his hand while she lit it, and then still retained it with one hand while she drew experimentally on the cigarette. She let it go and John took up his drink. Joan was talking about a dance they had been to.

"Do you boys go to dances much?" she said.

"Not much," John said. "We have occasional small affairs on the parade ground, just to satisfy the official mind. Nothing elaborate. The step gets a bit monotonous."

Elsie looked at Joan.

"It must be getting a bit late, Joan."

"It's getting on," Joan said. She looked down at Les. "You boys going to drink here all the afternoon, or what, Les?"

"Well, I don't know —"

"He means he hopes so," John said.

"I didn't say that."

"I think we better go, Joan," Elsie said. "It's getting late."

"What d'you think, Les?"

"Les and I," John said, "will still be here when closing time comes. You can't take Les from his beer."

"Come on," Elsie said. They got up. Les got up from the armchair.

"Well, see you boys again," Elsie said. They went towards the door. Les sat down.

"Y'know," he said. "I'm pretty full, John."

"I'm getting that way. But I'm not bad enough to get taken for a row by the amateurs. Here, I'll get another."

They drank and smoked, not talking. The room was warm, and heavy with smoke. It seemed close about them, as though distance was annihilated. The chairs were comfortable. They did not hurry their drinking. It was almost six o'clock when John said:

"Better get one for the road, and then we'll be turned out, I suppose."

They had the drink and went across the lounge to the passage. They went to the door. Outside it was getting dark. They went down the street.

ERIC LAMBERT

Homecoming

The narrator in this passage from Eric Lambert's novel The
Veterans *is Bill Farr, of the Australian Ninth Division, on
home leave after serving in the Middle East. He finds a good
deal to criticise as he observes life in wartime Sydney.*

AS soon as I got into the city I dumped the two
kitbags in the cloakroom of a canteen. Then, hands
in pockets, I started to roam the darkened streets of the
city, lost in a bleak wilderness of thoughts . . . Your
father's a big shot, Farr! Must be one of the top men in
the black market.

After a while I began to take stock of myself roaming
the city without hope or destination. I went from irony to
irony. If I had been somewhere like Tripoli or Cairo I
would have expected to feel lonely. But here I was in my
own city, and lonelier than I had ever been in my life.

For three years now life had seemed so perishable that

you resisted all unhappiness violently. So I began to look for something that I could call a diversion.

I turned into Martin Place. Slowly, I passed along the dim colonnade of the GPO, and there on the corner of George Street stood a Negro soldier.

He was one of the biggest men I had ever seen; six feet five if he was an inch. He stood quite still, as though he might never move again. Once in a book I had read that one must of necessity go somewhere, but he looked as though he had forgotten that necessity. His greatcoat was a tent; his shoulders belonged to a figure on a monument, and his great black head was as noble as a lion's. When I came closer I saw the whites of his eyes shining like moons. People passed him, like rabbits going round a tree.

He looked as lonely as I was — no, lonelier. At least I was looking for something, but he seemed as though he had known long ago there was nothing for him to find. The sight of him had arrested me. I stood gazing at him, then I made a swift decision. I walked over to him, looked up into his face, and asked:

"You looking for somewhere to go by any chance, mate?"

The whites of his eyes moved. He looked down at me and his lips murmured in surprise. Then he answered me:

"There ain't nowhere to go for me — except back where I came from."

"I can take you somewhere," I urged.

"Better not, Aussie," he told me sadly. "Only get us in trouble."

His voice was deep, like the sea rumbling at the back of a cave.

"I like trouble," I growled.

He smiled a little at this.

"Then you ain't had enough of it," he said.

But I wouldn't be denied; somehow I had made up my mind that wherever we went, we went together.

"Where have you come from?" I asked.

"Little joint up that way. Only niggers there."

"I'd like to see it," I said.

He gazed hard at me, with a mixture of wonder and doubt.

"You want to look at some coloured boys," he stated without reproach. "Ain't I enough?"

"If I want to look at black men, I've got a couple of mates just as black as you are — pure Australian."

"That so?" he said a little more easily.

"Yes, that's so. What sort of joint is this?"

"Just a little joint the army thought up to send us coloureds to." He looked at me more sharply. "You really want to see it?"

I nodded.

He turned his great shoulders around. "OK," he said. "What's your name?"

"Bill Farr. What's yours?"

"Jeb Steele."

And so we set off. As we walked along he glanced down at me every now and then, as though he was still a little puzzled.

The joint he had spoken of was in a dirty little lane off William Street, two rooms at the end of a foul, greasy passage. As we approached along the passage I could hear the sob and growl of instruments playing jazz.

The first room we entered contained a dozen or so Negro soldiers seated on chairs and lolling against the wall, shouting, arguing, drinking coca-cola out of the bottle, all of them very animated. Dark faces shone in the yellow light. As we entered there was sudden silence. A dozen pairs of eyes stared at me.

Jeb Steele moved in, dwarfing the room, dominating it. He smiled a little. His voice rumbled at them:

"Here's a nice Aussie guy wants to meet you fellers."

All of a sudden the tension went. A lanky boy in the corner smiled shyly at me. Jeb put a hand like a tennis racquet on my shoulder. A stout man leaning against the door to the second room with a trombone in his fist said:

"What's the name, boy?"

I told them, and murmurs of welcome went round the room. Smiles awoke along the wall. In the other room somebody rippled the keys of a piano. The man with the trombone regarded me gravely.

"You like music, boy?" he asked.

"Bloody oath!"

"Guess that means yes," he smiled.

He turned away, looking behind him. Jeb, who now held two bottles of drink in the one hand, guided me into the other room in the wake of the trombonist. There were three other players there seated around the pianist: a cornet player, a banjoist, and a clarinettist. They turned to look at me as the trombonist introduced me. I smiled at them, quite at ease and eager to hear the music.

"Howsaboy!" chuckled the pianist and rippled the keys again. Jeb went over to lean on the piano, having first handed me a bottle of coca-cola.

"What'd you like, boy?" asked the trombonist.

"Anything!" I told him.

He murmured something to the other players and made a noise on the trombone. The pianist hit the floor four times with his heel. They started to play.

I had never before heard such swagger and lilt to a tune. A man came in from the other room, walking rhythmically on his heels, then bringing his toes down lightly to the beat of the music, swaying his head and shoulders, turning his elbows in and out. His face was blank, absorbed. He was astonishingly graceful.

It seemed to me that swift, amiable music shared its origin with the smiles I had seen on their faces. The instruments declared the melody together, then the cornet took it up alone, flickering over the notes as if it were dancing for joy. It sang, chuckled, and turned somersaults. Then it gave way to the clarinet chortling high and sweet, next descending into sly little giggles. Just as the clarinet seemed to have exhausted itself with mirth, the trombone rescued the tune. Now it gurgled, roared out loud, and finished in a rich belly-laugh. The trombonist's right hand jerked in and out, his distended cheeks had the sheen of a purple plum, his eyes glared out like white marbles. He seemed lost in the mirth of his instrument.

With a last luxuriant sigh, the trombone finished its solo. The trombonist lowered his instrument, turning in my direction; and a great, shining smile grew out of his features.

The tune ended on a high note from the cornet. I broke at once into clapping. They seemed taken by surprise; they looked at each other, laughed, passed remarks to and fro. There seemed to be a swift heightening of jollity all around. Sensing it, I laughed back at them. Then they began another tune. They played one after another. There was one other tune that has remained with me. It was slow and sorrowful, with an underlying note of tragedy and reproach. The trombonist sang in a sweet, deep, husky voice that reminded me of a cello:

I'm black and blue

It seemed to utter every dark emotion the human heart had ever held: sorrow, bitterness, resentment, desolation, anger. It cried with protest:

My only sin
Is in my skin

When this tune ended I didn't clap. I wanted to say I was their brother, but I had no words.

It went on like this for half an hour. Just as the band had begun a new tune, all eyes went towards the door. Three whites had entered; Yanks wearing the armbands of military police, an officer and two sergeants. The music kept on, but the room had become watchful; the jollity seemed to be rushing out of it. The lieutenant looked at me, first with surprise, then sternly. The two sergeants stood enjoying the music. When it ended there was a curious silence. Also, there was venom in the air; I felt it as surely as if the officer had drawn the gun at his hip and brandished it; as he sent his eyes round the room, his expression was too cold even to be described as a sneer. The musicians rose and the room stood at attention.

"You boys behaving?" the officer asked the trombonist.

"Yes, sir," said the trombonist with a certain quiet dignity, although he looked a little comic standing stiffly at attention with the trombone under his arm. Behind the officer, one of the sergeants winked at him.

The officer turned and looked at me again.

"And how do you come to be here, Aussie?"

"I just strolled in," I replied.

"I guess you'd better just stroll out again. This ain't no place for you."

"It does me," I told him calmly. "I'm not strolling till I feel like it."

"You're liking it as from now. Need any help?"

I rose, swinging the bottle in my fingers.

"How'd you like to try?" I asked him.

Over the officer's shoulder, one of the sergeants said:

"He's one of them Ninth Division guys, Lootenant. They'd sooner fight than spit."

The officer lifted an eyebrow in a studied manner.

"Oh yeah, we were warned not to tangle with you guys," he observed, watching me through narrow eyes. "All I've got to do is order this dinge joint to be cleared."

The trombonist spoke to me in a calm, urging voice:

"Think you better go, son. You see how it is."

I shrugged and grinned. "That's settled it. I'll finish this drink if you don't mind," I told the officer.

"OK!" He waved an arm. "See you outside."

He left with the two sergeants.

As I finished my drink I felt every eye upon me. Then I turned to Jeb Steele and said:

"I'm sorry if I've got you into any trouble."

He smiled. "No trouble. Those guys come in every night."

I shook Jeb's hand, said good night to the others, who murmured a quiet farewell; but the trombonist accompanied me along the passage. Some of the anger in me was for the men I had been forced to abandon, for taking it all so quietly. I tried to provoke the trombonist directly.

"Fighting for democracy," I sneered.

"That's right, son," he agreed gravely.

Suddenly subdued, I told him:

"You wouldn't know what democracy's like."

He considered this very seriously as we stood in the end of the passage, just before parting. He rubbed his dark, round chin.

"No, son, perhaps not." Then from nowhere he sent me that beaming smile for the last time. "But I reckon I know what it *could* be like!"

As I expected, the three provosts waited outside, and the officer greeted me in a reproachful, but conciliatory, voice:

"You don't want to go into those dinge joints, digger."

"No?" I asked. "Why?"

"Less trouble keeping them on their own. It's nigger-lovers cause half the trouble back in the States."

"And what about the nigger-haters?"

"Lots of us are that, I guess."

"All nice and Christian," I observed.

He reached over and grasped my arm, determined on friendliness.

"Say," he laughed, "you don't have to be sore at me. Now how'd you like to see a real party, eh? Liquor, slits . . ."

"Where?" I asked. My first thought had been to tell him to go to hell; but then I remembered the lonely predicament that had sent me to the room I had just left.

"Up there a-ways. I take you in with me as my pal, and that makes it OK. What do you say?"

"All right!"

"Swell!" he said encouragingly. He turned to the two NCOs. "Take a look around, you guys. Be back in a half hour."

They mumbled and slouched off, after giving me an envious glance. The officer indicated a jeep at the end of the lane.

"Let's go! he said sharply.

We walked to the jeep and got in, he started it and swung into William Street. When he had got under way he began to talk. He told me his name was Hagen, and I gave him my own. I asked what kind of a party it was he was taking me to.

"Why, I guess you know about the squadron houses?" he replied.

I told him I had never heard the term before.

"An outfit is stationed here, like mine, or comes south on furlough," he explained. "They take over the house complete; everything's there — liquor, slits, food . . . The guys live there for the duration of their furlough; when they go back up top another outfit coming south takes over the house and everything in it. They call them squadron houses. Works swell, too. Keep guys in an outfit together."

"How do you get the girls?" I asked him.

He laughed and glanced sideways at me. "You kidding! This town's full of juicy young dames greedy for a good time and a fistful of dough."

"And you have both!"

"You wait till you get there," he promised. "They've thrown the joint open to a few friends of guys in the outfit tonight. I'm taking you upstairs to a swell party. Liquor by the gallon, and there'll be a stray dame or two if you're that way inclined. There are generally a few Aussies turn up — guys that our boys have palled up with."

"There's no doubt about you blokes," I told him. "You're highly organised in every department."

"Sure!" he agreed softly. I wanted very much to see his squadron house. I might even end up with a woman, if I got drunk enough to lose the fear I had always had of contracting syphilis.

He drove past King's Cross and into a quiet, dark street in Potts Point lined with tree-screened mansions, the sort of places inhabited by captains of industry down to their last hundred thousand. Hagen swung the jeep stylishly into a drive and drew up alongside a huge portico. A pair of double doors stood open, revealing a richly carpeted entrance hall with a wide staircase at the back. Hagen motioned me inside, and as we entered a girl half-staggered across the hall. She work a pink silk nightdress. Seeing us, she halted, giving Hagen a familiar leer from under disarranged hair.

"'Lo, Myra."

"Howzit, Gene!" She thrust a wavering finger at me. "Where'd you find that?"

"A better place than where they found you," I snarled at her.

She merely spat in my direction and continued across the hall into a room. Grinning, Hagen led me up the stairs.

"Don't mind Myra," he said over his shoulder. "She's a very willing dame, but the guys don't go for her the way they used to. She's liquored-up most of the time."

*   *   *

The room and all that it held seemed to close in on me; I felt almost a physical constriction. If I had decided at that moment to leave by the door by which I had come in, I would not have been able to fling off the aversion that held me rigid in the corner, and do so. To pick my way through those scattered, clamorous groups and couples, some lying down, some sitting, some standing, swaying, staggering, laughing, leering, grimacing, shouting — seemed for the moment beyond me. It was as though the atmosphere had become wholly tangible, upsurged, and pinned me up against the wall. I could not even identify my emotions: they seemed to be suspended . . . Disgust? I had seen worse scenes in the *burqa* of Cairo or the Rue des Soeurs of Alexandria, where all the heinous abuses of which the human body was capable had been paraded in a kind of frenetic ritual. Anger? Why? Australians over there had sought the same excesses and shut out violently the black reality of the war . . . No, if anything, I accepted the scene, felt it to be compelling me to remain as a witness — in order that the reality of homecoming might be complete; that I might not have one solitary illusion left within me.

Suddenly I felt light and reckless; I laughed aloud. It was as if I now stood outside of myself, observing the

spectacle of my disillusion and finding it too funny for
words. I turned to the buffet, reached between two
others and filled my glass, drank, refilled it — again and
again. They were heavy drinks: brandy, creme de
mĕnthe, kümmel, cognac; I did not discriminate, I merely
poured them into me. My mind grew numb, the scene
rosy, warm, blurred; the effect was pleasant, like that of
an aching tooth dulled by narcotic. The floor beneath me
commenced a soft, steep, dangerous swaying. I wanted
to sit down, to find company — perhaps a woman . . . I
took up my glass, a full bottle of whisky, and sought a
long divan. Up the other end were an officer and a girl,
who squirmed and screamed as he attempted to pour a
drink down the front of her dress; in the middle was an
Australian major who talked thickly and wildly to two
Yanks who sat near him on the floor. I tried to catch the
eye of one of those near me, but when a pair of eyes met
mine, misted with drink, they appeared not to see me. So
I listened instead.

"Jimmy boy," one of the Americans cried in loud,
watery tones, "you taking me to that beach you were
talking of tomorrow?"

It was the Australian major he had addressed; the major grinned witlessly and at length replied:

"No, shir!" A belching laugh. "Tomorrow's building
day."

"Building day? What th' hell's that?"

Hilariously, another man cried:

"Say, don't you know about Jimmy's building day?"

"Tell him, Jimmy," someone urged.

"You tell him," said the major boastfully.

"OK! Jimmy's in charge engineers' stores, see? He's
building himself a swell little bungalow out at a place called — what's it called, Jimmy?"

"Avalon."

"Yeah, Avalon. One day a week he takes what he wants from stores, loads the stuff into a truck and spends the day at Avalon."

The major swept an arm round in a wobbling gesture and mouthed vaingloriously:

"Everything in the bungalow out of bloody army stores — down to the lasht nail!" And he fell back wheezing and giggling to himself.

They burst into applauding mirth and the major sat up again and looked around him; his eyes caught mine, passed on, then came back again to peer at me; he raised and lowered his eyebrows as he tried to recognise me. He bent nearer and examined the colour patches on my shoulders. Then, seeming to understand them at last, he grinned, looking amused and a little contemptuous.

"Nnnnh-inth Division! Where'd you come from, soldier?"

"It's too long a story," I mumbled.

He looked at me silently for a few seconds; then he pulled himself together, became a little less drunk.

"Let's hear it, soldier," he demanded, and his voice was spiteful. His cloudy eyes, trying to keep me in focus, narrowed and widened. Then he seemed to forget what he had been saying, for he grinned idiotically and waved an aimless hand; he turned away to watch a woman further up the room who was dancing as several men clapped their hands in rhythm. Then, as if suddenly recalling me, he turned and pointed at my colour patch.

"Infantry," he said.

I nodded, and he lurched sideways until he leaned against me. For a few seconds he stared at me blindly. Then he said:

"Infantry! Get out of it! Don't be a bloody mug!"

I was dizzy now, and a little sick; I had company, but I

no longer wanted it. Above all, I did not want to talk of myself to the man beside me. So I answered him shortly:

"Someone's got to be in it."

"Let 'em be in it if they're mug enough! What's a young feller like you want to die for? It's bad up in those jungles, boy. Thass what it is!"

"You been there?" I jibed.

But my question did not offend him; he only seemed to find it ridiculous. His giggle brought another hiccup.

"Dice it!" he repeated.

For a moment I thought of a soft job, of never having to go wet, cold or sleepless again; never having to face bullets or shells again.

"It's not so easily done," I said.

At this his face spread into an awful smile of complacency. He leaned right against me and breathed:

"Boy, I know a couple of medical officers who'll board you unfit for fifty quid — for twenty, I'll claim you to my unit — a base unit — you know who I am, son?"

He revolted me: I hated him. He was not to know he had lashed at my pride, scorned all I had been through in the last three years.

"A house builder?" I suggested.

He frowned stupidly, not realising what I had overheard. The next second I had a violent urge to be sick; I stood up gawping, hand over my mouth. He pointed to a curtain in the wall nearby. I got to my feet, pushed through the curtain and went down a passage until I found a lavatory.

Once relieved, I straightened up, feeling weak and coldly sobered. Across the passage I saw another door. I crossed, opened it and met fresh air. Another wave of dizziness came over me as I felt the cool breath of the night. I clung to the door jamb. It seemed the only stable thing in the world; everything else whirled swiftly and silently.

Behind me the drunken tongue of the major stumbled over words I could not make out; I turned round to find him lurching towards me, his face convulsed.

"Bloody young bastard! House builder! What are you getting at? Where've you been snooping?"

I looked up, only half seeing him; despising him, dismissing him.

"Get out!" I said. "Go away!"

He steadied himself on the wall, glaring, snarling at me.

"Scoot! Before I call up the provosts and get you attended to. You bastard!" he breathed. "I'll have them bash hell out of you. You bastard! Do you know who I am?"

Wildly I shouted back at him:

"You're a dirty, thieving base-bludger!"

He exclaimed and came towards me. I straightened up and something shattered in my head; I seemed to see a wall of blood. I flung out my fist desperately and it met his face with a soft thud . . . The blood went. I was cold and calm again. The major sat on the floor holding his nose, murmuring over it. He looked silly and paltry . . . I walked outside.

I found my way on to a balcony, down a flight of steps, along the drive and back into the street. It was cold and forlorn and the wind filled it with dim whispers. I walked along without purpose, sick at heart, sick to the very core.

Part 2
The Military Life

So, emu-bobbing, bending, down the line of huts
We march at morning, picking up the litter —
Scavengers of dead matches, unhygienic butts
Of cigarettes, and papers in the gutter.
Strangling our ardour, halters of futility
Drag us upon emu parades, the Army wasting
Prodigal hours while soldiers, eager for the fighting,
Billions of butts in hand, bob on to victory!

T. Inglis Moore
from "Emu Parade"

LAWSON GLASSOP

Brawl On!

Mick Reynolds, the narrator from Lawson Glassop's We Were the Rats, *has no sooner joined the army at Ingleburn camp near Sydney than he is forced to defend himself in a camp brawl.*

AFTER we got back and had been dismissed on the company parade ground, I sat on the steps at the back of the hut and was conscious only of a pervading loneliness, of my feet that were hurting and of my utter weariness.

The other soldier in civilian clothes was sitting on the bottom step, and a few other fellows were lounging about. The soldier in civilian clothes stood up and went down to the latrine. He was soon back, and I noticed that he was white.

He sat down. "I can't do it," he said suddenly. "I can't do it."

"Can't do what?" I asked. The others were looking at him strangely.

"Take a coupler number nines," said one of them.

"I can't do it," he said again. "There are no partitions between the places. Everyone can see everyone else. It's disgusting. A soldier on one end throwing orange peel at one on the other. I can't do it."

Everyone gaped at him. "What's wrong with this galah?" asked somebody and another said, "Well wouldn't it rip you? What do you expect him to throw?"

"I can't do it," said the little fellow with the gleaming black hair and black moustache. "I won't do it."

"Don't do it," said one of the loungers, winking at his mate. "Just stay right where you are. Don't let 'em bluff you."

The little soldier sat down on the step near me, and after a while I saw his face become tense and he got up and went down to the latrine.

The loungers laughed. A soldier came towards the steps. As I stood up to let him pass one of my feet slipped and I fell forward. My shoulder struck his chest a hard blow, and he went sprawling on his back in the dust.

"I'm sorry," I said and, forgetting my weariness, went to pick him up. "I slipped."

The loungers laughed again. I could see his eyes gleaming as I reached out to help him up. He pushed my hand away and got slowly to his feet. He stood there for a moment, bent forward, and I could see his hands clenching and unclenching at his sides.

"I'm sorry," I said. "My foot slipped just as you went to pass me."

"God stone the bleedin' crows," he snarled. "Think ya bloody funny, don't ya? Think ya can make a mug outta me in fronter me mates?"

I sighed. "I'm not trying to make a mug out of anybody," I said. "I slipped. I said I was sorry."

"You'll be sorry all right," he said.

"Now listen," I said, "I'm not looking for trouble."

"Yer may not be bloody well lookin' fer it, mate, but ya'll bloody well get it."

Resentment was rising in me now, an insistent resentment I knew I could not suppress for long.

"I said I'm sorry," I said, and I noticed my voice was louder. "What else do you want me to do?"

"Ay, Eddie, would you like him to massage the thick head you got from drinkin' too much grog you scrounged from the sergeant's mess last night?" called someone.

Eddie did not look round. "You keep outa this," he said grimly, "or ya'll get a crack on the bloody jaw, too."

I noticed the word "too".

"I found out ya name," said Eddie. He was still standing there, leaning forward, and his eyes were still gleaming. "It's Howard Reynolds. Where'd ya get a pretty monicker like that from?"

"My mother gave it to me," I said quietly, and I heard some of the boys laugh.

Eddie's mouth closed suddenly. Then he said, "That's a pretty suit ya got on, too."

"It's paid for," I said.

The boys laughed again. Eddie's hands were clenching and unclenching. "Think ya smart, doan cher?" he snarled. "We doan want no bloody pansies in this battalion."

"Don't worry," I said. "They mightn't find out about you."

The boys guffawed, and I saw Eddie go slowly red. He came towards me, stopped in front of me, and pushed his face into mine.

"I don't like ya bloody face," he said.

He was tall, even taller than I was, and I was five feet

eleven. He had an ordinary face, the sort of face you would pass a thousand times in Sydney any day of the week. His blue eyes were hard now, and I noticed that he had a few pimples on his brown skin.

"I can't say," I said, "that I've fallen in love with yours. When you become a big boy you'll grow out of the pimply stage. I wouldn't worry if I were you."

A crowd of soldiers had gathered, and they roared with laughter. Eddie said nothing. He went white. Then he stepped back and began to undo the white tape at the bottom of his giggle jacket. His hands were trembling, and he fumbled with it.

"I joined the AIF to fight the Germans," I said. "It'd be a pity to kill one of my own countrymen first."

Eddie looked up with contempt blazing in his eyes. "Don't say pretty little Howard is a dingo?" he said.

"OK, soldier," I said, taking off my coat. "I'll take you apart to see what makes you get that way."

Soldiers were running from two lines of huts, and I could hear cries in the distance of "Brawl on! Brawl on!" A circle was formed and somebody took my coat. "Do this galah over," he whispered in my ear. "He's a king hit merchant."

I knew fellows who went out looking for what they called a "blue". Evidently this Eddie was one of them. There was a gloating leer on his face as he came towards me, his hands up and his fists still clenching and unclenching. How could you convince a man like that? It was like trying to reason with Adolph Hitler.

Eddie led with his left. I slipped it easily, but he ripped his right to the body. I dropped my left elbow mechanically, but it did not take the full force of the blow, and I felt my ribs stinging and heard the roar of the crowd.

Eddie was grinning. He thought I was easy. He came in

again, but I spiked him with a left lead that jolted him ludicrously back on to his heels. There was a new note in the noise this time, and I heard somebody call, "Take six to four and back blue pants."

Eddie bent his head and looked at me from under his eyebrows. He was sizing me up. He came in cautiously this time. I was deceived. Suddenly he let go with both hands in quick succession, his left to the face, his right to the body again. I expected him to try something else. I pushed his left aside, but his right got home and I felt the harsh impact of knuckles on my ribs. My feet, moving back, struck a tuft of grass and I went down. I heard the crowd roar. It seemed to be a long way away.

"Two's on Wilson," came the cry. "I'll bet a pound to ten bob Eddie. All right, Alan, ya set."

As I got up I saw Eddie's gloating grin hanging like a full moon in the sky. My God, I thought, what would Les Taylor and Tiger Farrell think of me if they could see me now? Knocked down into the dust in a brawl with a lout. Suddenly my resentment crystallized into a grim purpose. This knockdown artist couldn't do this to me. I was Mick Reynolds. One of the few things I could do was fight.

Anyhow, Eddie Wilson was ruining my new suit. My new blue suit. I had paid eight guineas for that suit only a few weeks before. I wanted it for after the war. No Eddie Wilson would do that to me. Instantly this defence of my suit became an obsession. Nothing else mattered. Eddie Wilson had probably never had a suit like it in his life. Well, by God, he was not going to ruin mine!

I walked straight into Eddie Wilson. I feinted with my left, and as he ducked I uppercut him with my right. I misjudged it slightly. It hit him on the edge of the mouth. He went down, and that mad roar, that blood-lust roar I knew so well, was pounding in my ears.

Wilson lay on his back. I did not see anybody else, only Wilson lying there. I heard somebody say, "What the bloody hell is all this about?"

"Get up, Wilson," I said. "I'll teach you to ruin my bloody suit."

"What the bloody hell is this all about?" said the voice again. I looked over my right shoulder. There was nobody there. I looked back at Wilson. Then I realised that the soldiers had vanished. I looked back again. They were gone.

I looked over my left shoulder, straight at Lieutenant Colonel Russell-Francis, the CO of the battalion. I shook my head, and looked again. He was still there.

"What the bloody hell is all this?" he barked. "Answer me, man. Don't stand there looking like a bloody idiot. What's going on here?"

I knew now why they called him Old Gutsache. His mouth always had the querulous expression of a man with a pain in his stomach, the peevish distemper of a dyspeptic.

"Nothing — sir," I said stupidly. It was an effort for me to say "sir"; I had never called anybody "sir" before.

Old Gutsache snorted. "Why the bloody hell you don't keep your fighting until you meet the bloody Huns I bloody well don't know," he growled. "Why the bloody hell are you dressed in those clothes?"

"I haven't been issued with anything else — sir."

Old Gutsache swung round and glared at a lieutenant standing behind him. "See this man is fitted out with his issue first thing in the morning, Briggs," he said testily. "What the bloody hell is this battalion? A hiking club?" He turned to me quickly. "What the hell's your name, soldier?" he barked.

"Reynolds — sir." I drew a deep breath and said, "Howard Reynolds."

"Hmmmmm. Pretty name that."

"So is Michael Hugh Russell-Francis."

"What's that?" he barked.

"I said, 'So is Michael Hugh Russell-Francis.' "

Old Gutsache shoved his chin forward and growled. "That's insolence, soldier."

"That's not insolence, sir," I said. "That's justice."

Old Gutsache reached up and stroked his chin quickly three times.

"I believe you're right," he said suddenly. "How the bloody hell did you know my full name?"

"Looked you up in *Who's Who*. You're a good soldier."

"Thanks," said old Gutsache. "Can I mention your name next time I see the general? What did you say your name was?"

"Reynolds. My father was in the Ninety-Third with you in the last war."

Old Gutsache's eyes lit up. "Well I'll be damned!" he said. "Mick Reynolds's son, eh? Should have recognised you at once. Mick Reynolds, eh?" He did not say anything for a while, and I knew he was back in France, slopping about in the mud with my father, going over the top with him, getting drunk with him on leave, bringing him in the time he got wounded at Villers Brettoneaux.

"Do you play cricket?" asked Old Gutsache suddenly.

"No, sir."

"Too bad. I remember once we persuaded Mick — your father — to play against a Tommy unit on leave. He was a hundred and fifty-six when we declared. Well I'll be damned. Mick Reynolds's son, eh? Another Reynolds in the Ninety-Third." He was off again, back in the past, and I thought there must have been some good in something that gave a man memories like these.

The lieutenant shifted his feet uncomfortably. Eddie Wilson had got to his feet and was wiping his mouth with his giggle jacket. I could see heads poking out of hut doors, and faces at windows.

"Who the bloody hell started this?" asked Old Guts-ache suddenly. "By Christ, I'll put you both on a charge. I'll crime both of you, that's what I'll do. What's your name?" he asked Eddie.

"Wilson, sir."

"Wilson, eh? Oh. You're the man who was in Bendigo jail when the Sixth Division sailed, eh? They thought a change of scene might do you good, so they foisted you on me. You're a trouble-maker, Wilson. I've a good mind to drum you out of this battalion, too. Get that?"

"Yes, sir."

"It was my fault, sir," I said. "I picked on Wilson."

"No, sir," said Wilson quickly. "I picked on him. It was my fault."

"Briggs," said Old Gutsache. "Privates Reynolds and Wilson will spend tomorrow on fatigue duty. Perhaps they'll get to know each other better in the salubrious atmosphere of the cookhouse and the latrines. That is all, gentlemen."

He glared at us both and stalked away, followed by the dutiful Briggs, who was saying "Yes sir, yes sir."

I looked at Eddie Wilson. Eddie Wilson looked at me. He grinned sheepishly. "Er — me name's Wilson," he said awkwardly. "Eddie Wilson."

"Mine's Howard Reynolds," I said, "but my friends call me Mick. You call me Mick."

Eddie smiled. I liked his smile. "I'll call ya Mick," he said. He held out his hand. I shook it. "I'm sorry," he said. "I thought ya was a bit of a queen. I done me block. Ya not crooked on me?"

"Forget it."

Eddie shifted his feet uncomfortably in the dust. I could see a purple stain on his chin where the blood was caking. "Ay listen, Mick," he said with the diffidence that is inevitable when you use somebody's Christian name for the first time, "I reckon where we're goin' a joker's goin' ter need a decent sorta backstop, and I was thinkin' — well, if ya doan mind — I reckon a bloke what can use his mitts like the way you done — that last one was a beaut — well, how about you an' me bein' cobbers an' sharin' what we gotta take, good or bad? Is she jake?"

He was looking at me eagerly, self-consciously. The last words had come out with a rush.

"Eddie," I said, "what I need right now is a friend. She's jake."

A cloud came over his face. "I've gotta give ya the dinkum oil," he said. "I gotta tell ya this before ya go sayin' ya'll be in it. I gotta be fair dinkum. Ya see, I got more red ink in me paybook than any joker in the Sixth Div. I was in the Sixth Div., see, but I was in the boob in Bendigo when they sailed. Nothin' serious it wasn't. Just a case of AWL, but I just wanted ter tell ya before ya said ya'd be me cobber." He was scraping the toe of one of his brown boots in the dust. "An' I won't have no money for a long time. I'll still be payin' fines for months."

"Eddie," I said, "she's jake."

"That's bonzer," he said, and when he looked up I saw the relief in his face. "Let's take a bo peep at what they got in the canteen. It'll only be milk, but it'll do. The bastards won't give us poor privates wet ones."

"Lead on, Macduff," I said.

"Mac who?" asked Eddie. "Me name's Wilson."

"Wilson or Macduff. Who cares?"

"I don't give a bugger," said Eddie.

"Neither," I said, "do I."

GEORGE TURNER

Discipline Begins with the Instruments of Discipline

Sergeant Peter Scobie is the central character in George Turner's novel, Young Man of Talent. *He finds that his hopes of promotion are dashed by the unexpected arrival of Lieutenant Keith Tolley as his new platoon commander at the isolated staging camp in New Guinea where he has been in temporary command. Moreover, Scobie finds himself immediately caught up in a bitter conflict with Tolley, who is determined to impose his own ideas concerning discipline on a unit he believes to have been pampered by the languid company commander Captain Midwinter.*

LIEUTENANT Tolley was not given to changing his mind, save under pressure and a crushing weight of evidence. His initial contact with Sergeant Scobie had been revealing, and he had seen nothing since to add grace to the poor opinion he had formed. He realised that Midwinter's peculiar attitude towards his men had a great deal to do with their behaviour, and was resolved to alter that behaviour soon and swiftly, and Scobie, the pivot of the platoon, was the obvious spot on which to lean the mass of authority.

Tolley's single-mindedness had often been a cause of comment. He knew it and ignored it, and his ability to ignore the unwanted was the measure of his singleness of mind. He did not lack ability to absorb new ideas; the restrictive factor was his unwillingness to discard old ones. What he knew, *was*, and for ever.

He sat at the table in the hut, noting the things that could, *should*, be done. The floor could be levelled better, and paved with sapling corduroy, and this footling table enlarged to twice its size and set on firm legs. This camp was semipermanent and he had to work in this hut, and every reasonable accessory was extra surety of the quality of the work. And this was a main trail, often used by senior officers of other units. Appearances counted.

The creased and dirty booklet on the table was, he found, the platoon roll. It seemed to be marked up to date. He glanced through it abstractedly, thinking the sergeant might at least have kept it clean.

Of course, the platoon had been without an officer for some months, and Midwinter was not the man to cavil over details. There were practical reasons why some lowering of standards must prevail in the field, but none to excuse downright laziness.

He was seized with a mounting tide of irritation. Midwinter apparently thought much of Scobie; well, he thought little of either of them.

That Peter entered the hut at this point in Tolley's emotional upswing may well have been a decisive factor in the shaping of events in the days that followed.

He laid down the roll book.

"Well, Sergeant?"

His careful stillness deadened the atmosphere. It was not even inimical.

"I've come to see what I can do for you, sir. Do you want to take a rest, or check stores and hand over right away?"

"Rest?" The word turned over in his mind as one loaded with significance. "I *have* taken over, Sergeant. The

accounting of stores should have been prepared and
ready when I arrived. A simple routine exists. Surely you
had instructions from the company commander?"

Laughton, Peter remembered, as Papa Barret, prepar-
ing to terrify his family with rolling, framed phrases.

He replied, "No, sir. I knew you were coming, but not
when. I returned only last night myself." That should be
enough for most men. Incautiously he grinned and said,
"No one worries too much about the formalities when
there's no crying need. After all, that takeover drill was
designed for trench warfare."

"No one worries? I do." Tolley knew precisely what he
was about. It is axiomatic that discipline begins with the
instruments of discipline, and the sergeant was his prime
instrument. "There is a right way to hand over command, and no other way except in extreme circumstances. I imagine you are aware of it."

This was a lecture, requiring no reply. Here was a man
to be approached with tact or silence — or to be avoided.

Tolley had said that he had taken over, and
demonstrated it as a fact without pause for doubt.

"We will inspect the platoon area at once. It will be a
complete inspection. Then you will parade the platoon,
which appears to be resting. After that you will prepare a
list of stores and hand it to me. I will look over the training syllabus at the same time."

With some trouble, Peter stifled speech. The last
sentence had been naked high explosive, and was better
left undetonated as yet. In justice, the man could scarcely
be expected to understand the sheer impossibility of the
idea. Training syllabus! Midwinter himself might have
staggered under the impact.

The situation, he supposed, was not overly abnormal,
but the main protagonist was unreal; he must adopt a
new frame of behaviour to deal with this man. So must

they all. With Tolley on the one hand, and Andy on the other, each breathing his particular brand of smoke, and Kane occasionally raking the ashes in the background, the future would test his craftsmanship to the utmost. He thought, incredulously, *All this in the space of a few sentences. I must be losing my grip. There's nothing wrong here at all. It's just his dead delivery — like being spoken to by a fish. That's better. There's nothing wrong. We're too new to each other.*

Tolley disillusioned him.

"Are you normally so tongue-tied, Sergeant?"

"No, sir." What else to say?

"How long have you held your rank?"

"Lance-sergeant for some months, sir, and sergeant a little over a week."

"Are all the NCOs similarly inexperienced?"

The gratuitous insult took a while to penetrate. It had something of the effect of a blow from a friend. He said calmly,

"You will find the corporals very capable, sir."

Tolley's voice livened faintly.

"I didn't ask you that. We will return to it later. You can conduct me on the inspection. We will begin with the perimeter — the weapon pits."

Weapon pits. Every new sentence was awash with disaster. Technically, he was entitled to count on their existence. Peter said baldly,

"We have no weapon pits, sir."

Tolley nodded, as one inured to surprise.

"None?"

"No, sir." He felt confident that he could make this point quickly. "This isn't an operational post. It never has been at any stage of the campaign. It is a camp maintained solely for the feeding and bedding down of troops passing over the range."

"I know the status of the post. Get on with it."

"It's just this, that the nearest enemy was more than a day's march distant when the place was first occupied, and has been retreating ever since. You won't find a weapon pit in any post within several miles."

"Not even for sentries?"

"No, sir. We mount sentries behind brush cover, with Tommy guns. It's the usual practice in rear areas here.'

He had considered himself on safe ground, and it had rocked under his feet. Tolley came in from an oblique angle that swept it away altogether.

"You are pointing out, Sergeant, that your experience in local procedures is greater than mine?"

That was monstrous.

"I don't make a habit of being deliberately rude, sir."

Midwinter's warning came back to him too late. The lieutenant's control was greater.

"Not rude, insolent. We will confine ourselves to the inspection." He took up his cap. "I begin not to expect too much."

It was hot outside under an enamelled sky. For once the platoon had not been required to provide a working party that day, and in the area only a few men stirred beyond the shelters. Most sat on their beds, writing, reading, playing cards, or just talking.

Peter wished futilely that he had given Kane some orders, any orders, for the afternoon, even if only to take the men into the scrub and hide them. As they passed Kane's shelter he broke away to say,

"Pass the word, Jim. Parade in about ten minutes. Muck order."

Tolley asked, "Why was that necessary? A parade is called or it is not. No warning is needed."

Peter protested.

"There will be a few out of earshot, washing clothes at the spring."

"You enjoy argument."

The disinterested tone was a slap in the face.

The unanswerable, basic truth was that the man was right. Technically right. There should be weapon pits, by standard procedure; there had been no need to warn Kane, by standard procedure; as for Peter's proneness to argument, that too might be termed standard procedure. But the capacity for extracting livable conditions out of an unnatural life depended on using the elasticity of the standard framework. He had no feeling for that. It might come later, before too much damage was done.

In the quick tour of the camp Tolley said nothing and missed nothing. He looked once at everything and turned aside. Only the latrine and the cookhouse, both reasonable examples of hygiene under difficulties, he surveyed at length, and passed by in silence. At the door of the hut he said,

"Call the parade."

The platoon assembled with permanent camp speed, and more presentably than Peter had dared hope. At least they all wore shirts, boots and hats; some had produced belts. He recognised the hand of Jim Kane, tidying three sections with hopeless speed, and thanked heaven for him, though that same heaven knew it was a shabby line-up. Why couldn't the man have called an informal get-together, or left it until morning, when he could have turned them out freshly shaven and in clean clothes? Weapons and equipment would have made some sort of a show.

It was not easy to foresee the impact of Tolley on this integrated group. Joe and himself, and all the NCOs, had been fairly easygoing men, but they got things done, which was what had been required of them. No doubt

Tolley would also get things done, perhaps even a shade more efficiently; but there could be balancing losses in the oneness of the group, built and maintained by unvaryingly even treatment over a long period.

It could be that Tolley would treat them better than he expected. It could be that the lieutenant had taken an instant and unreasoning dislike to himself alone, but he had no hope of it. He was too much the machined article.

In a state of confused rationalising he called the parade to attention, turned about, saluted, handed over, saluted again, and marched to his position in the rear of the platoon. He would have liked to have remained out in front, to observe their faces as the officer called the tune.

The performance was brief, and as wrong as it could be in so short a time.

Tolley stood the men at ease, and opened with a speech epitomising the personality he projected, a paced flow of economical sentences, flatly spoken.

"My name is Tolley. You are new to me and I to you, but a few days will remedy that. You will find me a strict commander, but not a hard one. I expect competent work and complete discipline, which are not too much to require. I expect that each man shall be as expert as good training can make him in the special duties which are his."

This was routine, the introductory words of any new officer, but it sounded learned by heart and delivered at this juncture because it was customary.

"To expect of you that you pull your weight is my right. Do your jobs and I'll do mine, and we shall have an efficient unit."

That word "expect" was much in evidence, but no hint appeared of what the platoon might receive in return for work, diligence and discipline.

Peter fancied the tone warmed slightly as now he entered on a phase nearer his heart.

"I have been here less than two hours, but I have seen much that needs attention, both for your benefit and for mine. I won't list these matters now; we shall *give* them that attention tomorrow. To that end, I wish to see all the NCOs in my office at 1800 hours."

Peter winced. *My office*, by God! He suspected a decree of banishment. The speech was plain, neatly packaged and tied, without a grain of ballast. It was ineffectual, because it meant nothing; he probably didn't *like* making it, because it was inessential, a formality, one of the inescapable "done things".

But an unpredicted, dismaying climax was at hand.

Tolley paused briefly before he continued.

"Regulations do not permit a batman to transfer with his officer, so I must recruit one from among you. If anyone wishes to volunteer for the job, take a pace forward."

Peter watched him intently. He had laid himself open to an inevitable snub. Didn't he know how men's minds work, their suspicion and wariness of strangers? Didn't he know enough to get his sergeant to find a batman for him? Did he, in fact, know anything beyond the duties and entitlements of his rank?

Not having heard of Palter's previous acquaintance with Tolley, he hoped the fool might rush in while others waited.

Nobody moved.

This was likely to be unpleasant, and regarded as a personal insult. He had not yet plumbed the impermeable nature of the man's sufficiency. The routine gesture would be followed by a stronger one.

He said, "Then I must detail one for the time being." He looked along the ranks to a youngster on the left.

"What is your name?"

"Willis, sir."

"At attention when you are spoken to, Private Willis!" The sudden cutting edge moved Willis like a spring. "That's better. You will act as my batman until further orders."

In the long hush Peter awaited an infallible fate, and hoped the boy wouldn't make too much of an idiot of himself. Willis said respectfully,

"I'd rather not, sir." The hush persisted until he had to go on, stiffly and unwillingly. "I'm not used to that sort of work, sir."

Tolley replied drily,

"It's hardly a case for expertise. You have been given an order. You will find nothing to strain your abilities in the execution of it."

He called Peter and had him dismiss the parade, and vanished into the hut.

They broke off quietly, but Willis came running.

"Peter!"

"Not so loud!"

"But, Peter, he can't — "

"Yes, he can. He's within his rights. Take it easy, son. It won't last for ever."

Willis was flushed and mutinous with the anger of an adolescence he had not yet grown out of.

"I'm not going to wash his bloody socks!"

Would they ever find a fresh objection? That seemed to be the ultimate stigma — to wash another man's socks.

"Listen, kid — "

"Can't I do anything about it? Is it he just tells me and I've got to?"

"I'm afraid so." He cast for a means of easing the sting, and was empty of ideas. "Do it for a start, anyway, and I'll try to get it changed."

Changed to whom? And how? And to make it worse, Willis trusted him.

"Do you reckon you can?"

"I'll try, but go quietly until we find our feet."

It was vague comfort, but it got rid of Willis though it left him with a problem.

He turned towards the hut, thinking, *It won't do, it won't do. He's going to tear my platoon apart. Was that what Middy meant?*

Quite naturally he thought "my platoon", who had never identified himself with them as a body. He had never permitted identification in his determination that no herd should ever swallow him. Now, angry and apprehensive, seeing and hearing and understanding so much more than they, he felt responsible and protective.

And, being a thinking introvert, he recognised the change in himself. It didn't improve his temper.

*   *   *

Clearly only one end to the affair was possible. One of them, probably himself, must be shifted from the platoon. But he would make a battle of it.

In one respect he resembled Tolley. He had an immense confidence in himself, and an immense lack of discernment of his own shortcomings.

He was so sure that his concern was purely for the men of his platoon.

He had forgotten Midwinter's dependence upon him — forgotten it entirely.

Tolley raged at his carelessness, assuring himself that he had only the interest of the unit at heart . . . As for Scobie, he had run wild for too long. He must be pulled back into line, beaten into it if need be, with every resource of discipline and authority.

He was more angry than he had been in all his adult years.

ERIC LAMBERT

The Barking Soldiers

After a period of home leave following their return to Australia from the Middle East, Eric Lambert's hero Bill Farr and his companions from the Ninth Division find themselves in North Queensland, where they have been sent to undergo jungle training to prepare them for the war against Japan. Their reactions to what they consider to be mere bastardry on the Army's part lead to the events described in this extract from the novel The Veterans.

WEEK after week ... Up before dawn, saddled with battle equipment and out into the wet jungle on a breakfast of one tablespoon of porridge, one wisp of bacon, one slice of bread. Our stomachs working with hunger, we hauled ourselves and our weapons up the muddy sides of mountains and among the tearing rapids of the Barron. Squatting all night in the mud in pits while the foliage dripped on our backs; moving at dawn on one mouthful of bully beef, one dry biscuit, one salt tablet. Always wet. Always hungry. Always stiff. Week after week ...

And we bore it all, complaining little. Maddening as it was, we tried to understand its necessity, even the shortage of rations. We relieved our wound-up minds with a sort of desperate, manufactured humour, even feigning the madness we felt that the monotony might bring upon us. "Troppo acts" we called them. We lost the condition we had grown in the fleshpots of the cities; we became lean, hard, chronically hungry, dull in our feelings, a little subhuman — and far less in love with life.

Then the truth began to emerge; the bastardry became discernible. We had been assured that our short rations were a part of our training, that our bodies had to learn to go hungry, but this was only half true. It became known that officers and sergeants were dining regularly on steak and eggs; through our grapevine, we learned that our scale of rations was much higher than what we got. Some people were working rackets.

First we told Tully about it, savagely and scornfully.

"Yers're doing all right in the sergeants' mess, aren't yers?" Lasher snarled at Tully. "Steak and eggs, and plenty of porridge and milk. You and the foggin' officers!"

Tully, as usual, was unshaken.

"Well, if I starved myself, it wouldn't make any difference to your rations," he smiled. "Why don't you kick up a stink? Get paraded!"

"Get paraded!" Lasher's scorn seemed to reverberate through his body. "Who to? The Skull?"

Tully smiled at him even wider. I began to have an idea he was deliberately goading Lasher.

He spread out his hands, saying blandly:

"There you are. You grizzle to me, but you're not game to do anything about it."

For a moment Lasher was speechless. Not game! Not game to front the Skull! Lasher's lips and eyes became slits, shone angrily. He rose, hurling away his cigarette.

"Parade me now," he sneered.

"Parade the two of us, you old coot," I challenged.

Tully grinned.

"OK. Make yourselves regimental, and I'll front you to the Skull."

The Skull was our name for our company commander, Captain Arnold Tuttle, MC. Like all the Tuttles of this world, he was easily described, easily understood — still more easily hated. The only son of an ambitious and determined mother, he had been raised on the doctrine that the world was a place made for Arnold Tuttle to get on in. His talents had never been anything more than moderate, but still he had got on, through a combination of self-denial, quiet cunning, and an ability to assume the credit for other men's achievements. He committed himself to nothing, was instinctively ruthless, appeared to feel for nobody. He had started as a private like the rest of us, but from the day he came into camp he made it clear that the ranks were only a stopping place on the way to better things. When we made trouble, Tuttle wouldn't be in it; when the company jacked up, Tuttle scabbed. When we were in the nearest town after women and booze, Tuttle was back in the tent studying army manuals. In the course of two years he had risen to a captaincy and gained an MC, which we always said his company had earned him. This was only partly true, because whatever else he was, he ws no coward and performed well in action in a heartless, uninspired way. Action was part of his job, and to get on he had to be good at his job, since he possessed neither money nor influence.

He sat behind his table in the company headquarters tent, listening stonily as Tully paraded us.

"Privates Daniels and Farr, sir. Complaining about the food."

The light shone on Tuttle's towering head, bald except at the temples: his eyes, the colour of syrup and seemingly all iris, had their usual disconcerting stare, despite being at the back of bony caverns. He drew back his lips and tapped with a pencil at a row of the falsest-looking teeth the Army Dental Corps had ever made.

"The food. . . . What's wrong with it?"

"Nothing," Lasher told him. "There just ain't enough of it. We're permanently hungry."

"Permanently hungry. There's tinned food at the canteen."

"What if there is?" I almost yelled at him. "Why should we spend our pay on tinned stuff because some bastard's flogging our rations?"

I might as well have commented on the weather; Tuttle just continued tapping.

"Have you any proof of that statement? Either of you?"

Lasher leaned over and slapped his stomach.

"Yair! Me guts!"

Tuttle ceased his tapping and regarded us without expression.

"I'll pass your complaint on to the quartermaster."

"What'll he do?" I sneered.

"That's up to him. Dismiss these men, Sergeant McTulloch."

"Dismiss" meant we had to salute.

"Squad — dis . . . *miss!*" growled Tully.

Lasher and I each flung up a hand in an exasperated wave and flopped it back.

"What sort of a 'dismiss' is that?" enquired Tuttle. "Try it again."

"Squad — dis . . . *miss!*"

We did it properly this time, since he was capable of keeping us there all day.

"That was a bright bloody idea!" rasped Lasher, outside. "That got us sweet foggin' nowhere."

Tully was grinning at him.

"I doubt whether Tuttle'll even mention it to the QM," he blandly remarked.

"Then why parade us?" I said.

But Tully only winked.

Two mornings later we were sitting in the tent awaiting a summons to fall in when Tully came in.

"Gooday, Tull."

"Gooday. How's the tucker these days?"

"Foggin' awful!"

Tully stared vacantly at the tent-pole.

"I was just wondering whether, due to the short rations — well, whether Twelve Platoon might be too weak to come on parade this morning," he murmured.

Lasher also gazed expressionlessly at the tent pole.

"There's a chance," he said.

"The other two sergeants were wondering the same thing about their platoons. The sar-major's a bit worried too. I think," concluded Tully, "you'd better go round your tents and check up."

Tully, Lasher and I exchanged long, hard looks that culminated in grins.

"See you on parade," said Tully " — I hope."

And he left the tent.

"Now what was all that about?" demanded Lucky.

"Never mind, pinhead," said Lasher. "Just keep quiet and do what you're told."

Silent Lew's features cracked into a great grin of pure enjoyment, and he made his most demonstrative speech to date.

"By hell!" he chuckled. "By hell!"

"Shut up, Lew! You make too much bloody noise."

Lasher and I left the tent and went our conspiratorial ways.

Ten minutes later, the company sergeant-major called:

"On parade, C Company!"

From the tents a chorus of pathetic voices replied:

"Too weak. Not enough tucker."

"All out, C Company!"

From a tent, the lanky form of Lasher half-emerged, on all fours. Wheezing, rolling a pair of piteous eyes, he said to the sergeant-major:

"Help! I'm dyin' of starvation."

He moaned and collapsed back into the tent. And from the company tents there came a chorus of terrible groans. Tully and the other two platoon sergeants, going around the tents, were greeted by the sight of groaning and prostrate men. Fighting their laughter, they reported the situation to the sergeant-major, who intoned:

"Most serious! Most serious!"

Presently, from the company HQ tent emerged Tuttle with his three lieutenants.

"What's this noise, sar-major? Why isn't the company turned out?"

Another wave of piteous moaning.

"They say they're too weak to move, sir," replied Tully gravely.

"Too weak?"

"Yes, sir. Something about not enough food."

"Tuttle woke at once," Tully told us afterwards. "His one idea was to stop the news of this business spreading. Tuttle's bloody career, you know! He turned and flew over towards the company mess like Phar Lap."

What ensued is battalion history, though our official history will not record it. Tuttle returned from the company cookhouse, and called his platoon officers into the HQ tent. Twenty minutes later, the company sergeant-major gave voice again:

"Fall in, C Company! With your mess gear! There's a feed on at the cookhouse!"

Lasher and Sammy made a sudden and remarkable

recovery; they sprang up like kangaroos and performed a victory dance in the tent. Putting his head out, Sammy cried:

"It better be good!"

A chattering, laughing, exulting company of us lined up with our tin dixies and marched noisily to the cookhouse, escorted by three grinning sergeants. And what a feed! Two rashers of bacon, a fried egg, tomato sauce, plenty of fresh bread and butter, and a tin of plum jam to every three men; not to mention a steaming hot brew of tea. The cook was cheered, the mess orderlies were cheered, and Tully was made to stay and have a cup of tea with us.

"You cunning old bastard!" Lasher told him.

"Me!" cried Tully, looking the picture of innocence.

"The Old Rock of Ages!" proclaimed Sammy.

"By Hell!" said Silent Lew. "By Hell!"

We got to know that our jungle training was to last six weeks, after which we were to go down to the coast to practise landing from invasion barges; but the Yanks with the barges weren't ready for us, so, since the higher command could think of nothing else, we had been traipsing round the jungle for twice as long as necessary. The tents began to mutter with rebellion.

One day our colonel, a famous lawyer, was strolling through the battalion lines with his sergeant-major, when a man put his head out of a tent and barked like a dog at him.

The colonel turned. "Was that for me?" he inquired.

"Arrh! Arrh!" yapped the man.

"Place this man under arrest," ordered the colonel.

The next morning the man and two armed escorts waited outside the battalion orderly room for the barker to be charged and tried. As they stood there, all three barked like dogs. The adjutant strode out enraged, and

placed the escorts under arrest. Four new escorts arriving to guard the three barkers, promptly began barking
themselves when told their duties. The colonel called the
barkers into his office and demanded an explanation. It
came at once:

"You're treating us like dogs. We're going to act like
dogs. Arrh! Arrh!"

The colonel dismissed them, and went to see the
medical officer, no doubt to enquire on the subject of
mass insanity. As he emerged, his ears were deafened by
the sound of the entire battalion, yapping like whipped
dogs.

"Arrh! Arrh! Ya-ow!"

It went on at intervals throughout the day, and for
many a day thereafter; it spread through the brigade,
through the division like a plague. At night, five hundred
men camped on one hill would all begin to bark in unison;
a unit on another hill would join in; and soon a gigantic,
hideous, animal din was ringing through twenty miles of
camps. And even after it had died away, throughout the
long, dark night, howl would answer howl among the
gullies and hills, like dingoes calling their mates. And
stately brigadiers and generals, entering a camp, would
find the guard turning out — not to present arms as their
exalted rank demanded, but to bark at them. Truck-loads
of troops, passing on the roads, yapped and yabbered like
frenzied curs.

"Arrh! Arrh! Arrh! Ya-ooooowr!"

In vain they crimed us, in vain they fined us, in vain
they sent men for a month's detention. We barked and
howled till our throats ached. A special Divisional Order
was pinned on all unit notice boards: "The practice of
barking at officers is unsoldierly and will cease
forthwith." And as we read the notice, we barked and
barked and barked. Ya-ooooowr! Arrh!

We were playing poker one night in the tent: Tully, Lasher, Sammy, Big Robbie, and I; Lucky and Silent Lew looked on. Under the murky yellow beams of a hurricane lamp we sat with a folded blanket for a card table. At the top of the lines in the HQ tent was David Bruce, duty officer for the night. The other two platoons were at the pictures. Twelve Platoon was duty platoon. About nine o'clock someone began to bark in B Company. Lucky strolled out into the night and barked back; from out of the darkness another voice yapped like a Pomeranian; someone in C Company countered, baying like an Alsatian who had cornered a burglar. Soon a hundred were hard at it; yaps, growls, snarls, howls and baying rang through the mild night air. In the entrance of the company tent David Bruce appeared, shouting angrily:

"Twelve Platoon! Stop that row!"

"I'll raise yer a zack," said Lasher. "Arrh! Arrh?"

"I'll see yer," said Sammy. "Arrh! Arrh! Ya-oow!"

"Bullets," said Lasher. "Arrh! Arrh!"

"Ya-ooow!" went Lucky and I.

"Hoh! Hoh! Hoh! Hoh! Hoh!" bayed Big Robbie.

"Ya-ooooow!" went the whole platoon.

"Twelve Platoon!" yelled Bruce. "Stop that row!"

"Ya-ooow!" went Twelve Platoon. "Arrh! Arrh! Hoh! Hoh! Hoh!"

"Sergeant McTulloch!" yelled David Bruce. "Report to me!"

Tully threw his cards down. "Hullo!" he said, and left the tent. A minute later Tully's voice cried:

"All out, Twelve Platoon! Tin hats! Rifles! Webbing!"

Twelve Platoon barked back at him.

"All out!" yelled Bruce. "At the double!"

In ones and twos we fell in, in three ranks. Bruce faced us, white and breathing hard.

"Twelve Platoon!" barked Tully. "Atten-shun!"

He handed the platoon over and awaited orders.

"Platoon!" cried Bruce. "Right turn! By the left, left wheel, quick march!"

And he led us out of camp. Muttering, we strode behind him.

"Quiet!" he shouted. "Correct those slopes! Pick up the step! Left! Right! Left!"

We swung savagely into step, hating him with all our hearts. Tramp! Tramp! Tramp! Along the dirt road in the moonlight.

"Correct that slope! Left! Right! Left! Swing those arms! No talking! Left! Right! Left!"

He took us a mile along the road, shouting at us all the time, and back into camp. He halted us, turned us to our front.

"Now bark!" he cried.

"Hoh! Hoh! Hoh!" went Twelve Platoon. "Arrh!" Arrh!"

"Ya-oooow!" screamed Sammy Fogg. Tully started to laugh, bent double, unable to stop himself.

"Platoon!" yelled Bruce. "Right turn! By the left, left wheel, quick march!"

And a snarling, mutinous platoon marched up the road again.

"Left! Right! Left! Correct that slope!"

Back up the road a mile, back to camp again. He halted us, turned us to our front. Like us, he was sweating and panting. He sagged with fatigue, we sagged; he glared at us, we glared back.

"Now bark!" he grasped.

"Arrh! Arrh! Arrh!" Sammy ran out on all fours, yapping; snapped at Bruce's ankle like a terrier. "Arrh! Arrh!"

"Right turn!" screamed Bruce. "By the left, left wheel, quick march!"

Staggering, he led us up the road again. "Left! Right! Left!" Did he think he'd break us! We swung into step like the Grenadier Guards, quickened our step, forcing him to march faster. A mile up, a mile back to camp. He halted us, turned us to our front. Officer and platoon stood panting, breathing gustily, hardly able to stand, like wild animals exhausted in combat.

"Now bark," he breathed.

For a minute there was silence — then:

"Hoh! Hoh! Hoh!" cried Lasher.

"Hoh! Hoh! Hoh!" went the whole platoon. "Arrh! Arrh! Ya-ooow!"

For a moment I thought David Bruce would cry. He stood and looked at us in utter defeat.

Then he became a man. He wrenched off his hat, threw it on the ground.

"You win!" he cried. "Oh, hell! You win!"

And he threw back his head and howled with us.

"Ya-ooooow!" went Davey and his men.

"Ya-ooooow!" went the rest of the battalion.

"Ya-ooooow!" went the Engineers.

"Ya-ooooow!" went the Artillery.

Soon a whole division was howling; twenty thousand men hurled their lamentations to the stars.

JON CLEARY

I Ran into the Gestapo . . . They've Got a Branch Here

Sergeant Greg Morley won the Victoria Cross during action overseas with the Seventh Division. This extract from Jon Cleary's The Climate of Courage *describes the aftermath of Morley's decision to go into the city of Sydney to get drunk, after his wife Sarah tells him she no longer loves him.*

THAT afternoon, while Sarah went over to Dee Why to see her mother, Greg went into town to get drunk. He showered and got dressed as if for a regimental parade. He put on his hat, admiring the thick puggaree that he had had specially made for him by an old Arab in Beit Jirja, and carefully turned up the brim at the side. He took a last look at himself, then took the Victoria Cross ribbon from his breast, dropped it in his stud box, and went out to get blind, stinking unremembering drunk.

He did it with a method that was unnatural to him, getting no enjoyment from it at all, taking a long time about it because he had never got drunk this way before, and at last he walked unsteadily out of the hotel and up through the crowded streets to Hyde Park. All the drunks go there, he thought. I'm not drunk, but I've tried, and I want to be with all the other drunks.

He found a spot free of drunks and lovers and shouting children, and lay down on the grass. Suddenly he didn't want to be with the other drunks, but to be alone. He lay flat on his back, his head pillowed on his hat, staring up at the clouds drifting across the sky. He could see nothing but the sky, but he was aware of the city all about him.

*   *   *

And why am I thinking about it? Greg thought. What do I care about its future or its streets or its pretty girls? I'm thinking about it only because I don't want to think about Sarah, the prettiest of all its girls. She came suddenly back to him, and then all at once he was drunk.

He lay in a stupor, tears running down his cheeks, and the forgetfulness he had been seeking had now come. People passed him by, looking at him disapprovingly, and none of them had pity. A bird perched on the toe of his boot and deposited its droppings on his gaiter. A dog came sniffing at him, then trotted on its way, disdainful and uncaring. The city had turned its back on him.

Dimly he was aware of someone sitting down beside him, talking to him, touching his pockets, but he had no way of telling who it was nor of speaking to them. A mumble fell out of him, but he had no idea what he'd been trying to say. Then the city fell in on him and the forgetfulness was complete.

When he woke he was in the back of a truck, and his right eye was swollen and painful. It was some time before he realised where he was, then he sat up and said he wanted to be sick.

A voice above him yelled, "Pull up, Les! The bastard wants to be sick!"

The truck came to a stop, someone helped him out, and he was violently ill in the gutter. Then he climbed back into the truck, he heard a gate or door slam, and the truck started off again. He sat for a while with his head in his hands, feeling the lump over his eye, then he straightened up and looked out the back of the truck. He was looking at the receding roadway through a screen of heavy wire.

"Are we off to the pound?" he said. "Is this the RSPCA cart?"

"Bloody funny." He turned and there was a big broken-nosed military policeman sitting opposite him. "A night in the cooler will knock some of the funniness outa you."

"That's all I need now," Greg said. "A night in gaol."

"You'll get it," said the MP.

Greg felt the lump over his eye. "How did I get this?"

"I give it to you. Any complaints?"

"None at all," said Greg. "As a shiner, it feels like a good job."

"Bloody funny," said the MP.

It was dark by the time the truck pulled up. Greg was pushed out through the wire gate by the broken-nosed provost. Another provost appeared out of the darkness and grabbed him by the arm, twisting it sharply up behind his back.

"No tricks like you played in the park, mug," the provost said. "Or you get the works."

"For Christ's sake, go easy!" Greg felt his arm was being torn from its socket. "I'm just a peaceful drunk. There's no need for standover stuff!"

The two provosts said nothing, but hustled him across the dark yard and into a room that at first looked like the office of a police station. Bars were on the windows and notices covered the walls. A warrant officer sat at a desk reading a copy of *Man*, and in a corner a corporal was seated in front of a switchboard, slicing an apple with a jackknife and reading an evening paper propped up against the switchboard in front of him. A barrier separated the sergeant major and the corporal from the rest of the room, which was bare but for three chairs lined along a wall. Some rifles hung by their slings from a hatrack, and something that could have been a straitjacket was tossed in one corner. The room had no look of comfort or welcome: it was designed to discourage visitors from coming again. On the wall above the sergeant major's head, like a picture of Justice, a little fly-spattered and dusty, was a photograph of General Sir Thomas Blamey.

"Well." The sergeant major took a last look at the pneumatic girls in *Man* and put the magazine face down on the desk. "Another drunken defender of our shores?"

"Drunk and resisting arrest," said the provost who held Greg's arm. "We picked him up in Hyde Park and he kept slinging punches all the way across to the truck."

"Me?" Greg said, then flinched as the provost twisted his arm. "Jesus, look out, you'll break it!"

"You should speak only when you're spoken to, sergeant. That's how you'd have it with the men under you, wouldn't you?" The sergeant major had a heavy blue-shaven face with a black moustache and dark blood-shot eyes. He had a trick of flicking his tongue over his teeth before he spoke, so that everything he said sounded cynical and disbelieving. "I suppose you really are a sergeant?"

"Am I supposed to speak now?" Greg said, and instantly realised his mistake: his arm was given another sharp twist.

"Let him go, Les," the sergeant major said. The provost let go Greg's arm, and Greg began to massage his elbow and shoulder. "Yes, you may speak now, soldier. *Are* you a sergeant, a drunken bum like you? And what's your name and Army number?"

"Lance sergeant Morley, G.W.," Greg said, and gave his Army number.

"Have a look at his pay book, Harry," the sergeant major said.

The broken-nosed provost went through Greg's pockets and came up with nothing. "Hasn't got a thing on him, except a dirty handkerchief."

"Come off it — " Greg said, and the broken-nosed provost slapped him across the mouth. Greg tasted blood and suddenly his temper blew up. He brought his fist up in a swing that would have hospitalised the broken-nosed provost had it landed. But the provost neatly parried it, stepped in and drove at Greg's stomach with a fist that seemed to have the weight and hardness of a rock. Greg went down, gasping for air.

"Pick him up, Harry," the sergeant major said, without rising from his chair. "And watch those slaps across the mouth. We don't want any broken teeth littering the floor."

Greg straightened up, his stomach sore, and looked at the broken-nosed provost. "I should have recognised you. Harry Delvico, isn't it? You always could only beat blokes smaller than you."

"Bloody funny. You want more of the same?" The ex-heavyweight boxer raised his fist, but first cocked an eye at the sergeant major. He had never been a top-line fighter, but because the country had been sadly lacking in good heavyweights for years, he had managed to get more fights than he was worth.

"That's enough for a while, Harry," the sergeant

major said, then looked at Greg. "There's nothing in your
pockets, soldier. And don't imply that the boys have
frisked you. If you've lost anything, then it happened
before you were picked up." Greg then remembered the
voice talking to him just before he had lapsed into un-
consciousness, and the hands feeling his pockets; but the
damage was done now and these provosts wouldn't be interested. "Let's have a look at your meat tags, soldier."

Greg undid his collar, felt inside for the thin chain that
should be around his neck, then grinned sheepishly.
"They're hanging on the handle of the shower at home.
I'm always leaving them around."

"Yes, we all do that, don't we?" The sergeant major
felt inside the collar of his own tunic and pulled out the
red and grey tabs on a length of tape. "I've got mine.
How about you, Harry? Les?" He looked over his
shoulder at the corporal munching on his apple. "And
you, Stan?"

"Never without 'em," said the corporal. "Army regulations say never take 'em off."

"There you are, soldier. Everyone has their meat tags
but you." The sergeant major flicked his tongue over his
teeth and looked up at Greg with one eyebrow raised.
"And you're the one that needs them most."

"Probably a deserting bastard," said the provost called
Les, and thumped Greg under the ribs. "How long have
you been AWL, soldier?"

"For Christ's sake, let's quit this play-acting," Greg
said, and got another thump, this time in the kidneys. He
kept the gasp of pain in his mouth and remained silent.
But for the taste of blood on his lips and the pain that now
seemed to be spreading right through him, this could be a
dream, or a military version of delirium tremens brought
on by getting drunk in uniform. After a while he said,
"Look, my name is Morley. Lance sergeant Gregory

William Morley, and my Army number is — " He gave his number and his unit.

The sergeant major flicked his tongue over his teeth again. "Sergeant Morley, eh? Where'd you grab that from? Don't you think we read the papers, too?"

"Where's your VC ribbon?" said the broken-nosed provost, Harry Delvico, the ex-heavyweight who could only beat smaller men than himself. "Don't tell us that's home, too, with your meat tags?"

Greg nodded, and the four provosts laughed. Harry Delvico slapped his thigh and his great battered face looked as if it would split with the roar of laughter that came out of it. The corporal choked on a piece of apple and had to cough it into a waste basket. Even the sergeant major relaxed his cynical mood and enjoyed himself. Greg looked at the four of them, hating them more than he had ever hated anyone in his life before, even the Germans or the Italians or the Vichy French or the Japs he still had to face, but he said nothing. His body still ached from the blows it had received, and he had learned his lesson.

"You look like spending more than a night in the cooler," Harry Delvico said. "You gunna have some trouble, soldier, proving who you are."

"Have you ever been in Holdsworthy, soldier?" the sergeant major said. "They tell me it's not as bad as the detention barracks in Jerusalem, but it's pretty bad." Then he sat forward quickly in his chair. "What's the matter?"

"I'm going to be sick," Greg said. The pain of his eyes, the fist in his stomach, the beer still left in his belly, hit him with a rush. He turned quickly and spun out of the room and was sick in the darkness of the yard. Harry Delvico stood by him, then when he had finished grabbed his arm again and pushed him back into the room.

"You'll clean that up before you get to sleep," Delvico said, and gave his arm a twist. "You'll be bloody sorry you ever got pissed, sport."

"Get him a bucket and a mop, Les," the sergeant major said. "Then we'll lock him up for the night."

"Wait a minute!" Greg felt his arm twisted again, but he was beyond pain now. "My wife isn't on the phone, but one of our officers is. Get him — "

"Shut up," Harry Delvico said, and twisted the arm further up Greg's back. "We've had enough of you for tonight."

Greg was almost crying now, but he kept on. "His name is Vern Radcliffe. He lives at Coogee. It's an FX number. Get him. Get him, for Christ's sake!" Delvico twisted the arm, his broken-nosed face shining with sweat and sadism; and Greg suddenly screamed and went limp.

"The bastard's fainted," Delvico said, and dropped Greg to the floor. He stood looking down at the limp bloodied heap at his feet. "Some of these —— oughta never joined the Army. Always making trouble for themselves and everyone else."

"Do you think we'd better call this bloke Radcliffe?" said the corporal.

"Why?" said the provost named Les.

"Well, just in case. What if he did turn out to be this cove Morley he claims to be?"

"This bum?" said the sergeant major and looked over his desk and down at the inert form of Greg. He flicked his tongue over his teeth with a loud sound. "Does *that* looked like a VC winner?"

"No-o." The corporal hadn't wanted to be a provost in the first place, but he would never have got two stripes in another unit and he needed the extra money. "But maybe this Radcliffe will come and identify him. Christ, it may take us a week to get this bloke to give us his real name."

"That's a point. See if Radcliffe is in the book and give him a ring." The sergeant major gestured to Harry Delvico and Les, and picked up his copy of *Man*, already halfway back to the overblown girls and the self-consciously naughty jokes. "Lock him up, and when he comes around give him an Aspro."

More than an hour passed before Vern Radcliffe arrived. Greg recovered consciousness just after he had been put in the cell, but he had lain quietly, glad of the respite from the thugs in the outer office. Once or twice one of the provosts came in to look at him, but he closed his eyes and breathed heavily as he had heard other drunks breathing in their sleep. They had left him alone and at last Vern had arrived.

Harry Delvico came to the door of the cell and swung it open. "Righto, on your feet! There's a Lieutenant Radcliffe our here says he'll have a look at you. We'll see how your story stands up now."

Greg got painfully off the stretcher on which he had been lying and followed Delvico down the hall. He stared at the thick neck in front of him and felt an almost over-powering urge to leap at it and wind a throttling arm about it. But sick and hazy though he was, he knew that Delvico was only walking ahead of him to tempt him into such foolishness, so that there would be one last excuse for indulging in another beating. Greg restrained himself and followed the ex-heavyweight into the brightly-lit office.

"God Almighty, Greg!" Vern's good-natured face was suddenly stiff with concern. "What's happened?"

"I ran into the Gestapo," Greg said, and didn't think he had ever been so happy to see anyone as he was to see

Vern. "We made a mistake, Vern. They're not only in Germany, they've got a branch here."

The sergeant major ignored Greg. "Do you know this man, sir?"

"Of course," said Vern, and looked at the four provosts with contempt wide open on his face. "He's Lance Sergeant Greg Morley, VC. He's a section sergeant in my company, and he's on eight days' disembarkation leave which doesn't terminate till ten hundred hours next Monday. What's the charge against him?"

"There won't be any charge, sir," the sergeant major said, and ran his tongue over his teeth, but nervously this time: "There's been a misunderstanding. He had no papers at all, not even his meat tags, and we've been having a lot of trouble lately with soldiers going AWL —— "

"Soldiers will always go AWL," said Vern, and it was the first time Greg had ever heard his voice rasp with such anger. "You'll never stop them, treating them *this* way." He turned to Greg. "Let's get some fresh air, Greg. This place smells like a concentration camp."

The provosts said nothing as the two men walked out of the office. At the door Greg stopped and looked back at the four big unmoving figures. Then very deliberately he filled his mouth and spat into the centre of the floor.

Outside in the yard Vern said, "The bastards! I didn't believe it could happen —"

"It happened, all right," Greg said. "I've just had a taste of what to expect if we lose the war."

"Dinah passed on the message. I was over visiting her mother at Hurstville. That's why I took so long to get here. We were just in the middle of dinner. Have you had anything to eat?"

"Not since lunch time. And I'm hungry. I could even eat a slice of provost."

"Where's Sarah?"

Greg hesitated, then said, "She's staying the night at her mother's. I don't get on well with the old lady and —"

They were out in the street now and Vern was unlocking the doors of his car. "You'd better come home with me. Dinah can give you a meal, then I'll drive you over home. You'd better have a bath at our place, too, and we'll put a dressing on that eye. And one last thing. I don't know how you got into this bother originally, but I don't think we'll let it go any further than the three of us. You, me and Dinah. Oh, and Sarah. Those provosts will keep their traps shut. If you were an ordinary soldier, I'd have an inquiry started into how those bastards operate. But you're not an ordinary soldier. You're a VC winner and you've been drunk — I can smell it on you — and whatever the provosts did to you, people don't like to hear about drunken VC winners. They like their heroes above reproach. So the whole thing finishes tonight. OK?"

"OK," said Greg, and settled his aching body back into the soft leather of the car seat. "It's good to know a man has friends in the world."

Part 3
In the Middle East

Far from the battle as his bones are laid
Crete will remember him. Remember well,
Mountains of Crete, the Second Field Brigade!

Say Crete, and there is little more to tell
Of muddle tall as treachery, despair
And black defeat resounding like a bell;

But bring the magnifying focus near
And in contempt of muddle and defeat
The old heroic virtues still appear.

Australian blood where hot and icy meet
(James Hogg and Lermontov were of his kin)
Lie still and fertilise the fields of Crete.

John Manifold
from "The Tomb of Lt John Learmonth, AIF"

ERIC LAMBERT

Victory at Tobruk

In this extract from Eric Lambert's The Twenty Thousand Thieves, *members of the Australian Ninth Division have taken up their defensive positions on the perimeter of the North African town of Tobruk to await the attack by General Rommel's Africa Corps. (The historical attack began on 13 April, Easter Sunday, 1941.)*

IT was Easter Sunday night. Once again the Nazis had withdrawn out of sight. Nowhere had they pierced the Australian defences.

The night was gentle and bright. Across the parapet Dick looked out over the stretch of desert where he had seen Nazis scrambling for three whole days. Their corpses were vague lumps on the stony ground. Under the starlight they had lost their meaning. So far the slaughter had seemed mainly an impersonal thing fought at a range of a few hundred yards. You could not discern the features of the man you killed. You pulled the trigger and a figure fell, like a puppet that had lost its strings. It was amazing how soon you ceased to be moved at the sight of a corpse. He felt glad for his encounter with the corpse at Mersa Matruh, for he believed that his thoughts on that day had prepared him for this and what else there was to come.

*   *   *

A few minutes afterwards the barrage began.

As they cowered deep in their trenches it seemed only a matter of time before they would be shattered. It did not seem possible that as much as a square inch of ground would be spared by the storm of thunderous metal that now fell upon them. The still, white desert that Andy and Dick had looked across only a few minutes ago now heaved in fountains of dust and smoke; shuddered, roared, and screamed a thousand times in a second. On either side of the trench the earth was convulsed. It leaped and trembled, threw them flat, deafened and mindless. Sand poured in on them from the ruined parapet.

Further along there had been a direct hit. Shrilly, a man called:

"Christ! Oh, Christ!"

Another voice appealed for a stretcher bearer. The wounded man howled unspeakably. Again the voice pleaded:

"For God's sake! His inside's pouring out!"

Shrilling metal that sang to a hideous background of detonations:

Crump! Zeeeee! Crump! Zeeeee!

Zeeeeeeeeeee!!!

Flashes that lanced at the seething smoke.

Dimly the cries of men.

Crash! Crash! Crump! Zeeeeeeee!

The sounds were thinning. It became possible to count them. With a last rumble the bombardment ceased.

The sudden quiet was wondrous. Plainly, a voice was heard whimpering like a child. Then the night air began to hum and rattle. It was the sound of approaching tanks. Soon they loomed up a hundred yards away, black and gigantic, lurching and clanking, gathering speed as they bore down. This time there was no doubt about their purpose.

They came straight through the wire like a great dark wave. The roar of their engines was all round; then they were on the infantry. The side of one of them loomed up near Dick and Andy. They cried hoarsely to each other and grovelled in the bottom of their pit. The world was blotted out as the tank passed above, half-burying them in sand.

The enormous black shapes were everywhere and right behind them were hordes of Nazis, pouring in on the shell-dazed Australians. Moonlight glinted on a sea of bobbing helmets. As Dick lurched to his feet a strange voice cried and a boot and the butt of a rifle came down past him. He brought his own rifle up quickly and the bayonet found flesh and creaked on bone. The Nazi croaked and clawed at his groin. Dick pulled the trigger and his rifle sprang free. He fired into another shape on the edge of the pit. It toppled on him, bearing him down. It was already a corpse, gushing blood from the throat, but he fought, terror-stricken, to get free of it as though it were still alive, kicking and pushing it aside. He reached his feet again firing without aiming at each shape he saw. Andy was out of the ruined trench, his rifle at his hip, three dead Nazis around him. Still they were coming through the shattered wire. They lurched, doubled, screamed and fell as the Bren guns poured a hail of bullets into them. Andy slammed another clip into his magazine as a Nazi came at him, his gun spurting. Andy sprang aside and met him in the face with the butt of his rifle. Dooley, still in his pit, hugged his Bren gun and exchanged bursts with a Spandau fifty yards away. Crane stood firing his pistol calmly into the mass of enemy. Out of the corner of his eye Dick saw Lucas empty a burst from his Tommy gun into a Nazi crouched to throw a grenade. Then, without knowing it, he had a grenade in his own hand, pulled out the pin and hurled it into an approaching knot of the enemy. Three fell, another staggered on blindly, hand to a bloody face. Dick ran forward and bayoneted him in the belly; it felt as soft as butter. Something hit his foot hard, finging it upward, out of control. When he got up again only the top of his right boot remained and his foot tingled dully.

The Nazis were thinning out. Andy was on his belly wriggling towards the Spandau. His hand came up as he threw a grenade. It burst in front of the gun and after the explosion a Nazi ran towards them crying hoarsely, his hands above his head. Andy rose deliberately to his feet and shot him through the stomach. Another Nazi began to run. Dooley arose in his trench, Bren at hip, and fired a burst into him. Tommy loomed behind Dooley and fired into the head of a wounded Nazi writhing near the gun. Lucas ran across in front of them, stood on the edge of a trench and fired downward into it. The Nazis still on their feet wavered, turned and commenced to run. Whooping, the Australians clambered out after them.

"Back to your posts!" yelled Crane.

"Back!" cried Lucas waving his arms frantically towards their pits.

A hundred yards to their flank a Spandau began to fire and tracers cut brilliant lines in the air. Away to their left the battle still raged. Out of the smoke to their rear came more Australians with a lieutenant leading them.

"What platoon's this?"

"Six."

"Where's Seven?"

"Over there."

They ran off towards Seven Platoon's position. The lieutenant called over his shoulder before they disappeared: "Seven Platoon's been overrun. Most of them dead!"

"Let's go and help 'em," said Tommy.

"Stay where you are, everybody!" rapped out Lucas. "Back to your own pits. Clear them and prepare for the next attack."

At platoon headquarters Percy Gribble tremblingly guarded seven Nazi prisoners. Dick and Andy hauled the dead Nazis from their pit and shovelled out the sand that the tank had pressed in on it. Crane checked their casualties hurriedly: three dead, seven wounded. Four of the wounded were walking wounded, the other three lay on stretchers near company headquarters.

A bullet had grazed Andy's temple singeing a furrow of hair. The bullet that had torn Dick's boot off had not entered the flesh, but his foot was painful to walk on. He hobbled over to their pit and sank down beside Andy. A delicious sleepiness crept over him. He shook his head and forced his eyes open. Slowly the lids closed, against his will.

"Do you realise," Andy was saying, "that there's a fleet of tanks behind us on their way to the town?"

"Yes," said Dick dully. "What about it?"

"What about it!" exclaimed Andy. "I just hope they don't come back this way — that's all."

"Don't care if they do."

Dick opened his eyes. Had he said those words or merely thought them?

The voice of Sergeant Lucas brought him awake:

"There's movement out front. I want a three-man patrol."

"I'll go," said Andy, rising.

"Me, too," said Dick, also rising.

"Don't be a bloody fool," Lucas told him. "You'll cut your foot to pieces." He grinned at Andy. "How is this young bastard?"

"He's out on his feet," replied Andy.

"Get down to company headquarters and see if you can get another boot."

Dick hobbled off. At company headquarters he found Henry Gilbertson.

"Hullo, young Brett! You too?"

"No, sir. Just got my boot shot off. I was sent to see if I could get a new one."

Henry sighed. "Boot shot off! Worse things have happened tonight. Come down here."

He led Dick down into a spacious dugout, and pulled a pair of boots from a heap of gear in a corner.

"Right or left?"

"Right, sir."

He watched Dick as he tried the boot on.

"Fit?"

"Good enough, sir."

"Had it?"

"Just about."

"Better get back before the shit starts to fly again."

"Thanks."

As Dick went to go, Henry touched his shoulder briefly and said:

"Those Huns outnumbered us five to one. You fellers are the salt of the earth. I'm proud to be with you. Believe me."

Dick was too surprised and confused to answer, but as he limped back he found his tiredness leaving him. He felt proud too.

Two hours later the Nazis attacked again. Met with a torrent of machine-gun fire, most of them died on the wire. The survivors turned and ran, and the Second X went after them. Before dawn came a few more tanks were seen to speed through gaps in the defences.

The sun came up redly, climbed the sky and, as it grew brighter, pitilessly revealed the thickly scattered corpses of the Nazis. At dawn the Australians stood-to but there were no further attacks. Away to the left flank of the Second X could be heard the sound of machine-gun fire. But there was not a live Nazi in sight, except for those being herded back to the prisoner of war cage.

*   *   *

The reports that reached Colonel Fitzroy over the field telephone that night all indicated victory. The Nazis had everywhere been repulsed. His elation generated a fierce energy. Pomfret knew he was seeing him at his best, and was glad.

In the early hours of Monday morning thirty odd German tanks were far inside the perimeter and making for the town. The telephone hummed with reports of their progress. Just before first light the colonel and his staff left the underground headquarters and manned emergency trenches on a mound immediately above. Standing together in a pit Fitzroy and Pomfret scanned the paling horizon. Nearby on their left flank a troop of twenty-five pounder guns was waiting to engage the tanks over open sights.

Dawn found several tanks feeling their way along the skyline. As the land lay revealed they moved into formation and swung towards the Second X positions. More of the ugly dark shapes came over the skyline. In all the morning the only sound to be heard was that of the tanks.

They seemed to come on incredibly slowly. They looked monstrous, deliberate, irresistible. The whole world seemed to be tensed for the clash that was to come. The engines had swelled to a steady roar. For the first time in his life the colonel thought about death.

He glanced at Pomfret, but Pomfret's features said nothing. They were just as they had always been. A sense of unreality, a strange resignation came over the colonel.

"Any moment now," said Pomfret with calm callousness, as though the man beside him had asked a question aloud.

Hardly had he spoken when the guns let go.

"There they are," Andy told Dick. "They're trying to get out again."

A few hundred yards away on their left Nazi tanks were making back for the perimeter and their own lines beyond. Two of them stopped and poured smoke as two-pounder shells struck them. One of them turned and its cannon flashed as it engaged the crew of the anti-tank gun. With a scream of steel it scored a direct hit on the two-pounder. Camouflage blown away, its shield shattered, the little gun lay smoking, its barrel tipped up in the air, a dead Australian slumped next to it. Over the skyline came two British tanks with guns crashing. The Mark IVs made swiftly for gaps in the wire. One was halted by a shell from a British tank; the others disappeared and the Australians stood up in their pits and jeered them outwards.

Andy chuckled. "I wonder how they felt when no infantry or artillery followed them in? All on their lonesome, with two-pounders everywhere and twenty-fives firing over open sights!"

Comparative quiet came over the battlefield. Dick looked out over the desert with its littered corpses, shattered wire, and wrecked tanks. They no longer meant anything to him. His mouth hung half open, his bloodshot eyes throbbed dully, his limbs seemed clamped into immobility. Stupid with exhaustion, he watched the Mark IVs disappear. Inwardly, he moaned for sleep like a child. Sleep . . . beautiful, blank, dreamless sleep . . . Oh, to be mindless and feel nothing!

*   *   *

A few days later the radios were hailing the victory of Tobruk. The announcers told of the tanks destroyed, the enemy killed or captured. For the first time on land the Nazis had been defeated, they told the world. Their impersonal voices could say little about the men who had won the victory.

The voices could not describe them as they washed the dust from their beards and shaved, or as they rebuilt the trenches crushed by shellfire or Nazi tanks; as they tenderly cleaned and oiled their weapons; as they took a mouthful from a water bottle or munched their bully and biscuits. They were not there to see a figure, as it watched out over the desert in the phantasmal glare, turn suddenly sideways then away again, as if he had half expected to find his dead mate still standing there. Only the soldiers knew the pain of their bitter, yearning images: of a wife or a girl; of things like children, gardens, dogs, pubs, beaches in the sun.

From Europe the radio voice of Haw Haw taunted them: "Come out, rats! Come out with your hands up!"

But the name given them in contempt they accepted and kept. They became proud of it:

The Rats of Tobruk.

JOHN HETHERINGTON

On the Run in Greece

Hugh Roberts, the hero of John Hetherington's novel The
Winds are Still, *is an Australian soldier on the run after the
fall of Greece to the invading German armies during April
1941. With five companions — one Australian and four
British — he has made his way across the Taygetos mountains to the Gulf of Laconia, where he hopes to find a boat
that will take him to Crete. The party's guide is a Greek
youth, Kosta, who has led them to a small chapel where they
have spent the night.*

IT was early afternoon when Roberts woke. He rolled
over, grunting as he felt cramp biting at his muscles.
His flesh was sore after pressing for hours on to the
stones of the floor. The chapel was so small that none of
the sleepers could move without disturbing one of the
others, and his shoulder touched against the man next to
him. It was McGurk, and he woke and lifted his head and
stared round the chapel, rubbing his hand through his
hair.

"Oh, Christ!" he said. "I was having a wonderful
dream. About a redhead in Cairo." McGurk dug sleep
from his eyes, yawning. "Maybe there's something in

dreams. I'd like to think I was going to catch up with that redhead again.''

"You're cracked, Duke," Roberts said. "Don't you ever take anything seriously?"

"Some things," McGurk said. "Lots of things." He looked round him. "Let's wake the others. It's time we talked about what we're going to do."

Roberts and McGurk shook the others and, one by one, they woke. The sun was shining outside, but little light penetrated through the skylight, and they sat huddled against the walls looking at each other in the dusk inside the chapel.

"First thing we've got to do is explore a little," Daly said. "We've got to know what's around us."

"You'd better leave that to me," Kosta told them. "Anyway, at the beginning. It's no use you wandering round and running into somebody and not being able to talk to them."

Roberts said, "No, Kosta. It's time you headed for home. You can't stay around with us."

Kosta grinned. "My father told me to stay with you as long as you needed me."

"You can't," Roberts said. "You bloody little fool, don't you know what would happen if the Jerries picked you up with us?"

"I know. They'd hang me or shoot me, I suppose. What about it?"

"This about it. You're not staying. Your family's risked enough to help us."

Kosta shook his head. "You can't send me back till I'm ready to go. That's all there is to it."

Roberts felt anger and admiration for Kosta struggling inside him. He believed that Kosta had already gone too far in imperilling his life; but he knew the hopelessness of trying to move any Boudaris from following out a decision once it had been taken. He looked at the others. Daly lifted his brows, McGurk shrugged, Blain and Tyler and Clunies sat with sober faces.

"All right, damn you," Roberts said. "If you won't go, you won't go, but I'm against your staying."

"That's fine," Kosta said. "I'm going out for a walk."

They watched him arrange his clothing and pat his hair into place with his hands, then walk to the door of the chapel and open it quickly and step out into the sunlight. They had a split second glimpse of the headland in the moment that the door was open, then they were shut in once more like prisoners in a cramped cell, with only the square of sky they could see through the skylight to indicate that there was a world beyond the stone walls about them.

Kosta was back sooner than they had expected him. He came into the chapel quietly and closed the door behind him and stood for a moment with his back pressed against it.

"Find out anything?" McGurk asked him.

Kosta left the door and came and squatted down among them. The light from the skylight in the roof was on his face, and they noticed for the first time that there was a dark swelling bruise below his left eye and a fresh cut on his cheekbone.

"You're hurt," Roberts said.

Kosta looked at him, and his face was tight and hard and white, except where the darkness of the bruise spread out under the skin.

"Not here," he said, touching the bruise. "Not my face, but inside. This is nothing."

"What happened?"

"I was going along the road and some Italian soldiers in a truck pulled up and wanted to see my papers. I got out the papers and handed them over, but I suppose the

Italians didn't like the way I looked at them. It's hard to hide your feelings all the time. The sergeant had the papers and he handed them back with his left hand and hit me with his right. There must have been a ring on his finger. He said, 'There, you little Greek mongrel dog,' and they got into the truck and drove away laughing and left me lying on the road." Kosta looked up and round at their faces. "Italians!" he said. "They're worse than Huns!"

"Let's see your face," Roberts said, but Kosta waved him away, saying again, "This is nothing."

He went on. "They did me a good turn, really. There was a man working in a field along the road a way, and he saw it all and came along to me after they'd gone and brushed the dirt off me and talked. He said, 'It's like that all the time now. The Italians couldn't beat us, but they're getting their revenge now.' I said, 'Why don't we do something?' and he laughed and said what was I doing about it, and I said I'd do anything I could to spite the fascists. He looked at me pretty hard then and said if that was how I felt I'd better meet him and some other men in the village tonight because they were organising to do something."

"There's a village near here?" It was McGurk who asked it.

Kosta nodded. "Under a mile away. It's called Loutraki, and this is the Headland of Loutraki. The cliffs fall away into a cove a little way along, and that's where the village is."

"Boats?"

"Just a minute. No big boats. Nothing big enough to take you to Crete. Only rowboats, but if there's rowboats there may be bigger boats calling there once in a while."

"How did you find out all this?"

"From this man I talked to. Grivas, his name is. I told

him" — his eyes went quickly from face to face, looking for a reaction — "I told him I had friends who wanted a boat. A biggish boat, I said, for a long cruise." He sensed their doubt of his wisdom in having talked to a stranger, and he went on, his voice rising a little, "When it's like this, you have to take a chance, you have to trust someone. I think Grivas is on the level."

McGurk said, "We trusted Embiricos and look where that got us."

"I know. But Grivas isn't Embiricos. Grivas looks at your eyes when he's talking."

Roberts said, "It's all right, Kosta. You're right, you have to trust someone, you have to start somewhere. Tell us about the village."

"I didn't go into the village. One thing, there isn't an Italian post there. The Italians send a patrol in two or three times a week. That's all. I asked Grivas if they'd had any bother round here about escaping British soldiers, and he said no. He said some British soldiers were caught in a cave about twelve kilometres along the coast a week back, but he hadn't heard of any others since right after the British army left."

Daly looked at Roberts. "What do you think we ought to do, Roberts?"

Roberts pulled at his underlip. "I think we ought to see this friend of Kosta's. It may be a plant, but it may be genuine. There's only one way to find out."

"All right. I'm with you."

Roberts looked at Daly and shook his head. He said, "No, Daly. Not you. We discussed this before, remember? The time I went to see Embiricos? Your skin's too fair. I'd never think you were a Greek. Even sunburned, you're still too fair for a Greek." He looked round at the others. Any of them could have passed for a Greek, with the possible exception of Clunies, whose bony facial structure was not characteristic. "McGurk and I," Roberts said. "We could get away with it."

Daly said, "You want me to miss out on all the fun. I'm the senior officer here. I've got a right to go."

"Don't be an idiot," McGurk said suddenly. "Rank doesn't matter when there's six of you in a hole like we're in. You'll bust up the chances of all of us if you're sticky about this, Daly."

Daly grunted, but he saw the force of McGurk's argument, and he sat in silence, tapping his teeth, while Kosta said:

"Grivas told me to meet him and the others at the coffee shop. I told him I mightn't come alone."

Roberts's conscience was still bothering him about Kosta.

"I'd be happier if you were out of it, Kosta," he said. "Today you got bashed. Next time it might be more than bashed. I don't like it. I don't think your father would like it."

"My father would only care if I left you to work things out for yourselves. Of course, I'm coming. There's a ten o'clock curfew, but that will give us plenty of time."

They ate sparingly that evening. Marika had given them all the food they could carry over the mountains, but their supplies were beginning to run low and none of them knew when they would be able to find more food.

Roberts felt excitement ticking away inside him like a clock as dusk fell. They were burning no light in the chapel, but the light of the early moon came through the skylight and etched a pale square on the floor and when they could see the stars through the skylight they made ready to go.

"Arms?" McGurk asked.

Roberts considered. "I don't know . . . All right, then. Pistols."

He assured himself that his own pistol was strapped inside his shirt. The hard bulge against his side gave him a feeling of security. McGurk did not have a pistol, but he borrowed the Luger that Daly had taken from one of the dead Germans in the cellar of the farmhouse, and tucked it into the waistband of his trousers where it was hidden by the hang of his coat.

Roberts and McGurk and Kosta let themselves out into the night. A breeze was blowing in from the sea, and Roberts filled his lungs with fresh air. It was like an intoxicant after the thick atmosphere in the chapel and he felt light-headed, as though he had been drinking wine.

They moved back along the headland, not talking, their feet whispering over the grass. Where the headland joined the cliff, Kosta turned to the right and struck off diagonally until he reached a beaten path. He led them along it, and presently they came to a sunken road, three or four feet below the level of the land around it. It was a fairly wide road, with a rough, stony surface. It led them down a gentle slope, and they had not gone far when Roberts saw, in the hollow ahead of them, a scatter of lights, and he knew that these must mark the village of Loutraki.

The slope ended and they reached level ground, and the road wandered back towards the sea and the lights of the village. They followed the road in among the cottages and down to the waterfront where there was a stone quay and a few boats were moored. There were two or three darkened shops facing the quay and one shop with an open door which spilled light out on to the cobbles. They went up to the lighted doorway and looked inside. The room was small, with a dozen tables crowded together. Not more than half the tables were occupied, mostly by knots of two or three men who sat over their coffee or liquor, smoking and talking.

Kosta said, "I can't see Grivas," but he stepped through the doorway of the coffee shop, and Roberts and McGurk followed him in.

There was a bar counter, and an enormously fat man, with a heavy black moustache and greasy black curling hair, sat on a high stool behind it, his heavy arms folded on the counter, his eyes staring without interest at the wall on the other side of the smoky room. He spoke as Kosta came level with the bar, and Kosta went across to him and they talked for a few seconds, and then the fat man jerked his head towards a narrow wooden stairway beside the bar counter, leading to the floor above. Kosta spoke a few more words, and then led the way towards the stairs. Roberts glanced quickly at the man behind the counter as they passed him and met the long, shrewd glance of his dark eyes as they rested on him and McGurk. Then they were climbing the stairs and presently they passed through a door at the top into a short, narrow corridor.

There were three doors opening out of the corridor, and Kosta halted at the second door and rapped on the panels. A voice inside spoke in Greek, and Kosta turned the handle of the door and they passed through into a room where four men sat around a plain deal table on which an oil lamp burned. Three of the men were young, but the fourth was older, about forty. He had a brown, lined face and a head like a ball, with the black hair clipped down to the scalp, and wide, strong shoulders. He stood up and greeted Kosta, then lifted his eyes to the faces of Roberts and McGurk.

He spoke to Kosta, and Kosta told them, "He wants to see your papers. Your army papers, showing that you are British soldiers."

Roberts took out his brown-covered Australian army pay book and McGurk his RAF identity card and handed them to Grivas. He inspected them, turning them over in his hands, then nodded and handed them back. There were wooden chairs against the walls of the room, and Grivas and the others pulled up three of these and set them around the table, gesturing to Kosta and Roberts and McGurk to sit down. They did so, and then Grivas, his hands lying with knitted fingers on the table, began to speak. He spoke for a long time, his voice a monotonous burr of sound.

When he ceased speaking, Kosta said, "M. Grivas says he understands you want a boat big enough to carry you a long way. He says he doesn't know why you want it or where you want to go, and he doesn't want to know these things. He also says it's difficult to find a boat now because the Germans and Italians have seized many boats, but he may be able to do something in two or three days if you will have patience."

"Tell him we'll have patience," Roberts said.

Grivas listened while Kosta translated the words, then nodded. He spoke again and Kosta answered, and two or three times Roberts detected the name Loutraki. When Grivas sat back, Kosta turned to them and said, "M. Grivas promises to send or come himself to the chapel, as soon as he has news for us."

"I suppose you had to tell him where we're hiding out?" McGurk said.

Kosta shrugged. "We've got to trust him. He's trusting us. There's no other way."

He turned back to Grivas and the conversation started between them again, but neither had spoken more than a few sentences when a staccato buzz, repeated three times, broke in on their voices. Roberts was watching Grivas's face, and he saw it tighten and the lids draw down over the eyes, hooding them.

Grivas spoke quickly in a low voice, and two of the

young Greeks got up and went to a cupboard in the corner of the room and brought out glasses and a bottle of brandy.

Kosta said, "It's a signal from the man at the counter. He arranged with M. Grivas to buzz three times if there was danger."

The young Greeks hurriedly distributed the glasses and filled them. Grivas raised his glass, smiling slightly, his eyes studying Roberts and McGurk especially. They sipped the brandy, which was raw but warming. Roberts noted with annoyance that his hand was trembling a little. He was wondering if this were a trap. He remembered his own suspicions of the afternoon and Daly's doubts and the doubts of all the others that Kosta had been wise to place their lives in the hands of a Greek he had met casually on the road. He was conscious of the pressure of the revolver against his body, and he wondered how long it would take him to push his hand inside his coat and shirt and loosen the revolver and start shooting if this were a betrayal.

There was a tramp of feet on the wooden stairway leading up from the lower floor of the coffee shop and the sound of the door at the top of the stairs being flung open. Then the feet came tramping along the corridor, and the door of the room where they sat opened. Four soldiers in Italian uniform came into the room. They looked at the seven men who sat around the table, and one of them, wearing corporal's insignia on his uniform, asked a question. Grivas replied, standing up at the head of the table. He faced the Italians with dignity and without fear. His voice was level and his words fell unhurriedly into the quiet of the room. The corporal grunted in reply, then came round the table toward Grivas, stretching out a hand. Grivas fumbled inside his coat and took out a folded white paper. The Italian took the paper and unfolded it and held it down in the light of the lamp to read it, and Roberts could see that the paper bore at the top, above some typewritten lines, a heavy black embossed seal.

Roberts looked across at McGurk. McGurk was watching the Italian corporal, and Roberts could not catch his eye. He knew McGurk's temper, and he was afraid McGurk would do something which would bring disaster on them. He willed McGurk to look at him, to hold himself in. But McGurk continued to stare at the Italian.

Then a surprising thing happened. The corporal shrugged and handed the paper back to Grivas, who laughed and clapped him on the shoulder and reached out for the bottle and filled a glass to the brim and handed it to the Italian. The Italian took the glass and raised it and drained it, then set it down and swung about. He said a few words to the soldiers who accompanied him, and they followed him from the room.

Roberts felt his nerves and muscles slacken, like taut wires suddenly relaxed, as the door closed. He looked at the others, and saw Grivas holding up his hand for silence. Nobody spoke as the tramp of feet receded down the corridor and then descended the stairway. Grivas went to the door of the room and opened it and looked outside. Satisfied, he closed the door and came back to the table and poured himself a drink. He gulped it down and sat back in his chair again, the tightness gone from his face.

Kosta gave a grunting laugh. "Well, that was something. You should have heard that. M. Grivas told the corporal he was having a meeting of enthusiasts who want to form a Young Fascist League and that he's authorised by the Italian commandant to hold such meetings. The corporal didn't believe him, but M. Grivas had a paper signed by the Italian commandant, and the corporal had to believe that. It seems that M. Grivas has made the Italians believe he's a friend of theirs. So what could the corporal do after that but drink Il Duce's health and look pleasant?"

"He might have done a lot of things," McGurk said. "I'm only glad he didn't."

The buzzer, operated by the man behind the bar counter in the room below, sounded again, this time in one long blur of sound, and Grivas spoke to Kosta and Kosta told them:

"That means the Italians have gone. M. Grivas says the village is used to these visits by enemy patrols now. Nobody worries much now, but tonight it was awkward."

Roberts stood up and said to Kosta, "Will you tell M. Grivas we are thankful to him? Deeply thankful. We know the risk he's taking, and these friends of his, too."

Kosta translated the message, and Grivas talked briefly in reply, speaking to Kosta but looking at Roberts and McGurk in turn.

"He wishes me to say," Kosta told them, "that you have no need to be thankful to him, because this isn't a personal thing. He isn't doing it for you, but for the British, because the British fight the fascists. He wants you to know this."

They nodded, and then Kosta said, "It's almost nine. We ought to be going. There's only an hour to curfew."

"Before we go," Roberts said, "ask if he can help us with food."

Kosta nodded, and he spoke to Grivas, and Grivas listened and talked briefly to the young men at the table. Then he turned back to Kosta, and Kosta told Roberts and McGurk:

"He promises to bring food when he comes with news of the boat."

They nodded their thanks, and Grivas rose and stretch-ed out a hand, first to Roberts, then to McGurk. The three young men also shook hands with them, and one of the young men went across from the table and opened the door. They walked to the door and out into the corridor and heard the door close behind them, and they went down the narrow stairway into the coffee shop where the men still sat at the tables and the fat, black-moustached Buddha still perched behind the bar counter. He glanced across at them as they passed him on their way to the street, and he raised his brows almost imperceptibly but did not speak. They went out of the light into the darkness of the cobbled street and walked away from the quay where the boats swung at their moorings and back along the road they had come.

Roberts tried to stifle the small flame of hope that had begun to burn inside him. He knew that they were still far from getting a vessel that would carry them to Crete, that optimism now could be dangerous and illusory. But the flame continued to burn, warm and bright and steadfast.

RICHARD BEILBY

Retreat to Sphakia

Sergeant ("Gunner") Lewis and his platoon commander Lieutenant Whiteside are the two main characters of Richard Beilby's novel Gunner. *As members of the Australian Sixth Division, they are caught up in the allied retreat from Canea to the embarkation port of Sphakia during the closing phase of the Cretan campaign, at the end of May 1941. The character Yorgo is a Cretan who has lived in America and who speaks English like an American gangster of the Al Capone prohibition era.*

T HE platoon left the village without delay, making good time back to the bridge. The woman's body still floated in its reedy bourne but the men passed it with no more than a few incurious glances.

Gunner listened to the firing: it was no closer, no further away, but it seemed to have slackened. It came to him then that Crete had fallen and everybody who had survived thus far wanted more than ever to survive. Even the few bombers over Canea appeared in no hurry to press their spite, just lazing across a perfect sky, making somnolent sounds. Nearing the bridge he hustled from his place at the rear of the file and caught up with Whiteside, matching his pace to the man's stride.

Whiteside glanced at him, worry and impatience pinching his thin face.

"What is it, Sar'nt?"

"What about water, sir?"

"What about it?" Whiteside didn't look at him, just tramped, stolidly, his face set.

"This joint we're making for — what's it called? Sphakia? It's over the mountains you said. That's a long way. We ought to fill up here while we can."

Whiteside stumbled momentarily on the incline of the bridge, recovered his step and said curtly: "That won't be necessary, Sar'nt. The men can draw rations and water when we get back."

"Back where? Company headquarters?

"Of course. Where else did you think?"

"To Sphakia. You said it was every man for himself."

"I know what I said, Sar'nt. We've been recalled to headquarters and that's where we're going."

"I don't think that's such a hot idea, sir."

Gunner looked away, not wanting Whiteside to see his face: he saw that the flight of bombers had split up now, some of them wheeling widely. Behind him he heard the tramp of boots mounting the hump of the bridge, stamping a hollow quivering out of the tightly compressed stones: he hoped that the men hadn't heard what had been said. Then Whiteside's voice came to him, loaded with that Pommy inflection which he disliked.

"I'm not interested in your opinions, Sar'nt. We're obeying orders."

Like hell we are, Gunner thought furiously. We're playing good soldiers just to suit some shit-pot notion of yours. He tried to remember whether the Boy-Bastard had used the word "recalled" back there in the village but all that came back to him were the salient facts, "the battalion pulling out," "show finished", "generals got

out", "Sphakia", "the navy". Stuff Whiteside and his
military traditions. Now that the game was over the important thing was to get out. "Every man for himself."
That was plain enough. They were off the bridge now,
moving along the road, boots scuffling dryly. Gunner saw
that the bombers were swooping low over the trees but
they were too far away for him to make out what they
were after.

"Just what were those orders, sir?" he asked suddenly,
adding rather too respectfully, "If you don't mind my
asking."

"I do mind," Whiteside said stiffly, plumping his feet
down heavily as if he was trampling something
distasteful. "I resent it very much. It seems to me you're
questioning my decisions rather more than your rank
warrants."

"I'm sorry." Gunner's tone was hardly penitent. "But
don't you think it would be a good idea to take a look at
things before we go barging in?"

"And what does that imply?" Still Whiteside didn't
turn, merely presenting a haggard profile that resented
with all the jealousy of his class and military rank.

"Well —" Gunner drew a deep breath, choosing his
words carefully. "The way I see it, it would be an hour
since you got that signal and it would take a runner about
an hour to reach you, plus the hour it will take us to get
back to HQ. That's three hours. The way we've been
dog-dancing around lately anything could happen in that
time. The battalion could be gone by the time we get
back. You said they were pulling out right away. We
could be walking into strife for all we know."

Whiteside turned on him, smiling unpleasantly. "We'll
get to Sphakia in time if that's what's worrying you,
Sar'nt, but we'll get there as a military unit. We might be
retreating but we're not a rabble yet."

Gunner stiffened, glaring. "That's not what I meant and you know it — sir!" He came down hard on the "sir": Whiteside heard the challenge and reacted sharply.

"Sar'nt! This has gone far enough! I knew you were a barrack-room lawyer but I didn't think you were a defeatist. Now close up the rear and let me do the thinking."

Gunner held his ground and they continued to trudge shoulder to shoulder glaring at one another.

"Sir! If you're saying . . ."

"Sar'nt! I don't like your tone."

"And I don't like what you're trying to make out about me!"

"That's enough! I don't want to have to put you under arrest."

"Thanks for nothing!"

"Watch it or I'll have your stripes."

"That'll be a new experience!"

"Sar'nt Lewis, I'm ordering you to keep quiet. If you don't I'll charge you with disobeying an order in the face of the enemy."

"And I'll be glad to front up — if we ever get off this bloody island!"

"So that's it. You think because we've got to get out there's no more discipline."

"I think fuckall! You called me a defeatist!"

"Get back to your place! That's an order!"

Abruptly Gunner swung away. The army was too big, too experienced in disciplining men for one man to fight it. You had a hard job throwing any charge that had the phrase "in the face of the enemy" tacked on to it: that was a courtmartial offence. He would have saluted then, smartly sardonically, projecting his animosity at Whiteside but he heard the men talking excitedly and there was a familiar sound that swelled ominously.

"Sir," Father Dennis reported worriedly. "Aircraft right, heading this way!"

The plane was a Junkers, with its side-hatch open, flying so low that it looked as though its undercarriage would rake the trees.

Whiteside spun around, taking a couple of backward steps, yelling: "Take cover!" But already the file was breaking up, men diving for the ditch. Gunner slammed himself against a tree, keeping his face turned down: he heard scuffling sounds amongst the roots and guessed that it was Whiteside getting down. He felt a quiver of amusement that their argument should end like this. Then the plane was above him, cowing him with its sensation of colossal malevolence hunting him: one square tipped wing had dipped and a slight alteration in the engine note warned him that the thing was changing direction. Then through the backwash of sound, Whiteside's voice came, inordinately thin.

"Sar'nt! Look down there!" He was pointing, not with arm outstretched but cautiously, a finger aimed like a pistol over the mossy roots.

In front of them, in an open space where the ground sloped quite steeply to a small depression, a swastika flag had been laid out, its corners weighted with stones.

"Jesus Christ!"

Gunner sank to his haunches, appalled by the realisation that whoever had spread that flag could be watching him now, sights aligned on him. His flesh crawled and he balled himself as small as he could amongst the roots, fumbling the Tommy gun around, cocking it with his hand over the mechanism to muffle the snick. He held his breath, dreading a shot, hearing the plane buzzing around the edge of his consciousness while he stared into the declivity.

It wasn't large, just the sort of place which collected the run-off from winter rains, not marshy, yet with sufficient subsoil moisture to support thick grass and deter the not so greedy olives. On its other side the ground rose gently, thickly timbered, with that dark lupin-like growth which always flourished rankly under trees. The plane was far out now, still banked, holding to its circular course.

"See anything?" Whiteside whispered.

"Not yet, but they'll be down there. And they'll be a moral to be on to us by this."

"Not necessarily." Whiteside's voice was weirdly calm, disagreeing, stirring all the ghosts of past dissentions. Crouched shoulder to shoulder they argued softly.

"It wasn't there when we came past the first time."

"You mean nobody saw it, Sar'nt."

"Hell! Somebody would have spotted it."

"Nobody saw it this time — until now."

"We were watching the plane, that's why. It beats me why they haven't given us a burst before this."

"Perhaps they were like us, watching the plane. That's what the flag is for, isn't it — a supply drop?"

"Or to let their mate up there know not to bomb."

"There's nothing in the area worth bombing, only us."

"What now then?"

Whiteside looked up at the plane. It had almost come right around, side-slipping slightly, correcting, setting itself on a course that would bring it directly over the flag. Without taking his eyes off it, Whiteside whispered: "We wait until that chap was finished hanging around."

The plane came in on a gravelly rush of sound. While it was still some distance away a dark cylindrical object was ejected from its open hatch to fall through a couple of lazy somersaults before a flutter of white streamed from it, filling out and at once the canister slowed, swinging down in stately arcs. The pilot had estimated the drift to a nicety. Penduluming gracefully, the canister skimmed the topmost branches, dragging through the trees on the other side of the hollow before hitting the ground in a tangle of white lines, bouncing a couple of seven-league strides, over the flag, to crash into the trees on the nearer side. There was a crackle of breaking foliage, the white fabric sighing gustily, settling limply over branches. The plane had lifted away. Catching Whiteside's eye Gunner grinned.

"Spot on, eh, almost in our bloody laps."

Whiteside smiled fleetingly as if loath to betray any excitement. "These chaps are really quite good you know."

Leaves were floating gently through the shafts of sunlight and somwhere a bird was calling distractedly. Gunner saw that the canister had lodged against the roots of a tree, its lines festooning the branches like a broken web: it was near enough for him to see lettering stencilled on its dark green side. He heard the faint rasp of metal on webbing as Whiteside drew his revolver, then the man was nudging, pointing.

Down in the hollow where trees cast filigreed shadow on the grass, a man was standing. He looked formidable and bizarre, big-headed in his flat-topped helmet, big-bodied in the tiger-pelt of his camouflaged jump-smock which was buttoned under the crotch: he had discarded his overalls, probably because of the heat, and his knees and muscular legs were bare, startlingly pale, like an overgrown small boy fisting the stubby Schmeisser across his waist like an evil toy. In the shadows behind him there was a dark trough where he had lain in the thick growth: he was like a figure that had stepped out of a picture, leaving a vacant silhouette. Instinctively Gunner levelled the gun over the roots but Whiteside signalled him to hold his fire.

The German completed his survey unhurriedly, the muzzle of the machine pistol coordinating with his gaze: he had tinted motorists' goggles clipped around his helmet catching the sunlight like baleful Martian eyes. Raising his left hand he beckoned and there was a commotion in the thick growth under the trees as a second man stood up and stepped out of the picture of tree trunks and shadowy green. He was shorter and dark and he might have been older: he was also more cautious, hunching, looking around as he joined his companion. He wore his overalls with the sleeves rolled up above his elbows while his jump-smock was unbuttoned, flapping about his thighs like a dustcoast: he looked like a factory hand except for the Schmeisser and the stick grenade in his belt and the revolver in a buttoned-down holster at his hip.

"What about it," Gunner whispered without taking his eyes or his sights off the men in the hollow.

"Wait! See if any more show up."

The Germans showed every sign of being alone, not looking back, striding briskly, in a hurry to do what had to be done and be gone. For a moment they were out of sight in the dead ground at the foot of the rise then their helmets came bobbing into view, their footsteps loud, big hobnailed boots tramping without stealth. Gunner concentrated on the younger man, sensing that he was the most dangerous, quicker to react, more bellicose. He also wondered how much longer Whiteside was going to wait.

Reaching the canister the Germans halted. The older man kicked it irritably, spitting out a few disgruntled words: he looked very tired and something in his tone proclaimed him to be a habitual grumbler. His companion glanced at him contemptuously, speaking curtly: his youthful face was mottled by sunburn and tight about the mouth and eyes, an indoctrinated hardness drawn tautly over his boyishness. Producing a knife he set about cutting the 'chute lines, the Schmeisser swinging handily across the chest. The older man watched him, his gun slung across his back, one hand resting on the revolver holster. He would have lit a cigarette but his companion checked him with a sharp rebuke: sullenly he put his cigarettes away and began tugging at one end of the canister. Together they heaved the thing upright and shoved it sideways, clear of the tree: it fell heavily, something inside it knocking hollowly, then it slid and slewed and rolled down the slope.

"Doesn't appear to be any more of them," Whiteside whispered and Gunner nodded. He felt they had waited too longer for already the Germans were down the slope, trees intervening.

Rolling the canister out on to the flat ground they wasted no time in getting it open, one entire side hinged and folding back. Kneeling the older man reached into it, laughing as he held up a biscuit-coloured stoneware bottle with a finger-loop. The younger man had taken out a metal framework, unfolding it, snapping locking devices, attaching two circular objects and a bar with a crosspiece assembling, in that short space of time, a two-wheeled cart with rubber tyres and drawbar. Wheeling it alongside the canister, he spoke to his companion who stowed the bottle away and closed the flap. Together they lifted the canister on to the cart and while the older man took up the drawbar the other retrieved the Nazi flag and draped it over the cart, arranging it so that the swastika could be seen from the air. Joining his companion at the drawbar, they commenced to drag the contraption away.

Whiteside stood up, holding his revolver in both hands, shouting: "Halt! Hands up!"

It was as if he had commanded the world to stand still.

Gunner had an impression of an eerie heart's beat span of immobility, bright sunshine and crepitant woodland sounds and in it the two Germans leaning in attitudes of arrested strain. Then everything erupted in violent action. The older man flung himself flat on his face, the younger wheeled, bringing his Schmeisser up with a wicked flutter of muzzle flashes: bullets thrashed and thudded amongst the trees, the reports sounding fractionally later. Then Whiteside fired. And Gunner fired, seeing his burst plough wide through the grass. As he corrected, the German fired again, sweeping the slope with a protracted burst: the furious staccato of Schmeisser and Tommy almost drowned the banging of Whiteside's pistol. Then somewhere away to the right a single rifle crashed, followed by a spatter of rifle shots and shouting: the rest of the platoon was joining in. Dust spurted around the cart and the Nazi flag jerked spasmodically while the air was full of the back and forth slamming of bullets clipping leaves from the trees. The younger German swung away and pitched forward on to his face.

Yet the firing continued for the remaining man was on his back, his Schmeisser raking the slope. Whiteside ducked angrily jerking his empty pistol. As he did so, Littlehorse walked past firing from the hip while Gigglepiss stood beside a tree firing: Pepsodent knelt, jerking at his rifle bolt while Father stood, taking careful aim. Suddenly Yorgo tramped grimly into view, looking like a comic opera brigand, except for the Schmeisser spraying from his hip. The German arched belly upwards, heaving over on to his face. Then there were only echoes beating themselves against the slopes and the clatter of rifles being reloaded and two dead men in the long grass.

Climbing stiffly out of his nest amongst the roots, Gunner felt a sense of elation at the thought of having survived again. Men seemed to be everywhere, moving restlessly between the trees, talking excitedly. Even Whiteside was affected, reloading his pistol, poking cartridges into the chamber, closing the weapon with a flamboyant cowboy flick of the wrist, holstering roughly.

"Come on, Sar'nt," he called, a terrierlike cockiness about him as if they had dealt the German army a stunning blow. "Let's see what they've got in this billy cart."

They found plenty that was of use to them. In a compartment at one end there were cans of food and medical supplies but several bullets had penetrated the canister, smashing bottles of antiseptic so that most of the dressings were soaked with a pungent brown fluid. Discovering the stoneware bottle, Ev grunted frustratedly, holding it up to show its shattered lower half: reverently he touched a finger to a drip, tasting it lovingly.

"Schnapps," he pronounced dolefully. "The only bloody thing worth having in this grab bag and you trigger-happy ning-nongs blow the arse out of it."

The rest of the canister contained weapons, a small mortar and racks of bombs, rifle and machine-pistol ammunition and several gas-operated carbines as well as a sniper's rifle with a long barrel and telescopic sights.

"Say, dat's some gun." Yorgo eyed the weapon covetously. "Wid dat I could bump off Ironheads real good up in dem hills where I come from."

"You'd better have it, then."

Gunner held out the rifle.

*   *   *

Lighting a cigarette, Gunner watched Littlehorse wrecking the mortar, battering the range indicator and bubble housing with his rifle butt: Tarzan had the muzzle of a carbine in the fork of a tree and was levering on the stock. He heard Ev joking with Yorgo as they divided the rations. "Tinned ham. That'll put lead in your pencil, if you've got anybody to write to." Gunner saw Pepsodent removing the pistol from the dead man's holster.

"Hey! Cop a slew of this! I got one of them Parabellums!" Standing astride the corpse, Pepsodent waved the pistol jubilantly: slipping the clip from the butt, he worked the action, triggering the firing pin on the empty chamber.

"Put the damn thing away before you shoot yourself," Gunner shouted . . . and because he was looking that way he saw Pepsodent jerk upright at the exact moment that he heard the rattle of firing.

It seemed to blast up out of the ground, frighteningly close, so rapid that the reports seemed to overrun one another. He also heard the killing sound of bullets slamming into flesh and bone. Pepsodent went up on his toes, back arched, the pistol spilling from his hand as a great force took him, spinning and hurling him sideways in an ungainly sprawling of arms and legs.

Throwing himself flat, Gunner saw that the younger German was propped on one elbow, the clattering Schmeisser hugged to his shattered chest: recoil pummelled him viciously, shaking the gory mess of his body, making his head wobble weakly. Swinging the Tommy, Gunner saw that Father and the other men were in his line of fire: as he shifted his position he saw Whiteside tugging at his holster and Ev flat on the ground amongst scattered cans, while Yorgo had the sniper's rifle swung over his shoulder, charging insanely. Perhaps the German saw him coming. Perhaps it was the kick of the Schmeisser, knocking him backward, continuing to traverse in a stuttering arc that stitched bullets through the canister and across Yorgo's chest, whanging away off the barrel of the shotgun behind his shoulder. Spatters of blood exploded from Yorgo's frilled shirtfront and he appeared to pause, looking most surprised, then he lurched onward, momentum carrying him a few more sagging steps before he crumpled and went down quite close to the German. The firing ceased as suddenly as it had started.

"For Crissake somebody see to Peppie," Gunner bawled, hoisting himself up in a scrambling rush.

He knew that Yorgo was dead before he reached the man. Nobody could have that meaty cratering of exit holes across the back and still live. He lay with his cheek against the earth, his eyes wide and there was blood and dust on his great moustache: his headcloth had come off, revealing him to be completely bald. Bending over him, Gunner smelt the yeasty salt-sweat oil-and-raki odour of his flesh, vaguely animal. An eye for an eye, he thought dully and he touched a forefinger to his brow in a sort of a salute, murmuring: "*Pallikari*, that's what you were, feller, real *pallikari*."

The men had gathered around Pepsodent's body, a troubled conclave muttering dire profanities that would be his only obsequies. Pepsodent lay, wild-eyed, a hank of hair over his brow, mouth opened, cracked lips turned back, pink ridges of hardened gums and blabber tongue as if death had interrupted one of his obscene tirades.

*   *   *

They came out of the uplands, halting for a breather on a rise: it wasn't high, just the usual Cretan topography of steep incline, scree and scrub and toothy rocks but it afforded an unimpeded view of the Sphakia road.

Hundreds of tired defeated men were struggling along that dolorous road. They moved as creatures in a herd move, inchoate without order, following the herd's mass instinct for direction, with currents and surges of lesser movement swirling fractiously in their midst. There were Australians, New Zealanders, British, Greeks, Palestinians and Cypriots; in khaki slacks, in shorts and pullovers, in Greek tunic and puttees, in British battledress, in Australian uniforms, in worn out, cut down remnants of uniforms: men in helmets or slouch hats, berets, forage caps or Kiwi "lemon squeezer" hats, bareheaded men and men with bandaged heads. Most of them carried pieces of equipment, haversacks, rifles, basic-pouches or a few possessions, stuffed into a respirator bag: some had nothing but rolls of blankets or groundsheeted bundles. There were wounded amongst them carried on stretchers and rolling their pallid faces to the sky or half-carried by mates, the blind being led, the lame on crutches, even a man with bandaged stumps of feet being carried pickaback. A few civilians plodded amongst them, distraught dark-faced family groups burdened with suitcases and bundles and shepherding bewildered children: they made eddies of pathetic colour in the dark flow of troops. Abandoned equipment littered the ditches, rifles, helmets, gasmasks, packs and officers' valises, ripped open and ransacked, even a blitz buggy, riddled with holes and nose down in the ditch. Here and there groups of dejected men sat beside the road or stretched out in the meagre shade while several were poking around in the ditch, turning over the discarded packs: several had started a fire and were brewing tea. The rest streamed on, moving with the fretful clamour of the herd, strident voices, metallic clatterings and the harsh massed crunch of boots tramping southward to the sea.

Gunner stared aghast. This was every man for himself . . . this rabble! He was shocked and ashamed, suddenly hating the statesmen and politicians and the bemedalled planners whose muddlings had brought this humiliation upon soldiers. Nobody could do this to men and still demand their loyalty. Behind him he heard the rest of the platoon cursing luridly. Then Littlehorse essayed a hollow joke. "Looks like there's a beer issue on somewhere." Whereupon Gigglepiss came in. "Yeah, at Sphakia. Navy rum — if we get there on time." Nobody laughed.

HARRY GORDON

The Desperate Months

Harry Gordon's The Embarrassing Australian *is the biography of Reg Saunders, who in 1944 became the first Aboriginal soldier ever to receive a commission in the Australian armed forces. In the following extracts, the author describes the conduct of the men of Saunders's battalion during the retreat to Sphakia in May 1941 and Saunders's success in avoiding capture by the German forces until his escape from Crete on 7 May 1942.*

IT was something between a retreat and a rout. While units like the 2/7th Australian Battalion took up rearguard positions along the road and continued to fight a war that had already been lost, other troops swarmed and straggled south across Crete along the one road that led towards Sphakia and possible safety.

There was little food and not much water, and through most of the brutal, bleeding march across the mountains the men on the road were open to strafing and bombing from the air. Badly wounded soldiers, in filthy, blood-stained bandages, made the trek on foot: men with limbs blown off staggered along, numb with suffering . . . some of them using rifles as crutches.

"Several cases of amputated arms, gross injuries of limb and trunk, even a case of perforated wound of the chest, were known to have walked a distance of thirty miles or more to the point of embarkation", an army medical officer wrote later. "The last part of the journey consisted of a precipitous descent down mere goat tracks at night time. No tribute can be too generous to the qualities of men such as these."

And General Freyberg reported: "There were units sticking together and marching with their weapons . . . but in the main it was a disorganised rabble making its way doggedly and painfully to the south. There were thousands of unarmed troops including the Cypriots and Palestinians. Without leadership, without any sort of discipline, it is impossible to expect anything else of troops who have never been trained as fighting soldiers. Somehow or other the word Sphakia had got out, and many of these people had taken a flying start in any available transport they could steal and which they later left abandoned . . . Never shall I forget the disorganisation and almost complete lack of control of the masses on the move as we made our way slowly through that endless stream of trudging men."

Behind these beaten, dispirited troops, Saunders and his comrades covered pass after pass along the road, hungry and belted almost constantly by enemy planes and mortars. Even after their last rearguard, when their only job was to get to Sphakia, they moved in military formation — and often fought off men from other units who tried to break into their ranks.

They were proud, but more than a little embittered. They felt, like many of the New Zealanders, that they were better fighting soldiers than the Germans, but that they had been given little opportunity to demonstrate the fact. They also felt that they had often been poorly disposed: in Crete the high ground usually controlled the low ground — and the Australians sometimes found themselves occupying lower ground than their opponents.

Once, as they crossed the island, members of the 2/7th were confronted by the unlikely sight of three thousand Italian soldiers, marching against the tide, frantically waving white flags. They had been taken prisoner by the Greeks during the Albanian fighting, and now they had been released. The battalion diarist took official note of their appearance, with the cryptic observation: "No ammunition to spare on them."

*   *   *

On June 4 a count was made in Palestine among those who had escaped from Crete. This was the breakdown on the battalion strength:

	Officers	Men
Unit strength, as at April 10, 1941 when battalion sailed for Greece....................	33	726
Lost in Greece......................	2	150
Battalion strength on landing in Crete	31	576
Lost in Crete.......................	24	511
Total of the remaining members of the battalion who were engaged in the Greece and Crete campaigns.......................	7	65

Those who were left on Crete were bitter men, with some reason. The Greece evacuation had been a comparatively smooth, well organised affair; from Crete, though, much of it was a shambles. The troops had fought strenuously and well, and throughout their retreat they had had to cope with a rabble on the roads, plus an acute shortage of food and ammunition. The 2/7th war diary makes it clear that they were let down often by men who were farther from the fighting.

Saunders described the retreat this way: "The pressure was tremendous. Each night the Germans were horribly close, but too exhausted to close in on us. They would sleep until daylight, and we'd have to move as hard as we could in the dark to put some distance between them and us. On almost no food and no sleep, it wasn't easy.

"For two days, we ate no food of any kind. I believe some of the boys came to a stream, and literally fell into it with all their gear. Some drank so much that they had to be lifted out. As we waited above Sphakia, a few of the lucky ones caught chickens and ate them raw . . . entrails and all. Our bunch were carrying cans of bully beef and biscuits, but for the last couple of days we were without water — and the result was that we just couldn't eat . . .

"At times, we were almost running to keep up with the battalion. Every one of us knew that it was a race against time, as it had been in Greece, and that anyone who stopped had had it. But still some men just slumped exhausted beside the track. 'I've had it', they'd mutter. And there was nothing we could do about it.

"On the forced marches we moved mainly in threes; the CO had impressed on us that we must stick together as a unit, and sometimes we were forced to lash out at the disorganised stragglers who tried to break in among us. They probably felt, or had heard, that only real units would be evacuated from the beaches. It wasn't until the night before we were supposed to be evacuated that we even saw the sea. We were in single file on the goat track that led down from the hills to the beach — and each platoon sergeant impressed on us that we had to know the man in front of us, and keep out all others. We kept on the left; other troops on the right.

"About a quarter of a mile from the beach, we could see an English officer on the roof of a house, trying to get these other troops into some sort of order. At one stage he threatened to shoot them unless they took some notice of him. 'If there's complete order', he said, 'You'll all get off the island during the night.' They pressed on panicki- ly, in complete disorder.

"Below us on the beach were milling masses of English and Greek troops. I couldn't see any officers, and there was absolutely no discipline . . ."

The men on the beach were from all sorts of outfits — gunners, searchlight batteries, engineers, field am- bulance men who considered that their work was done and who were desperate to get onto some sort of transport headed for Egypt. With them were Greeks, Jews, Palestinians, Cypriots. They were terrified for the most part, and lawless. They rushed food dumps and water supplies.

It was tragic that units which had borne most of the burden of the retreat should find, on arrival at the beach, that there was no transport to get them off the island. Brigadier Vasey later reported on the failure of most of the 2/7th to get away:

"The route (to the beach) lay along a wadi and a very narrow track which ended up winding through the village of Sphakia. When some little distance from the beach it was found that this road was blocked with men sitting down and many officers challenged anyone approaching wanting to know what they were. Other officers represented themselves as MCOs (Movement Control Of- ficers) and eventually one of these said only single file was allowed through from that point, and that the 19th Australian Infantry Brigade would have to wait . . ."

Sergeant Harry Thomas, DCM, who had guided the battalion to the beach in Greece, led two companies of the 2/7th in pitch darkness to the beach road. They were deadbeat now . . . some had to be threatened and cajoled to keep on marching.

When they finally reached the water's edge, still in formation, Saunders and his mates found that only one landing craft was still waiting — and it was mostly filled. Lieutenant Colonel Walker sent a few of his men to the craft. An officer on the last barge reported watching the battalion standing "quiet and orderly in its ranks" as it waited on the shore.

"I was supposed to have been on the next bargeload off," Saunders wrote later, "But there wasn't any. The last barge left not twenty yards from me. I guess, like the rest of the boys, I was too fatigued to worry much about it . . . even as we stood and watched the barge go with some of our mates aboard. Food and water seemed the most important things then; it must have been a fortnight since we had had anything other than catnaps and B and B (bully beef and biscuits)."

As the last barges pulled out, New Zealand troops both in the barges and on the shore began to sing the "Maoris' Farewell". The Australians began to sing the English words . . . "Now is the hour, when we must say farewell." The men who had been saved by a matter of minutes and the men who were virtually lost sang it together, and tough, unshaven men wept a little. It was the sort of scene that would undoubtedly have looked hammily, stickily sentimental in a Hollywood war film; on the beach at Sphakia it was spontaneous and natural. For many men on the beach, it was a hymn of unlikely hope.

At 3 a.m. the following day, the 2/7th Battalion — still one organised unit among the mobs which prowled the beaches — learned that the Navy had moved off from Crete's shores.

Lieutenant K. R. Walker, who escaped the same day, later reported: "The CO addressed us and told us that the Navy had moved out and would not be back again, also remarking that we had at least arrived as a complete battalion. He told the men they could stay on the beach and try to get away, or else follow him and fight and keep together. The men cheered and shouted that they would follow him. We then collected rations and distributed them, and then marched into Sphakia to get water . . . the intention was to march out and make our way further along the island, where we could rest and obtain a few supplies, in the hope of being picked up by Naval ships.

"At about 6.30 a.m. we heard that rabble in the town were burning arms and ammunition and hoisting white flags everywhere. The CO went to investigate, and found the order had been left by General Weston that the force had been surrendered, and all arms and ammunition had been destroyed. This order was carried out. The CO then decided it would be best to break up into small parties."

When it was first learned that officers and men on the beach and in Sphakia were flying white flags, several of Lieutenant Colonel Walker's men had debated whether to shoot them. When Walker learned of General Weston's message — which directed the most senior officer available to "make contact with the enemy and capitulate" — he decided that resistance was hopeless.

Lieutenant Colonel Walker, as the most senior officer, climbed to the town of Komithades with his adjutant, Capt. H. K. H. Goodwin, and found an Austrian officer, to whom he surrendered. "What are you doing here, Australia?" asked the Austrian in English. "One might ask what you are doing here, Austria?" replied Walker. "We are all Germans", said the Austrian.

Down on the beach, Saunders and other members of his company had been assembled in caves. Their commander, Major W.V. Miller, advised them that they were now members of a surrendered army.

"I've been told that every man must destroy all arms, papers and paybooks," he said. "After that it's a question of every man for himself. The CO says you can either wait for the Germans to pick you up, or strike off in groups in the hope of picking up a boat. There's nothing else to tell you except . . . good luck."

There were several similar conferences in the caves that fringed the beach. One company commander closed his address with the advice: "Life is sweet . . . it's worth fighting for."

Then, for the first time, the battalion broke up into little pieces. Some headed left along the coast, some right, and some decided that they'd have more hope hiding out in the hills for a few days, until the "heat" was off. Saunders, and a group of about fifteen men, which included Mick Baxter, filled their water bottles, collected what rations they could, hiked to an olive grove about three miles from the beach — and hid for the rest of the day. That night they climbed gingerly down the slopes to a beach east of Sphakia, and flashed a torch out to sea. They pressed short bursts of light, long bursts, and every now and then tried to send messages in morse code. All night they signalled, until finally the battery was flat — and they attracted no attention.

* * *

The story of the hundreds of troops who lived for varying spells under the German occupation of Crete is largely unknown. Curiously, since it was an adventure of some proportions, there has been comparatively little published about this little corner of the war.

Here you had a force of desperate young men, unarmed and moving either singly or in batches of two and three, hiding out by day from the German Luftwaffe troops and the Hitler Youth garrison troops who succeeded them, venturing out only at night to get food and exercise. They had the great sympathy of the Cretans, large numbers of whom were shot as hostages because they were known to be feeding or guiding the fugitives. And they had the aid of a hilltop grapevine between shepherds — a sort of bush telegraph — that communicated all sorts of intelligence on German troop movements as fast as any network of walkie-talkies.

Saunders, who stayed on Crete for eleven months after the surrender was among one of the last batches to be taken off. He found that his colour worked against him in some senses — he was almost certainly the only coloured man on the island, and was obviously a marked, easily identifiable figure — but that his native bushcraft and his ability to move, comparatively unnoticed, at night, were distinct advantages. These latter attributes, plus his toughness, later made him immensely valuable in the New Guinea jungle as a guide and scout.

After digging up some food in the sand at Suda Bay, Saunders visited a village the Australians had been quartered in briefly during their stay on the island. There a priest took up a collection in church, the proceeds of which were used to repair his boots and those of a batch of Englishmen hiding out nearby.

Later, at a town called Lubini, he linked up with two other Australians — Les "Dodger" Vincent, from the 2/1st Battalion, and George Burgess, from the 2/3rd.

One night recently, Saunders and Vincent, who now runs a small mixed farm outside Sydney, sat around Vincent's kitchen and sipped muscatel and talked about their days together at Lubini.

"Mostly," said Vincent, "we would thieve rather than let the villagers give us food. We knew that if they gave up chickens and eggs, as they wanted to, they'd be victimised. But at Lubini they insisted that we come into their homes and eat from communal bowls with them. They'd even try to give us their children's milk."

"Their courage and generosity never ceased to amaze me," Saunders said. "It went beyond just being helpful to another human being. Sometimes I used to ask them why they were doing it, and the answer boiled down to two reasons, really. Firstly, they hated the Germans intensely — and as the Germans looted towns and wiped out whole villages, this hatred became progressively more intense. Secondly, they seemed to be terribly impressed by the fact that we had come so far to fight a war which concerned them more than our own people."

They talked with tremendous affection about the villagers at Lubini, who harboured them in the certain knowledge that if this fact became known to the Germans, every male would be shot dead. The people of Lubini had learned, via the shepherds' lines of communication, of the fate of the village of Skines — which had been blown up with high explosive because it was believed that several escapees had stayed there overnight. They knew about the day at Galatos, when all the women of the town were lined up in rows naked from the waist; those with bruises on their shoulders were judged to have used rifles, and accordingly shot dead. They knew about Fournies, where all the male population were put to work digging a mass grave, then executed.

And they knew that the Hitler Youth guards who had moved in were more cruel, less honourable towards prisoners, than the paratroops who had taken part in the actual fighting. The Hitler Youth lads were aged around seventeen, and they conformed to the most ferocious Nazi specifications; one of their favourite punishments was reported to be making an offender jump higher and higher over a strand of barbed wire.

"Of all the Cretan peasants, the most impressive I met

was a woman called Vaselichi Zagarachis," Saunders
recalled. "She was about thirty-five with classical
features and magnificent flashing eyes. She walked
straight as a gun-barrel, and had courage to match. Her
husband was a little man, a rank coward, and her brother,
Casteli, was a member of the Greek Evzones . . . the
blokes with the little frilly skirts.

"There was one bad time, when the village of Lubini
was crammed with German troops, and we were camped
in an olive mill about five hundred yards away. It was the
warmest place in the district we could find to sleep.
There were Dodger, George Burgess, who had broken
out of a prison camp, and Arthur Lambert, a New
Zealand soldier who had bumped into us. Below us we'd
watch the Germans lounging round, smoking cigarettes
— and at night the village kids would bring us up some
smokes and some eggs.

"Vaselichi brought some food up to us one night — it
was white, soft cheese, riddled with maggots, but we
thought it was wonderful — and she found that Lambert
was running a high fever and shivering badly. He was obviously suffering from yellow jaundice.

"By this time, we were speaking fairly fluent Cretan.
Anyway, she decided that Lambert should sleep in her
one-room house in the village. Burgess and I helped her
down with him, and, under cover of the darkness, we got
him into Vaselichi's house. We were in a neighbour's
house afterwards, having a meal, when somebody burst
in with the news that the Germans were making a house-
to-house search of the village. They must have heard that
we were in town, because they'd clamped a cordon all the
way round.

"We had a quick conference and decided that the only
thing to do was try to break out. If we did that we knew
that there was a good chance that they wouldn't continue

the search and find Lambert. So Burgess and I put our heads down and ran. The shooting started at once.

"Burgess jumped down a six-foot bank, and I streaked off the other way. I went so fast I reckon I passed the bullets. Burgess apparently twisted his ankle when he jumped, and was caught. As we expected, all the commotion had the effect of halting the search, and Lambert was not found.

"Next morning I saw Burgess and two Greek soldiers being marched into a house which had been taken over by the German commander. The women of the village, Vaselichi included, spat and screeched at the armed Germans in the escort. I've never seen such brave people. They knew there must be reprisals, and they still weren't afraid to express their hatred and contempt.

"One of the Greeks was a major. The pair of them were working with the underground which assisted escaped soldiers, and brought in supplies for the resistance movement."

While Saunders watched from his perch in the tree, the two Greeks were tied to kitchen chairs in the town square. Then seven Germans in rimless helmets lined up fifteen yards away and shot the sitting pair to death, while the villagers screeched their disapproval.

Unaccountably, the Germans decided not to shoot Burgess with the Greeks. He lived in their compound for a week or so, made a break, and linked up again with Saunders at the olive mill. He told Saunders that he had been well treated, and given good rations.

Soon after, Saunders and his comrades moved on from Lubini. Because of its quite open sympathy to the hunted troops, there were several savage acts of vengeance by the Germans. Later the mayor was shot dead and a number of houses burnt to the ground.

*   *   *

It was against this sort of background that Saunders lived on the run for eleven months. On Christmas Day 1941, living in a cave in the White Mountains, he had the worst Christmas dinner of his life . . . a couple of black olives, soaked in oil, and a chunk of dry bread. Mostly, though, he lived on honey, broad beans, eggs, occasional slabs of goat flesh and ewes' milk.

In one village, before he had mastered the language, he rubbed his stomach and rolled his eyes wildly to express extreme hunger; the large Greek woman to whom he made this fine gesture replied: "Don't worry about that, son. I speak good English." In another, a dignified, elderly Greek to whom he had indicated thirst, wordlessly escorted him to a shed which housed an eighty-gallon vat of excellent wine — then gave Saunders a battered old army mug with which to attack it.

He lived mainly in caves, prowling at night like a hunted animal. He grew a beard, and he wore the same set of clothes from the day of capitulation — June 30, 1941 — until his escape on May 7, 1942. And on the night he was taken off the island he was, not surprisingly, covered with lice.

Part 4
The War in the Jungle

Clammily cold,
Like the touch of a nightmare snake,
Each vine clings hungrily as I pass
But must not, can not hold me from my goal,
Which may be here: or there: or in the bole
Of that web-footed tree.
Everything is mad. The trees grow feet
And corkscrew themselves up to the sky,
Unable to escape the dragging vine
That holds them firm within its fetid bed.

Death I can face,
But hidden, creeping fate
That lurks behind each tree and palm,
The ultimate in hate,
Defeats the routine calm of conscious nerves.

Eric Irvin
from "New Guinea"

KENNETH SLESSOR

The Twilight War: The Fight in the Jungle

This dispatch, written by Kenneth Slessor while he was still the Australian official war correspondent, was issued by the Department of Information to all Australian newspapers towards the end of 1943.

The Jungle

It is war in the twilight, this crazy, deadly, sweating, stinking, cat-and-mouse campaign in the swamps and undergrowth, the rainforests and the mud, the huge mountains and cruel tracks of New Guinea — a war that is being fought by silent armies, not only in the literal twilight of the dripping jungle subways, but in the twilight of the news as well.

Its communiques are as bald as clinical reports. Its maps are vacuums, its placenames difficult to spell, impossible to remember. Its forces, by comparison with the swarming divisions locked in combat on the European battlefronts, are insignificant. The war correspondents who can penetrate to its front lines are relatively few.

The men who fight there are relatively laconic. The light has played on Egypt, Greece, North Africa, Sicily, Italy, the Russian infinity, and the world has followed the successive waves of battle in those countries with a detail that is almost painfully minute.

There is no searchlight on New Guinea. For this is a different kind of war, and it is being fought in the shadows. It is different in almost every way that you can imagine. To soldiers who came straight from the great desert battles, with the sand of the Middle East still in their boots (as many of the Australians now fighting in New Guinea did) the contrast at first seems almost fantastic. The whole foundation of military "do-and-don't", which guided every moment of their lives in the desert, has been overturned. Their movements, training, habits of life, camp routine, sleeping, foodstuffs, weapons — all have undergone an abrupt and violent transformation. The very uniforms in which they fight, dyed as green as Robin Hood's to match the intense verdigris of the jungle background, are like no others in the world.

Here are no stony pans of sand and emptiness, where concealment is almost impossible. In this war, concealment and surprise are everything; and a man can hide himself completely, if he wants to and knows how, at a range of a few yards.

Here are no easy roads or open spaces, on which motor transport can turn almost at will. There are no roads, no tracks, except those beaten out painfully by the sweat of the fighting men themselves, or by the snout of the faithful bulldozer. There is no room or surface for the million wheels which, on other battlefields, have changed the face of warfare. Hence, there can be none of that quicksilver switching of men and material, from pressure point to pressure point along the battleline, which distinguished the struggle in North Africa. There can be no ferrying of vast stores and ponderous equipment, such as kept the highways of the Middle East black with interminable convoys.

All that a man takes to this war he must carry on his back. What he can't carry — stores, ammunition, replacements, reinforcements, food and water — must often go by air, to be lobbed by parachute, or landed precariously on makeshift ribbons of clear ground, torn from the heart of the jungle. So there often isn't much food or stores or reinforcement, and a soldier has to learn the human minimum and how to survive on it.

For the same compelling reasons, there are no huge concentrations of men and armour pitted against each other here. It is not a battle of armies; it is a private and personal war of man against man, of small patrols and scattered sections, bursting out of nowhere into nowhere, hiding stealthily in ambush, suffering in silence, shooting and melting away again, sinking for weeks on end into the anonymous green infinities. There are no massed divisions on this front, because it would be as impossible to get them there as for them to operate coherently.

On the other hand, here, for one of the few occasions of the war, the infantryman is king. Tanks can be used, and have been used, for severely limited tasks in severely limited areas, but the rest of the picture is dominated by the infantryman with artillery support. The jungle makes some things possible which, in other fighting zones, could scarcely be considered. It turns a relatively small force into a formidable battle-unit. Cover is so easy and so universal that encircling movements can be accomplished at incredibly close quarters. But movement itself is slow, difficult and exhausting. There can be no lightning marches here, no rapid feints and thrusts of the European kind. Distance is measured, not by lines on maps, but by painful hours of sweat and plod and climb. Ten miles is not ten miles; it may mean ten days.

It follows that the supreme factor in such campaigning is not sheer weight of metal or superiority of numbers or equipment. It is the quality of the fighting man himself, tested to the last ounce, to the last atom of bravery and endurance. It is the fighting man himself who wins this war. Never before has the issue of defeat or victory, life or death, been imposed so directly on the individual.

Australians and Americans, plunged into this obscure struggle for survival, have long since found that their enemies are not the Japanese alone. Even to get within bayonet length of the Japanese is often a physical challenge which only a young athlete could hope to endure. The jungle has deadlier adversaries than the Japanese. It hits back at the fighting man with savage claws, with matted roots and vines and thorns, with tiger-toothed branches and barbed undergrowth; it mocks him with tremendous ribs of mountain, with vertical peaks, deep torrents, agonies of rock and marsh; it soaks him to the hide with whipping rain, it saturates him with sweat, it burns him with incandescent heats and fevers, it cakes him with a pulp of loathsome mud.

It is full of malaria, ague, dysentery, scrub typhus, obscure diseases; full of crocodiles and snakes and bloated spiders, leeches, lice, mosquitoes, flies, all the crawling, creeping, leaping, flying, biting reptiles and insects that even suck human blood (and in the morning you make a habit of knocking your boots to shake the scorpions out). Its breath is poisonous; it stinks of rotten fungus and dead leaves turning softly liquid underfoot; mould and mildew put their spongy paws over everything; shoes, papers, clothing, sprout with grey beards, and there is a mottling of brown measle-spots on the cigarette which sags from your mouth, if you've been lucky enough to find a cigarette.

Sometimes it's so wet that wood won't burn until it has been dried by the little flame which you keep smouldering almost permanently, like prehistoric man. Sometimes it's so hot that sweat trickles like brine over the lips. Sometimes it's so cold that your bones seem to chatter. Sometimes it's so high that your ears hurt, you can't hear properly, you have to keep opening and shutting your mouth. At the end of the trail, the Japanese wait with knives and bullets. But the jungle enlists a thousand enemies before this last enemy of all. It is unending, unrelenting, unforgiving. It is maleficent. It is not made for man.

To comprehend this kind of country and this kind of war, you must abandon all visions of tropical islands, white beaches, waving palm trees, tinkling music, romantic moonlight. New Guinea is not that kind of island at all. To begin with, as a bomber's-eye view quickly reveals, there is literally almost not a square foot of this territory (itself bigger than Great Britain or Italy) which is not crowded with pushing, swarming, groping vegetation. There is a viscid and sticky earth under the green chaos, but you can't see it. Trees, bushes, scrub, lock their leaves and branches overhead as if to keep a secret. When they diminish, the kunai begins — a tide of surging waist-high native grass, tough and sharp as metal. Roots clot the riverbeds, vines run through the foliage and loop themselves over the boughs, like the black wires of a mad telephone exchange.

Sometimes there is a plantation of coconut palms, with light filtering in watery slopes through their limp leaves, and bald grey coconuts, like a Golgotha of skulls, heaped where they have fallen (bombs are not the only missiles which a soldier has to dodge from the sky here). But even the tiny clearings, the native gardens, glittering with yellow croton flowers and scarlet hibiscus, are hemmed in by the ridges and razorbacks, rising steeply to enormous mountain ranges, so high that shelves of floating cloud bisect them.

Clambering up these precipices, sometimes above ten thousand feet, loaded with forty or fifty pounds of battle gear, is physical torture; slipping and sliding down them is worse misery. Some of the ridges are so steep that thousands of steps have had to be gouged from their sides. At times, the ascent is so sheer that a man scrambles desperately on all fours, or claws with hands and feet to naked rock faces, his boots fumbling and scrabbling on the brink of an abyss. This is painful enough when it is not raining, which is seldom; in the wet, which is often, it is a nightmare road to war.

Over every inch of this kind of track, the myriad vital articles needed by a fighting force in the field have to make their journey, even more arduously than the troops themselves. At one stage in the Kokoda fighting, 1500 native porters were needed to carry supplies for 600 soldiers. But not only have rations, equipment and ammunition to be carried to the fighting line. The wounded have to be carried back. With heartbreaking difficulty, but with incredible and gentle care, they are lifted and lowered on rough jungle-stretchers over cliffs and gorges and swirling rivers, through matted scrub, black slime, primeval forests; sometimes, when the earth falls away in dizzy perpendiculars at the side of the trail, they have to be passed from hand to hand around the hairpin corners, like a human bucket-chain. In the country around Mubo, 16 natives were allotted to carry each wounded man, and it took 216 of these "boys" to carry out 8 wounded from one skirmish.

At sundown, the jungle is drowned abruptly in

darkness. It is the slab darkness of a seabottom five hundred fathoms deep, lit only by the flickering morse of the fireflies, flashing and dancing like flakes of wandering phosphorus. In the fighting areas, not a torch can be shone, not a match struck, not even a cigarette allowed to glow in the cup of your hand. It is a blackout so complete, palpable and all-enveloping that each man feels himself isolated from the human race, a solitary and invisible speck in the black infinity.

The darkness seems to last for an immeasurable period. Nerves become filed, noises distorted or magnified, the night filled with a thousand presences unheard in daylight. Flying foxes bump and flap through the treetops with a heavy, thumping wingbeat. Birds utter a monotonous faraway reiteration to which the mind fits human words. A shot cracks and echoes in the distance from a sentry whose finger twitches on his Owen gun at every rustle of the leaves.

It is in this landscape of perpetual struggle, primitive exposure, of savage hardship and unceasing nervous drain, that you must imagine yourself, to gain even a refracted picture of the conflict in New Guinea. You toil and march and fight in it, without a break of even a moment, without escape without contact or signal with the world you left behind. You dig slit trenches with blistered hands, and crawl on your belly in them half-a-dozen times a day. You are never quite dry. Your skin is itchy with the weals of insect bites. You are as gaunt as a telegraph pole (there are no fat men in the jungle). Your clothing smells rancid from the soaked sweat and dirt of two or three weeks' wearing, without change night or day. You have no sleep sometimes for forty-eight hours on end.

You grow a beard, but not a fashionable one. You eat bully beaf at every meal (when you get a meal) — bully beef hot, bully beef cold, mashed with biscuit, stewed, fried or curried, but still intransigently bully beef. Sometimes you don't eat at all. Your drinking water has to be shaken up with disinfecting chemicals, and it always tastes like medicine. You swallow little canary-yellow pills of atabrin, the antimalaria drug, every day except Sunday, and they gradually tinge your body with a film of jaundice yellow. Your boudoir is a shallow hole in the ground — and the digging is hard here, the earth tough as iron and webbed with roots and boulders, by no means the yielding sand of the desert. Your bed is a groundsheet and half a blanket, and even in the firing line you must crawl under a net from the clouds of disease-laden mosquitoes.

All this before you may even see the human enemy, or exchange shots with him. That is the kind of war it is, and that is the kind of country, not made for man. For such a special sort of warfare, a special sort of soldier is required. He must be young, strong, lithe, resilient, battle-cunning and weather-grilled, with nerves half steel and half elastic; he must be cautious and reckless, disciplined but unorthodox, crafty and patient in ambush, audacious at the end of a bayonet. Otherwise he would be lost before he could give battle.

The Japanese war commanders knew what these conditions would be long before they set forth on their grandiose adventure. For months, perhaps years, in advance, their picked warriors were trained with diligence and enormous thoroughness in guerilla fighting, drilled and conditioned to withstand the rigours of the jungle. Since their assault was premeditated to the day and minute, they had all the advantage of this early start.

What answer have the Allied forces of Australia and the United States contrived? The next part of this article describes, with necessary reservations, how Australia's jungle fighters have learned to beat the Japanese at the ruthless game which they chose to play.

The School

The Japanese were in New Guinea. That was the fact, as cold and solid as a cannonball, which hit Australia in March 1942.

To most Americans, as to most people in Great Britain, New Guinea is just a wild name in an imaginary ocean, five thousand or ten thousand miles away. To Australians, New Guinea is neither imaginary nor far away. It is something much closer, much more familiar, as near and actual as Martha's Vineyard to New York or the Isle of Wight to London. It is the mat at the Commonwealth's front door.

On this mat, in March 1942, Japanese soldiers were wiping the jungle mud from their boots, massing their supplies, oiling their guns, getting ready to deliver that crashing knock on the door itself which would mean the invasion of a British continent. From a trickle of early landings, they had streamed down in swollen and still-spreading hordes on Lae and Salamaua and the Markham Valley, like cannibal ants descending on the carcase of Port Moresby itself, the heart of Australian and American defences in Papua. From Port Moresby to the Australian mainland is barely 350 miles.

Useless at this fifty-ninth second of the eleventh hour to seek reasons, to excuse or blame or ponder on the might-have-beens. The fact was there; so were the Japanese. The crisis had to be faced squarely and at once, without the loss of a moment; without, also, that bulwark of specialised equipment and trained men which a more leisured strategy might have considered vital.

The crisis was faced. Within a few weeks, the encroaching fringe of the invasion tide heard the first bullets whistling from Allied patrols. In July, another Japanese force landed at Buna, 140 miles down the coast from Salamaua. An ominous lull followed for the next two months. It burst in September, when the first full-scale Japanese land attack was launched on a point 32 air miles from Port Moresby. This, with a calamitous and quickly crushed landing at Milne Bay three weeks before, was the highwater-mark of the Japanese advance towards Australia. In another fortnight, the tide was going back. The Australians had driven the Japanese from their ridge at Ioribaiwa in the Owen Stanley mountains, and the invaders were in full retreat to their strongholds in the rear. By November 1942, with the recapture of Kokoda, the Japanese had been pushed back to Buna, and there was at last an uneasy breathing space.

For the Allies, if not for the Japanese, it was a time for permanent decision and revision. The Australian and American commanders had learned a lot during those desperate seven months when the fate of Australia, and possibly the fate of the Pacific, hung in the scales. Now, with appalling clarity, they realised to the full what they had merely anticipated before — they were pitted in a life-and-death struggle against a perfectly prepared, highly skilled, long trained, and implacable foe. Their own men had been flung hurriedly into battle in this wilderness of peak and jungle, savager than almost any other fighting country in the world. They had come without special training, special knowledge, special weapons or equipment.

All these, the Japanese had. For a year before entering the war, their assault troops (picked by hand for precisely such an adventure as this) had been toughened in mimic jungle fighting on the islands of Formosa and Hainan. They knew all the tricks, and they had all the necessary material. To this point — and the Allied commanders knew it well — the Japanese had been beaten back by sheer blind heroism, by haphazard equipment and makeshift stratagems, by the impromptu resource and endurance of men who fought as best they could and knew how, but who lacked any organized foundation of technical knowledge, special gear or physical conditioning. Even their desert khaki uniforms, designed for sand and open spaces, put them at the mercy of the Japanese, whose green garments, camouflaged helmets and dyed faces merged almost invisibly into the background of the jungle.

The commanders came to a decision. In this battle for the survival of the fittest, their own troops would have to be trained, equipped and camouflaged, not merely as well as the enemy, but better than the enemy. The fight on the Owen Stanleys had convinced them that the Japanese forces of cunning, tough and expert jungle warriors could be countered only by men who had been trained in the same school. If the conflict was to be this kind of muddy scuffle, a man-to-man contest with rifle, bayonet or grenade, then the Australian would have to prove himself the better man — better at cunning, better at stealth, better at a stand-up fight or at all-in throat-cutting. The Japanese must be outwitted and outfought.

There was only one answer. The troops would have to go to school again — to a school like no other in the academy of war, with no previous model, devised only from bitter experience and experiment. There they would have to train themselves as quickly as possible, as arduously and painfully as if they were under fire, abandoning all formal textbook principles of attack and defence.

The notion that any Australian can fight efficiently anywhere has been encouraged only by the fact that the average Australian soldier responds quickly to an emergency. It is a false assumption, and it dies hard. Other things being equal, the Australian soldier without proper training or equipment will be killed in the end by an enemy who has both.

Again, it is too often supposed that the typical Australian soldier comes straight from the sunlit spaces, with acquired or inherited assets of bushcraft and open-air physique. In the Australian forces, there are just as many men from office desks or factory workshops as men from the shearing sheds and cattle runs. And no man, however eager his spirit, can expect to walk from a department store into the jungle with any reasonable hope that he may scramble through somehow to survival. Sir Thomas Blamey, Allied commander-in-chief of land-forces, has criticised those people who too easily assume that Australian soldiers are inherently invincible. "With appalling self-confidence," he once declared, "they say that the city-bred Australian is a born guerilla fighter."

It is true that many Australian soldiers begin with the natural advantages of vigorous health and strong, limber bodies, a legacy bestowed by the national privileges of good food, high living standards and open-air sport in the sun. Those who come from country life often have other special attributes, such as a knowledge of the bush, an instinctive pathfinding sense and the ability to travel long distances in rugged country with a minimum of carried food or water. They can shoot and ride and endure hardship.

But all this is not enough. Indeed, it has been found too often that even the most aggressively healthy athlete is as vulnerable to illness or disease as the man who was a physical weakling before he joined the army. The hundred arts and devices of living and fighting in the jungle are not instinctive or inherited. They have to be learned and relearned from the tortures of experience.

So the troops were sent to school again. It was a queer kind of school, not at all the place for refined young gentlemen — in some ways more like a lower class running amok in the teacher's absence, with the pupils hurling firecrackers, climbing walls and rafters, and beating each other over the ears with hockey sticks. That was its outward appearance. Actually, each of these pupils was painfully acquiring an eccentric education, not to be found in any textbook, which in a very few months might save his own life or terminate an enemy's.

The qualities which the instructors tried to impart were not many, but for jungle soldiers they are vital. Carefully planned courses were organized to develop the troops' ability to live without food or water for long periods; to accept wet, cold and mud as part of the day's routine; to resist disease by obeying the simple rules of jungle hygiene; to lie under cover, lost and doggo, for weeks if necessary; to move silently and kill expertly. They were taught how to conceal and camouflage themselves, how to cover up their tracks, how to creep through undergrowth unseen and unheard, how to pounce on the enemy and kill him secretly with knife or strangling-rope or bare hands. They learned jungle tactics, the arts of infiltration and ambush. They practised sniping. They mastered the science of travelling in pitch-darkness without making a sound; already in the Middle East, many of them had learned how to find their way silently and unerringly at night, but that was in open country, and the jungle, with its tangled maze of roots and branches and trip-vines, is quite another matter.

By keeping stationary in cramped and unnatural attitudes for hours on end, they trained themselves for close-quarters sniping. By taking their own curious pride in discomfort and rough living, they learned not only how to live *in* harsh country, but also *on* it. They acquired the ability to exist healthily on monotonous rations of the smallest bulk. Most importantly, by working and training constantly in a hubbub of high explosives and whistling bullets (supplied diligently by the school), they tempered their nerves to withstand the shock and noise of battle, enabling them to think and move with coolness and restraint under a stream of machine-gun fire.

From this kind of school, negating in many of its precepts the whole system of orthodox soldiering, they went back to the jungle and the Japanese. They went to the jungle, and are still going, not as valiant neophytes, improvising as they fight, but as trained graduates with a confident technique to fortify them. The Japanese found themselves confronted by skilled and toughened fighting men, as practised in this underworld of slime and shadows as themselves, but craftier, deadlier, and even more ruthless . . .

JON CLEARY

No Way to Fight a Flaming War

It was August 1942 when troops of the Australian Seventh Division first encountered the Japanese forces advancing along the Kokoda trail towards Port Moresby. In this passage from his novel The Climate of Courage, *Jon Cleary describes an ambush staged by a group of his AIF characters and the resulting confusion when Japanese pressure forces the group to retreat into the jungle.*

I wish we'd get some mail," Greg said. "It's been ten bloody days now since we got any."

"There should be some coming up today," Bluey said. He had come up last night from BHQ with four native carriers bringing rations. He hadn't arrived till just on dusk and he had decided to stay at company headquarters rather than go blundering down the mile of track in the dark. Vern hadn't objected when he had asked if he could come out on this standing patrol with them: he had recognised it as the desire of an old soldier to pull a trigger again. "I heard twelve bags of mail arrived at Brigade yesterday."

"I must have quite a wad waiting for me," Mick Kennedy said. "I got four sheilas writing to me."

"All suing you for maintenance, I'll bet," said Joe Brennan.

"There's too much talking." Vern's voice came out of the darkness, a disembodied whisper. "Shut your traps."

The darkness was so impenetrable that no man could see any part of himself; their eyes were just aching nerves that saw nothing but the blackness that was worse than blindness. There were no dimensions to the world about them but those offered by touch and sound; and they hadn't been blind long enough to be able to trust their other senses. The watery mud in which they squatted sucked and squelched as they moved to ease cold cramped muscles; the rain dripped in a fine steady stream through the invisible trees above them; and always there was the cold smooth feel of leaves like dead fingers brushing against their faces.

The platoon had been out here since yesterday morning acting as a standing patrol in front of the battalion position. All day they had been watching the track along which the Japanese were expected to advance, but after twenty-four hours there had still been no sign of movement. In another hour, just before dawn, they were to be relieved by a platoon from B Company. A Company would retire down the track for forty-eight hours' rest — unless the Japanese moved again within those forty-eight hours.

The battalion had been in action now three weeks without any respite at all. It had landed at Port Moresby and climbed up the long tortuous Kokoda trail, through the rainforests of the Owen Stanleys and down to join the single militia battalion that had been fighting a desperate but losing battle against a Japanese force that outnumbered it four to one. Every day reinforcements had been expected, but none had arrived. And every day the small force had been pushed farther back up the narrow trail that was the only way through to Moresby and the key to the conquest of New Guinea.

Casualties had been heavy. Enemy bullets and mortars had taken their toll, but the Japanese were no more destructive than the jungle. Fifty per cent of the men evacuated had been suffering from malaria or dysentery or, in one isolated case, scrub typhus. Haggett, the company 2 i/c, had been killed, and two others officers had been seriously wounded and sent back. Vern was now 2 i/c of the company and Jack was acting platoon leader.

Vern, sitting in the mud, so cold and wet that he was unaware of his sodden clothes clinging to him, felt someone slide towards him.

"That you, skipper?" It was Jack.

"Yes. How's it?"

"Bloody, as usual." Jack's voice was another whisper in the whisper of the rain. "I've had the shivers all night. I think I'm in for a bout of malaria."

"You'd better get to bed as soon as we get out of here. I don't want to lose you, too."

"Bed? Christ, is there a dry spot anywhere in the world? Three bloody weeks, and none of us has been dry in all that time!" Vern heard him slap his hand against his Tommy gun. "This is no way to fight a flaming war!"

Jack's voice had risen slightly, hissing through the rain. Vern put out a groping hand and patted Jack's arm. "Steady, feller."

"Sorry, chum. I've got a touch of SOL, I think. I keep thinking what a lovely war it was in the Middle East."

Then Vern heard him move away. Vern stood up, stretching his aching limbs, and looked at the luminous dial of his watch. He stood looking at the faintly glowing circle for a full minute, almost as if relieved to find that his eyes

could see. There was another hour to go till dawn. He
listened to the soft murmurings of the men, vague
sibilant murmurings that were like the gentle escape of
steam from valves. He knew most of them were like
himself: too tensed, ready to explode in anger or hysteria
unless some relief arrived soon. These past three weeks
had been worse than the whole accumulated time in the
Middle East. And what was worse was, that for the first
time in the experience of all of them but Joe Brennan,
they knew they were losing. They had fought for three
solid rain-drenched unending weeks and every day but
yesterday they had lost men and given ground. A feeling
of defeat had crept in and it was beginning to sap them
more than the chilling never-ceasing rain and the malaria
and dysentery and the fear that clotted each brain like a
malignant growth.

Vern had listened to them talking among themselves
yesterday. Mick Kennedy had started it. "Christ
Almighty, what's the use of it all? Why don't they drag us
out, get us back to the mainland and let's wait for the
bastards there? At least we'll be able to see 'em! Three
weeks, and I've seen the bastards once! That's all, just
once. The day we used the bayonet down at Eora
Creek."

"Where's everybody else, that's what I wanna know,"
Joe Brennan said. "Even in Greece we always knew
there was someone else around. They didn't help much,
but you didn't feel so bloody lonely. Outside of us and the
Thirty-Ninth, who else is in this war?"

"The Japs," Charlie Fogarty had said, and the men had
laughed quietly and gladly, easing their nerves.

"I wonder where the flaming Yanks are?" Mick had
said. "It's nine months since Pearl Harbour and we're
still fighting the war for 'em!"

"They're waiting to win it for us," Dad Mackenzie had

said. "We'll start the roll-back and then Bullshit MacArthur will step in and be the hero."

Vern had been glad Alec Putnam had not been around to hear the next ten minutes' abuse of the Americans. Sometimes he had wondered himself what was delaying the arrival of American forces in New Guinea. The Japanese had landed at Lae and Salamaua early in March and it must have been decided weeks ago by the Allied Command that the battle for Australia was to be fought in New Guinea. Alec had sometimes hinted at the extent of unpreparedness in the United States and Vern had tried to be fair in his judgment. But for a man who had been at war for over two years and had been on his way to a theatre of war within two months of joining the Army, it was hard to understand or forgive the tardiness of a nation, some of whose spokesmen had criticised Australia's part in the war and asked if she was worthy of American aid. Vern would be glad to see the Americans when they arrived, but he knew there would be some like Mick Kennedy whose welcome would be tinged with bitter sarcasm.

If the Americans were here now, or even some more Australian battalions, which for some reason were still being kept on the mainland, these past few weeks might have been a different story. On the only occasion when they had had a hand-to-hand clash with the Jap, on the day at Eora Creek when they had gone at him with the bayonet, they had more than held their own. But two sadly depleted battalions, no matter how often they used the bayonet, couldn't go on holding their own with an enemy that never seemed to diminish.

He remembered what Joe Brennan had once told him about the Germans in Greece: "There were just too many of them, that was all. They licked the soul-case out of us. But man for man, all things equal, I think we could have licked 'em. Trouble is, things ain't equal and haven't been since the start of this bloody war.''

That had been sixteen months ago and things were still not equal.

The Japanese came up the track with the piccaninny dawn, ahead of schedule. There was still no hint of daylight in the latticework of sky beyond the trees, but more just a lessening of the darkness. They had learned that the Japanese didn't like to move in darkness and usually waited for first daylight. But this morning he was on his way early, possibly eager to get going again after yesterday's respite.

"Someone on the track, boss," Charlie's voice was just a breath in the darkness. "A mob of 'em."

Vern strained his eyes till they pained him, but he could see nothing but the black wall of trees that seemed only a yard from his face. Then suddenly he saw the dark wedge of greyness, almost a light blackness, that was the bend in the track. He saw the black bobbing heads and heard the soft slush-slush of feet, then he opened up with his Tommy gun.

Above the sound of the guns he heard the screams and high-pitched, almost girlish shouts of the Japanese and he felt a wild fierce exultation that swept away his fatigue and despondency like the Tommy gun in his hands shattering the invisible bushes before him. The negroid silence had fled and now the paling morning was a welter of deadly sound. There was the short snap of rifle fire, the deeper chatter of the Tommy guns, the sharp flat bursts from the Bren; and still the shouting and squealing that was so much like that of raped schoolgirls.

Abruptly Vern gave the order to retire. "Mick and Joe, stay with me on the Bren! The rest of you beat it!"

The men stood up and slid away. In the gathering daylight filtering down through the trees like a mist Vern saw them go. The Japanese had begun to return the fire now, but they were still seeking the target and the bullets were thudding into the trees three or four feet above the men's heads. Fred Talmadge took his section out, then Jack came slipping down beside Vern.

"Greg's taking the other section out now." He stopped for a moment as right beside him Mick opened up again with the Bren. "Did you hear the firing over on the right flank? There it is now! The Thirty-Ninth must be copping it, too." All at once there was a distant succession of thumps. "The bastards are using mortars, too!"

"Righto, it's time we got out of here," Vern said, and gave the word to Mick and Joe. "You two buzz off. Jack and I'll toss a couple of grenades, then we'll be after you."

Mick hoisted the Bren to his shoulder, turned and went scuttling away in a crouch, followed by Joe. The Japanese fire had dropped lower now but was still too far to the right of Vern and Jack, ploughing into the empty bushes where Greg's section had been a minute before. Vern and Jack pulled the pins from a couple of grenades, tossed them, heard them explode, then got up and went at a run up the track.

They hadn't gone fifty yards when they heard the firing in front of them. They came round a bend in the track and Greg was shepherding men into the bushes. "Come on! Get a move on!" He spun round as Vern and Jack came slipping and sliding up the muddy trail behind him. In the grey morning his face too looked grey. "They got in behind us! They're right across the track, moving in on the company. We almost walked into our own blokes' fire!"

"Can't we take them from the rear?" Vern said.

"There's too many of them. We'd never get through

them, not with these other bludgers farther down the track trailing us.''

"Have you lost anybody?"

"Some. I don't know how many — look out!'' Vern dropped flat in the mud, seeing Jack fall beside him, as Greg let go with his Tommy gun above their heads. Vern swivelled round and saw the Japanese coming up the track. Oh, Christ, there are millions of them, he thought; and felt his gun jam, clogged with the mud in which he lay. Beside him Jack was firing with a savage intensity and behind him he could hear Greg slamming another magazine into his gun and cursing at the moment's delay. Desperately he worked to clear his own gun, fear frantic as a flame within him, his fingers scrabbling like despairing claws. A bullet clanged against his helmet, jerking his head sharply, and then he heard Greg cry out.

"He's got it!'' Jack gasped. "Get him out, for Christ's sake!''

Vern swung on his belly in the mud, slinging his gun by its strap across his back, and grabbed the cursing prostrate Greg by the shoulders. "Can you get up?''

"No, it's my ankle! Leave me and get out yourselves!''

Vern didn't answer. He lifted Greg, rolled him over on to his own back, then slowly began to crawl through the mud, off the track and into the thick bushes at the side. He moved slowly and with effort, Greg's weight pressing him flat into the stinking black mud, so that he seemed to be breathing nothing but the thick foul miasma that covered the treacherous sliding earth, a human tortoise crawling under its human shell.

Then there was the roar of two explosions and he guessed Jack had thrown two more grenades. Then suddenly Greg was lifted from his back and looking up he saw Dad Mackenzie and Fred Talmadge staggering away up through the rising bushes with Greg held between them. He got to his feet, felt Jack fling an arm about him, and together they went plunging up the hill.

At the top of the hill the rest of the men were waiting, eight, ten, twelve, he wasn't sure how many. One or two were wounded, and one man was sitting down holding his face in his hands as if he were weeping. Below them in the jungle, on three sides of the hill, firing was still going on. Away to their right the mortars were still thumping away and nearer at hand, where he guessed the rest of A Company to be, there was the woodpecker sound of two or three Japanese machine-guns. The firing was steady, and when more mortar bombs began to fall with their dull door-banging noise only two hundred yards away, he knew this was a major attack by the Japanese.

"We'll keep moving," he said. "Down the hill and straight ahead. Anybody hit?"

"I've got a slug in my shoulder," Bluey said. "And Charlie copped one in the face."

Vern looked down at the man holding his face in his hands. "Let's see, Charlie."

Charlie Fogarty brought away bloodstained hands to reveal a smashed and bloody face. The bridge of his nose was broken, the bone showing through as a jagged white fang, and it was impossible to distinguish his eyes from the raw bleeding flesh that hung down over them. There was a gasp of sympathy from the men looking at him.

"I can't see," Charlie said, and his soft voice was numbing and cold as a sliver of ice against the ears of the other men. "They've shot out my eyes and I can't see!"

"Where's your field dressing?" Vern found it and ripped off the covering. He wound the bandage round Charlie's head, trying to be gentle but knowing he had to hurry. "That'll do for now, Charlie. Soon's we get away from here, I'll dress it properly. Come on, up on your feet. You lead him, Bluey. How's your shoulder?"

"It'll keep," said Bluey, and took Charlie's hand as he might that of a child. "This way, mate."

Vern looked at Jack. "Can you carry Greg on your back, just still we get off this hill? We'll see about making a stretcher later."

"Why don't you leave me?" Greg's voice was thin with pain. "Don't waste time — "

Jack swung Greg on to his back. "You talk too much."

Then the party had gone sliding down the other side of the hill, slithering in the mud, tripping on roots, grabbing at thick lawyer vines, crashing against trees; while from down on the track where they had been a few minutes before there was suddenly a chorus of exultant high-pitched yells, a final mad burst of firing, then silence.

Vern looked at Dad Mackenzie. "Sounds like our blokes have had it."

Then he and Dad went sliding down the hill after the other men. At the bottom of the hill they were waiting in a straggling line along a faint native pad that ran roughly east and west. "Which way, skipper?"

Vern pulled up, gasping for breath, hesitated a moment, then said, "We'll go east."

"That may take us back to the Japs, skip," Jack said.

"We'll have to risk that," Vern said. "I lost my map case back there on the track, but I had a good look at it yesterday. West of here the country gets pretty wild. If we get in there we might never get out."

"We mightn't get out anyway," Mick Kennedy muttered.

"We'll see about that," Vern snapped. "Anyone who wants to chuck it in, had better do it now. We don't want to be handicapped by bludgers."

"I'm no bludger," Mick said.

"Well, then, stop whining," Vern said, and looked

around at the others. "Righto, on your way. You up front, Joe, as forward scout."

The party moved on. It had stopped raining now but the sky was still grey and sagging with water. The path was downhill and sometimes, when the screen of trees above thinned out they could see across to a spur of mountains in the west. There the sky was a trailing curtain caught in the grasping peaks; nearer, a small stray cloud or two floated above the mat of the jungle like grey carpet fluff. On either side of the narrow pad the jungle was a green wall covered with rotting fungus and tangled lianas: it was like walking down a back alley of some ancient forgotten city. Underfoot the path was a slop of mud that covered their boots above the ankles and in which thick leaf mould floated as a slippery trap for the unwary foot. Water dripped from the trees in a steady irritating whisper and always, so that it had now become part of the men's sense of smell, there was the heavy clogging stench of vegetable decay.

They had been walking ten minutes when Vern, at the head of the column, stopped and held up his hand. "Joe's coming back."

A moment later Joe came round a bend in the track with Major Caulfield, Father Chase, Alec Putnam and Herb Nutter. Caulfield had lost weight since they had been in New Guinea and now looked a tired older shadow of his former strutting self. Vern wondered if he himself had aged in the same time. It seemed years since he had said goodbye to Dinah and the kids.

"I wondered if you'd made it, Radcliffe." Caulfield hadn't lost his arrogance of voice, even when he whispered as now. "This all you managed to get out?"

Vern felt a stab of temper, but he checked his angry retort. "This is the lot, sir. What happened to the company?"

"I don't quite know," Caulfield said. "Captain Putnam and I were on our way down to you when the business started. We could go neither backwards nor forwards, so we had to duck into the bush. We were caught between two parties of the Japs."

"Goddamned embarrassing." Alec's face was drawn with strain, and blood flowed from a deep scratch down one cheek, but he still managed to look wryly cheerful.

"I think the company's had it," said Father Chase. "Or most of it, anyway. They were on us before we knew what was happening, then they'd gone through us and were on their way to BHQ. It was the same old story, but worse this time. There were too many of them."

Herb Nutter moved past the officers. "What's the matter, sarge? You cop it?"

"In the ankle," Greg was standing on one leg, leaning against Jack. His eyes were dull with pain and his voice was a shredded whisper. He had gone yellow beneath his tan and looked ready to faint.

Herb patted the small extra haversack that hung on one skinny hip. "I'm supposed to be a stretcher-bearer, only I lost my stretcher. But we'll fix your ankle up later, sarge. And Charlie, too. What happened, sport? Wasn't you looking where you was going.

Charlie smiled weakly but said nothing. There was something unreal about the flash of his teeth below the bloodstained dressing about his eyes. He was breathing through his mouth in soft hissing gasps.

"Who have we here?" Caulfield said, and looked along the line. "Radcliffe, Putnam, the padre, Savanna, Morley, Brown, Talmadge, Mackenzie, Kennedy, Fogarty, Nutter. And Brennan back down the track. That makes thirteen of us, a nice lucky number. Have you got a map, Radcliffe?"

In the scrambling retreat of the past few weeks

Caulfield had gradually lost or discarded most of his paraphernalia, but Vern couldn't resist the slap. "Haven't you?"

The barb went home. Colour flooded into Caulfield's face, but all at once he turned away and went stumbling down the path. Vern and the men stared after him in amazement, then they saw him lean heavily against a tree and begin to vomit.

"The poor bastard's sick," Bluey said.

"I didn't think his stomach was capable of it," said Dad Mackenzie quietly and without sympathy. "He must be nearly human, after all."

In a minute or so Caulfield came back. There was a scum across his eyes and his freckles were black in the paleness of his sagging face. "Malaria, I think. A bad dose of it." He shook his head and shut his eyes instantly in pain. "Christ, I've got a headache!"

"If he asked me for an aspro," Mick Kennedy murmured, "and I had one, I'd drop it in the mud and make him look for it."

Father Chase looked at him and said softly, "Ever heard of the milk of human kindness, Mick?"

"It curdles when I look at him, padre," Mick said. "I got no Christian feelings towards that mongrel. So don't expect 'em of me."

The men stood watching Caulfield swaying in the middle of the path with his eyes shut. At last Caulfield opened his eyes and made an effort to draw himself together. "We'd better get on, Radcliffe. You take the rear. I'll lead. Ready, men? March!"

"Listen to the drongo," Dad muttered. "Thinks he's back at Ingleburn."

Vern stood by the side of the path watching the men file by him. There was a sameness about the look of their faces: the Japanese and the jungle had given them a common expression: it was a look of exhausted resignation. They had lost their enthusiasm for the war and would fight now only for their own survival. Ideas and causes, patriotism and antifascism, were buried somewhere in the black slime of the past three weeks.

They were bent forward under the weight of their packs, some a little more than others. Herb Nutter was carrying Greg's pack besides his own, and Father Chase was carrying Jack's. Bluey's was hanging from his un-wounded shoulder, canting him to one side. Vern took it from him as he went past.

"I'll take this for a while, Bluey. You look after Charlie."

"Thanks, skipper," Bluey said. In action the men always stopped calling Vern by his first name. Out of ac-tion, on leave or in the privacy of a camp tent, he was their friend; but as soon as they were back in the serious business of war they automatically looked upon him as their commander. It was a relationship that might not have worked in a good many armies, but it seemed to work in the AIF.

Vern fell in behind the file of men. They went plodding, sometimes sliding, down the path, a line of un-distinguishable brothers. Some were in khaki and others in green, some in shorts and others in long ducks tucked into canvas gaiters; but sodden and mud-covered, hun-chbacked under their packs, all with the same glistening steel-topped heads, it was almost impossible at a glance to tell one from another. The jungle had completed the Army's efforts at regimentation.

DAVID FORREST

Beyond Bobdubi Ridge

David Forrest's fictitious Eighty-Third Battalion is a militia battalion, and the honourable role played by Australia's militia in the battle for Salamaua during the New Guinea campaigns of 1943 is one of Forrest's main themes in this passage from The Last Blue Sea. *In the character Chilla Troedson the author acknowledges that not all soldiers were able to withstand the mental pressures of jungle warfare.*

THE jungle and the ranges were ancient and without end. There was day, and then there was night, and this was how time had been measured in the jungle since man first walked upon the earth. There were no months, and no years, and no seasons, but only day, and then night.

Rain swept through the high ranges and the fogs seeped through their forests and the undergrowth: and under the passing of many feet, the Missim Trail began to break up, boots chopping the fetid ground into sludge, and in the sludge tree-roots caught at feet and became steps on the side of the mountain.

The sun had never shone there, and a man did not walk

on earth, but thirty feet above it, on thirty feet of decay laid down by the forest over scores and centuries of years: and in the decay caverns lurked, with their roofs of muck supported by the roots of trees, so that occasionally, under the pressure of climbing feet, the roof collapsed, flinging a man through the ground into danger of being staked or even more gravely injured.

The sun had never shone there, and the forest grew in a mantle of moss and fungus and slime; and in the forest, moss hung from branches and roots and trunks and vines like putrid, grey fairy floss. The mosses dripped with water and slime, and the roots of the trees were as much in the air as they were in the ground. That part of them that was visible writhed and twisted in the air like a witches' ballet stilled in a grotesque climax, as though captured in a photograph to be seen for all the rest of time.

The whole ancient rotting forest perched precariously on the sides of the mountain. The ranges and the moss and the forest and the slime went up and up into the sky, into the realms of the aeroplane. The rarefied air made a man's ears pain, and burned his lungs and his throat raw and then almost numb, while he struggled over the mountain under sixty or seventy pounds of weapons and ammunition and gear.

His hands groped for tree-roots and vines and his feet flailed in the putrid sludge, and his hands slid on the slimy timber when he grasped at it for support.

When he could not climb on his feet, then he crawled, like a beetle, living intimately with the sludge and the smell of it till it soaked and plastered his body and cargo and uniform with additional weight; plastered his face, got in his ears; lived intimately with it, smelling it, tasting it, sleeping in it, till his green uniform turned black: lived in it with the fogs and the rain; and at night, curled in a ground-sheet and a damp half-blanket to fend off the freezing cold.

So the Missim Trail climbed into the clouds, and when it reached its pinnacle it fell down through the moss forest and a man slipped and stumbled and tripped and fell down the trench of sludge and tree-roots and slimy handholds. Then when he thought that he had taken leave of the moss forest, then the Missim Trail almost broke his heart, for the ranges rose again, in a massive wall, as great as the one he had traversed.

He dragged his heavy feet after him, and sometimes he crawled, and sometimes he slid backwards from a breaking, rotten handhold, losing height he had gained: and his universe contracted about him until it encompassed himself and the twilight and the muck he lived in. On the wide steppes south of Moscow, the Russian Army fought for Orel, but he had forgotten that Russia existed. The bombers flew to the invasion of Sicily in the Mediterranean, but the Mediterranean, too, had disappeared from his mind.

In the United States, in Detroit, white men and negroes fought out a race riot with rifles and machine-guns; and in Australia, politicians abused each other concerning the Brisbane Line, a returned soldiers' organisation denied membership to militiamen, and people complained about the shortage of petrol and beer and butter: but he dragged himself up the ranges, and when he crawled in the forest, he finally forgot even the land that he came from.

There was the Trail, and the nature of it; and beyond the Trail, in front of it, behind, to the side, there was no existence: and once, a wounded commando came over the Missim in the other direction; no longer, it seemed, a man but a bit of debris spat out of war, like a derelict ejected from civilisation.

"Make way for the wounded," and the cry echoed through the silent forest, carried from voice to voice in a croak. "Make way."

The debris moved like a jerky puppet, and one saw that he was young, young as Ron Fisher, but weary with a great age upon him. This was what Ron Fisher remembered, that as the debris passed him by, it winked.

Then from the top of the eastern wall of the ranges, the Missim Trail fell down from the sky, for thousands and thousands of feet, down into a wild, twisted land of ranges and chasms and razorbacked ridges: and a man understood why the enemy believed the Kuper Ranges to be impassable, and why a man who set out from Bulwa weighing twelve stone should be less than eleven when he came to the end of the Missim Trail.

The days and nights went away, one by one, until they receded, indistinguishable from each other in a blur of time; and somewhere in that time, the Eighty-Third Battalion came to Missim and went down to the Uliap Creek, which runs, burbling and swirling, along the foot of the dark green ridge of Bobdubi.

On the other side of Bobdubi Ridge was the Komiatum Track, leading from Salamaua to Mubo and Wau. Bobdubi Ridge protected the Track like a shield, and the enemy were on the Ridge, on Old Bobdubi and Old Vickers, on the Triangle and Gwaibalom, Orodubi and Sugarcane Knoll.

The companies of the Eighty-Third Battalion began to disperse in the jungle west of the Uliap, covering off, as it were, against their objectives; Don Company for Old Vickers, A Company for the Triangle, B Company for Orodubi.

Bobdubi rose above them, high and green, but they could not see it for the density of the jungle. They could not see the Ridge, but they knew it was there, and it came into their lives, subduing their voices, colouring their thoughts, and because time had almost run out, they wrote home, borrowing stubs of pencils from one another, writing on miserly preserved pieces of letter-paper which the jungle humidity had already begun to attack.

When they had written their letters, they prepared: a day, a night, and then another day, and in the late afternoon they moved down through the undergrowth to the bank of the Uliap Creek, there to wait for the sun to come up. There, in the hour before dawn, while the rain thundered upon the jungle, a young soldier in Seven Section shot himself in the foot, and Sergeant Townsend carried him away to the Regimental Aid Post as though he carried a baby to its mother.

At that same hour, southeast of Mubo, the American regiment landed in Nassau Bay, and on the heights around the Mubo Gorge, ten miles south of Bobdubi Ridge, the troops of the AIF stirred themselves to another jungle day of twilight and fighting.

Beyond Poppendetta, on the Buna airfields, the bombers and the fighters rolled out on the runaways, and while they stood there, bombed up and waiting, the night went away, and the morning came.

*   *   *

Colonel Wilson was coming back from Sugarcane Knoll. He said goodbye to the commando major and called to his escort, and they went down the long track along the Uliap, west of Bobdubi Ridge: past Nambling and Orodubi and Gwaibalom, past the Triangle and Halligan's Spur and Old Vickers.

He had gone to Sugarcane Knoll because it afforded a tactical view of the valley behind Bobdubi Ridge. From a study of his map, he had been prepared for the view, and the more distant view of the valley of the Francisco River, and beyond that the stern, green razorbacks of Kela Heights guarding Salamaua from sight. In the south, he had been prepared to see the clouds and the ranges, and the black bulk of Mount Tambu reinforcing the enemy defences of Mubo.

Colonel Wilson had not been prepared to expect the sea. The sea was a shock, it seemed so close. It was close, and then, vast and clean, it stretched away from him, a great noble lake that went out to the horizon and met the sky.

The sea was a shock, and he went down the long Uliap track, remembering the sweet and bitter day that the battalions came out of the swamps of Gona and saw the sea.

How does one find the sea? Take Bobdubi Ridge and cut the Komiatum Track. Then when Mubo has fallen, and Mount Tambu has fallen, and there is no enemy left to the south and west of the river, then cross the river and fight him on the Kela Heights: and from the Kela go down to Salamaua and walk on the white sand, and trail your fingers in the water and marvel that the sea is soft and cool and clean.

That is how one finds the sea.

One has to fight for the sea, and I am getting old, and tired. I have learned something that is known only to the men of Bardia Morning, that a road can be too long, and that if you travel it far enough, all that you have left to fight for is the sea and the last of your self-respect.

That is the truth, and now I must go on a little further, and find the sea.

The jungle was a mass too large for the eye to comprehend: a mass of trees, creepers, shrubs and undergrowth. This afternoon the jungle was still, so that from Old Bobdubi in the north, to Sugarcane Knoll in the south, no sound arose and no breath of wind came to stir the leaves or the fetid heat.

The leaves stretched so far, and rose so high above a man's head, that they were the fourth dimension, the jungle.

The jungle appeared empty.

On Halligan's Spur, in the riot of leaves, on the Spur where it begins to turn towards the Triangle, Nine Section lay in ambush.

The jungle was far from being empty.

The admiral stared through the leaves along the track. To his left, Peter Mitchell nursed his rifle and waited. To his right, Nervous Lincoln, who was on his first patrol, watched the track in trepidation. Ted Thorn dozed, as did Mitch and Ron Fisher.

That three of the six of them could doze was a supreme, sweet paradox of the war on the ridge. Ron Fisher treasured the lying in ambush, for then he escaped from the hunting, avoided the unpleasant, forgot the terror of the leaves, slept as he could never sleep at night in the perimeter. He dozed in the ambush, far from guns, from knives in the night, far from strain and Butcher O'Grady.

The ambush was a valve, releasing the pent-up pressure, for the mind desires to forget, and forget it does. Forget how Carnal Knowledge slid down in the mud, making that dreadful noise in his throat. Forget the horrible suspicion one formed on looking into the eyes of Lieutenant Cislowski, wondering whether he is a particle of Colonel Maitland's estate, finding the doubt proved. Forget how a man clung to the mud while grenades pounded about him, forsaking self-respect for naked fear. That is the most shattering blow of all, and a man *must* forget, as he must forget the terrible temptation to leave his comrades for safety.

The mind takes a memory and sifts it, discarding the obvious, the detail. In a few days, a man has forgotten the noise Carnal made, but the memory of it was horror, and a thin stratum of horror sinks down into the mind. There is a layer in the mind that Jigger ran through fire to aid Old Miserable; and another that Lalor died, and that layer is of pity so infinite that a man feels very old at the age of nineteen.

When the mind had accumulated a certain number of layers, they constituted experience, and from them, one came to wisdom and understanding; setting out on a long road to the rediscovery of the simple truths of life; or if one was very young, like Ron Fisher, discovering them for the very first time, and taking them to himself as his father must have done, long ago, between Sinai and the Wells of Beersheba.

In the forest, on the day when the jungle was so still, from Old Bobdubi to Sugarcane Knoll, a hand nudged the dozing Fisher. At the touch, serenity fled, and slowly his head came up from his hands folded across the gun-butt. His eyes, watching through the leaves, began to grow hard, and any pity that may have been there was submerged.

He had never seen a live Japanese before, and now there were ten of them, one behind the other, coming down the track from the Triangle. That they were men did not occur to him. They were something less than men.

He moved infinitesimally, wriggling and bracing himself behind the Bren gun, his eye finding the foresight in the aperture of the other, finding the enemy scout lined in both. Let him come, right up close. The closer they are, the harder they fall.

It was the Bren gun that would begin the ambush. He wriggled again, cuddling the gun-butt. The other five men waited upon his judgment. For twenty-five seconds, he led them, transcending rank and age and discipline.

His heart was thudding painfully against his ribs. He was aware of every bone and muscle and fibre in his body. He was alive, and entire, and he was going to live for a thousand years.

Do unto those, as they do unto you.

Steel and sound streamed out of the Bren gun, waking up the forest, punching the enemy into the mud, shredding all their lives and emotions in one great, gigantic flash of knowledge of death, and after the flash, there was nothing.

"Come on," said Ted Thorn, and Nine Section was gone, sliding and slipping down the side of the Spur, away from the place where they had waited in peace, and which would be for some little time the most dangerous place to be in all New Guinea.

They came home again to the perimeter, to the rain and the mud and the knives in the night, to the conversations conducted always in whispers, to the waterlogged weapon pits and belongings that were never dry, to the undergrowth and bully beef and Lieutenant O'Grady.

*   *   *

Chilla Troedson stared down through the fringe of undergrowth at the track where he would presently have to lead the way. He stood there, staring, hating the leaves, feeling the terror of the unseen upon him.

He stared in dread, and began to quiver. The leaves of the jungle and the last of his self-respect fought madly in his mind. They made a battlefield of him and he could stand no more. His mind began to crumple, not courageously as history would have it, but pitifully, as it befell in the world of leaves.

He shook and could not control himself and the leaves of the jungle swept over his mind, degrading him, sneering at his futility, smearing his repute, smearing his courage.

Before his eyes the leaves and the track swelled to obscene dimensions, swelling up and rushing over him. Then he almost laughed, so that his jaw quivered and the last shred of control left to him clamped his teeth together in silence.

He could not know that there were only two more days of the battle for the valley.

"I —— " he croaked, and shut his mouth, but it did not avail him.

With a great, shuddering sigh he surrendered.

He said huskily, "I can't do it."

And avoided the gaze of his men, *his* men, who looked to him for leadership. They stared, woodenly, knowing dimly that he was finished. He avoided their gaze, for in it there could be only contempt and derision. They hoped dimly that he would lift his head and look at them so that he would see that they did understand.

That was the most terrible part of all, that they did understand, but he thought they sneered.

Snowy Higgins squeezed his shoulder and began to walk toward the track, the track and the leaves that his mind loathed and shrank from; the track, the only track they knew, that led to Salamaua.

"It's the leaves," said Troedson, and began to weep.

"It's the leaves," thought Snowy, and started to walk down the track.

He was scared, and lonely, and the track went into the valley and the Komiatum. The sea became very dim.

Westinghouse and the Golliwog were sitting side by side in the lean-to.

"Same old answer," said Westinghouse. "It's the leaves."

"He's got to go back," said the Golliwog.

He thought, it's the leaves . . . and disease . . . and O'Grady.

Ron Fisher approached the lean-to quietly and the Golliwog's dark, killer eyes seemed to dissect him particle by particle.

Ron Fisher raised his eyes to Westinghouse. "It's no good, sir. He won't go."

He added with a sigh, "He's got to go back."

The Golliwog's eyes moved, ever so slightly, as though several trains of thought suddenly came together and fused into an unexpected unity. Troedson had brought the ideas together, but the Golliwog forgot about Troedson.

His voice was so soft it was arresting.

"Corporal Fisher?"

Ron Fisher glanced down and found himself unable to look away from the dark, compelling eyes.

Lieutenant Westinghouse sat quite still, pinned by the soft words, afraid in the silence that followed them.

"Corporal," said the Golliwog softly, "are you ready to carry out any order I ever give you . . . regardless of the consequences?"

Ron Fisher stared in fascination. He thought, this man's never been more deadly in his life, and he's a killer.

When he spoke he could feel his throat tight around the words. "Yes, sir."

Oh God, what have I said?

"I'm handing out a lot of dirty jobs tomorrow," said the Golliwog. "They're really dirty. I've got one for you."

He threw his tobacco-tin to Ron Fisher. "Here, roll yourself a smoke."

They crouched in the valley and waited, not knowing the final horror approaching them in the leaves.

Mitch grumbled, "The Golliwog must really want this information."

Ron Fisher nodded and studied the undergrowth.

He thought, "I don't like this. If they're not back in five minutes, we'll go in after them."

He had three men forward, three to one flank, and five including himself at a point where he could control the movement.

The group of five men waited for the three men forward to come back. They had no illusions, for they had seen the Golliwog's eyes when he issued the order.

"Trouble," thought Ron Fisher broodingly. "Trouble. I can feel it."

He brought in the three men from the flank and began to lead them forward after the front patrol.

"In this particular respect," the Golliwog had said, "this is an order which you will not question. You will find the enemy. If he finds you, you will run. Regardless of the consequences. This order will be obeyed to the letter."

Ron Fisher crept through the undergrowth. The three men followed him. He was within grenade range of the Komiatum Track, and if the reports were correct, within the area of a battalion of infantry temporarily encamped.

A bird flew wildly up from the jungle in front of him and he froze there, in the unwinking silence.

The silence exploded.

The major wanted the information. It was needed, to help tear open the road to the sea.

Of the three men in the forward patrol, someone had to escape, or they and all the platoon died for nothing.

"Run!" Stanaway screamed, knowing he had to die.

"Run!" he screamed in desperation, and hurled himself at the nearest Japanese. His rifle-butt crunched against a skull and the man flopped into the mud. They all came at him then, beating him with rifles, uttering strange screams and cries and clawing at him.

He stood erect in the middle of the track and threshed at them with his rifle while his comrades ran. They ran, obeying the Golliwog. They ran, by his order stripped of the only rationality left to them, that they never leave a man on a track. They ran, demented.

They left him to fight in the valley. He stood erect in the grey jungle mud, and arms cracked and heads stained the butt with an obscenity of blood and grey matter and pieces of bone.

His chest heaved and his shoulders spread as he chopped and swung and threshed. He had lost his hat and half his shirt and the blood streamed down his face from a sword cut.

The butt whirled and stabbed and struck and the crunching nausea was lost upon him and his enemies, for in the whirlpool of his rifle there was no haven for reason.

He stood, alone, defending the track, having chosen to die, and his comrades brought the information to the Golliwog at the Triangle.

"It won't be long," said the major softly, and turned away, knowing from their eyes the price these men had paid for the scrap of information he had needed to complete the division's plan.

He began to walk, down the Uliap track, aware of their

eyes, watching him, staring; executed eyes, naked to all the world.

He thought tightly, "They would have done it for no one else but me."

The jungle closed about Major Ellerslie and gave the eyes privacy. They had need of it, as he did.

Morning would bring them the knowledge that they were never going back to the valley: but only death could ever erase the day when they last walked east of Bobdubi Ridge.

PETER RYAN

Behind Japanese Lines

Fear Drive My Feet is Peter Ryan's account of his experiences as a young Australian patrolling behind Japanese lines in the isolated and rugged country north of the Markham River in New Guinea during 1942-43. Some of the hardships and dangers which Ryan constantly endured are vividly described in the following passage.

W E set out on 30 May over what was assuredly one of the worst tracks in New Guinea. It was incredibly steep and rough, through moss forest all the way. We all, even the Kiakum men, suffered violent headaches which seemed to split our skulls in half. Probably they were caused by the very great altitude. To cap our miseries, leeches were swarming everywhere. The whole surface of the ground seemed to be covered with their tiny waving shapes, smelling blood and stretching out for it. We dared not sit down, but we halted every twenty minutes or so while I scraped them from under my gaiters and the boys picked them from between their toes. Despite our exertions in climbing, we shivered all the way. When almost in sight of Kawalan, the first Wain village, we met with an obstacle that was almost enough to make us turn back. A landslide had carried away a large section of the hillside, where the track had once been, leaving a rock-face without a foothold of any description, a sheer drop of fifty feet or more. After half an hour's search in the bush the boys found enough vines to fashion a rough rope ladder. We tied it to a tree, and hoped for the best as we lowered ourselves into space, bumping hard against the rock from time to time as the rope swung round, and scraping the skin off our knees and elbows. We left it hanging there, hoping that no one would come along and move it. If they did, the only way of getting back to Kiakum would be to make a two- or three-day journey through Wampangan and Bawan.

There were only two men in Kawalan village when I arrived, and not a sign of the women and children. I questioned the two men about this, but they declined to say where the others were, and both affirmed that there were no Japanese in Boana. I was not at all happy about this "ghost town" of several dozen empty, silent houses. After a while one becomes very sensitive to the "atmosphere" of native villages — there is an air about them which tells you whether everything is as it should be. In this case I had the strongest possible premonition of something being wrong, and so as soon as it became dark we crept quietly out of the house we were occupying, and spent the night at the edge of the surrounding bush.

In the morning the tultul of Kawalan appeared mysteriously out of the blue, and he too assured us that there were no Japanese at Boana, nor would he give us any hint of where the rest of the Kawalan people were.

I still did not believe what these people had said about Boana, and decided to investigate. Telling Watute and Pato to approach it down the left side of the Bunzok

Valley, I went off with Dinkila down the other side. We were to call at Bandong en route to prepare the cargo I wished to take back to Kiakum. If one of us were blocked the chances were that the others might get through and see what was happening.

Bandong I found almost as empty as Kawalan. In spite of the assurances of the few old natives who were there, the people were not merely away at work in their gardens, for every cultivated patch we passed was deserted. Something mysterious was happening. But what? In the hope of solving the mystery Dinkila and I set off for Sokulen after only a short pause to regain our wind.

We had covered about half the distance when a native lad about twelve years old came panting up behind us. He brought a message from Watute, saying that he and Pato had discovered that Boana was inhabited by a strong force of Japanese, and that almost every native in the Wain had gathered there at the summons of the enemy commander, who intended to announce new Japanese government of the area. Watute and Pato were still investigating, and they suggested that I should wait for them in Kawalan, and not take the risk of proceeding to Sokulen.

Dinkila and I turned back towards Kawalan, but did not go into the village. Instead, we camped in the bush on the side of a small hill near by, commanding a good view of the track along which Watute would come.

Late the following afternoon we saw him limping up the hill, and it was Dinkila who first spotted the fact that he seemed to have lost all his belongings except his rifle, bayonet, and ammunition. When he reached us, mud-caked, scratched, and weary, he had a grim story to tell.

Pato and he had decided to spend the previous night in a house at Wampangan, intending to go to Boana the next day disguised as bush kanakas, he told us in a bitter voice. Two natives who had come up from Lae with the Japs heard of their presence and betrayed them to the enemy. A party of twenty Nips attempted to trap them in the house, but they heard them coming just in time, and managed to escape by tearing up part of the light bamboo floor and dropping down beneath the house. In the darkness, and with all the shooting and confusion, Watute became separated from Pato. He did not know where Pato was now — but feared he might have been killed or captured. The Japanese got onto Watute's track and chased him up the valley. They had heard about my presence there, and were out for my scalp too. He thought they were still a few hours behind him, but whatever happened we should get out of the way quickly.

As there was not a kanaka to be seen anywhere we had to abandon all thought of taking extra stores back to Kiakum. Before darkness fell we had made a few miles along the road back, and when we could see to walk no farther lay down to sleep in the bush at the side of the track. It poured with rain all night, soaking us as we huddled together for warmth.

At dawn next day we moved on. We had no means of knowing whether the Japs would continue the pursuit past Kawalan when they found us gone, but after we had struggled up our vine-made Jacob's ladder we cut it away behind us and felt reasonably safe. It was about three o'clock when the house at Kiakum came into view, and we hurried down the hill for the last few hundred yards, with only bad news for Les, and a bitter blow to give the rest of the boys, who had been very fond of Pato.

We drafted a radio message to headquarters to give them our latest information on Japanese movements. According to Watute, the patrol now at Boana was surveying the overland route the enemy proposed to set up bet-

ween Madang and Lae. They would shortly leave for
Kaiapit, in the Upper Markham, travelling through
Sedau, Sugu, and the Erap, by the same route as that
taken by the party we had so narrowly missed last month.
Their destination, Kaiapit Mission, was being watched
by an old New Guinea resident, a goldminer called Harry
Lumb. He moved about the district in much the same
way as Jock and I had patrolled the Wain, and knew the
area and its natives intimately. I had last met him in Wau
some weeks earlier, when he had just discovered a case
of canned beer in somebody's abandoned cache. We
drank a few tins, and then buried the remainder at the
foot of a tall dead pine tree. "There it is now — a nice little drop for our next meeting," Harry had said with a grin
of satisfaction as we piled earth on top of it. Then we
parted, he bound for his post at Kaiapit, I on my way
across the Markham.

I had thought of Harry as soon as Watute said the
Japanese were bound for Kaiapit, and now mentioned it
to Les.

"Do you think Port Moresby will warn Harry Lumb?" I
asked. "He's quite likely to be poking round that Kaiapit
country now."

"Sure to, I should think, when they get our news that
the Nips are bound that way. Why? Do you think we
ought to suggest it?"

"No. I suppose they would do it as a matter of course,
and we have to keep our radio messages as short as possible."

And so the message went without any suggested warning to Lumb. I wished later we had put it in.

While I removed my wet and stinking clothes, Tauhu
cooked a meal and Les sat down at the radio and tapped
out the message. I was so tired that I ate more or less
mechanically, half asleep. I thought in an idle sort of way

how pleasant it would be to return to the old humdrum life of the Wain of last December. It had seemed so dull then, but what a welcome change it would be now.

We spent most of the night trying to decide what to do. The position, as we saw it, was briefly this: the native situation was very bad. The kanakas had thrown in their lot with the Japanese, having apparently decided to regard them as the new rulers of the island. We could remain alive only by hiding in some quiet spot like Kiakum. But that would achieve nothing. The alternatives were to attempt to escape back across the Markham and admit failure, or to try to cross the Saruwaged Range and see what was happening on the north side. We had heard that two men, Lincoln Bell and Fairfax-Ross, were somewhere on the Rai coast, and we hoped we might be able to find them, and perhaps help them.

"Anyhow, if you ask me," said Les, "getting back across the Markham just now is not only inglorious — it's impossible!"

"All right. That leaves the Saruwageds. What about it?"

"Yes — let's have a go at it."

So it was decided that next day we should try to cross the range, and if we failed we would consider trying to get back to Wau. Following our usual plan of keeping the native members of the party well in the picture, we sent for Kari and asked what he thought of the idea. He said he was quite prepared for the crossing, and he was certain all the others would feel the same way.

"All right," I said. "Tell all the men to pack their gear at dawn tomorrow."

We talked of our chances of making the crossing. I remembered how Jock had described the mountains, though the track he had used was a different one and lay ten miles or so to the east. If anything, the range was a trifle higher where we were going to try. All day long the mountains were covered with clouds, but at dawn and sunset the summits were frequently clear. Often we had risen early at Kiakum to study the bare windswept rock-faces, the sheer precipices, and the yawning cavern-like valleys that scarred the sides of the range. Here and there, like white threads, streams coursed down. We knew our task would not be easy, but the valley of the Sanem River seemed to offer the best approach, and the Kiakum people said the range could be crossed from there, though none of them would admit to having made the crossing. Probably they feared we would ask them to come as guides.

In the morning, to the great grief of our friend the village idiot, the Kiakum people lifted our gear to take it to the village of Mogom, the most northerly habitation in the Sanem Valley shown on our map. North of that was unexplored, and we had no idea whether people lived there, or whether it was just a barren waste. Even if it were inhabited, it was likely that the people would be so wild and shy that we would be unable to establish contact with them, much less induce them to undertake the long and arduous carry across the range.

We left Kiakum with some regret. Our quarters had been comfortable and the people friendly, and it had been a place of wild, magnificent beauty. We would probably never see it again in our lives, and we felt sad to think it as we looked ruefully at the plot of ground we had already turned up to make ourselves a garden. The plot seemed a symbol of man's incurable optimism, even in the face of every possible reason for being pessimistic.

Part 5
The War in Europe

Death walks abroad. In shelters underground
A million souls, united in their dread
Are drowned in waves of terrifying sound
Through years of time, as bombs burst overhead;
Vast fires rage to light for miles around
Wrecked cities of the homeless and the dead.

Kevin E. Collopy
from "Reaping the Whirlwind"

D.E. CHARLWOOD

Mission Accomplished

D.E. Charlwood flew as a navigator with a mixed RAF and RAAF Lancaster crew, operating against targets in Nazi-controlled Europe from Elsham Wolds, a Bomber Command aerodrome in Lincolnshire. This is one of several accounts Charlwood gives us in No Moon Tonight *of operations in which he took part during the winter of 1942-43.*

THE ground crew have shut the rear door, sealing us within the fuselage. Down the long, dim interior I can see the bulkhead and the armour-plated door; then the stretcher at the rest position; then, in the empty, ribbed belly, the legs of the mid-upper gunner dangling from his turret. Beyond him, where it is too dark to see, sits the rear gunner, most isolated of us all.

It is five months today since we came to the squadron, sufficient time for us to have brought more detachment to these hours than we had imagined possible. For the fourth successive night the target is Essen; the time of take off 1715. In the semi-darkness rain is pattering insistently on the metal shell encasing us. Through the wet windscreen the outer world is distorted as though by tears — its multitude of lights, its vague, squat buildings, its low-hanging cloud. As we begin trundling to take off position the nearer lights assume a new order, forming a long line on either side of a straight, wet road that narrows in the indefinite distance and leads God knows where. Naked gooseneck flares are out, the flares that can best be seen in such weather as lies tonight over the whole east coast.

At the take off position there is no waiting. The same words are spoken as on every night.

"You've got your green, Skipper."

"Thanks, Doug. Everyone OK?" A pause follows that seems very long. "Here we go then."

Whatever we may be in other hours, in this moment of take off, as we part from the earth, a different spirit holds us. In the voices that have spoken I could swear that there was a momentary realisation, called out by the intensity of the hour. What the realisation may be for each man, I do not know; but I feel that in it there is an awareness of his love for the men with him and, more than this, a moment of widened vision in which all danger, and death itself, assume their ultimate proportions, which are far less than the proportions we have given them in daily life. We feel on our bodies the forward surge of the aircraft and on our eardrums the assault of the engines. The instruments on my table begin vibrating as though in alarm. We lift from the earth; leave the lights; pass over the barracks. Behind us the flarepath shrinks rapidly.

I write, "Airborne 1715."

"Undercarriage!"

"Undercarriage!"

On the familiar order and reply Doug retracts the wheels. Obscure in the failing light I can see the village.

Somewhere among the huddled buildings the girl of the fair, upswept hair is listening. That we stood so close an hour ago I can barely believe. We are in cloud; now out of it; now deeply into the main layer. We are wrapped about in mists that erase from our minds all sense of whereabouts. To me we have become nothing more than a mark on the white expanse of my chart, which we shall remain until the journey is over.

For a long time we climb on instruments until, at ten thousand feet, the cloud about us is diffused with light. Like a diver rising from the sea, we emerge into a region of waning sunlight and clear skies. About us a floor of cloud is flushed by a sun that has not yet set. Arched above it is the dome of the sky, quickly darkening. In this Arctic region nothing else exists.

There is still half an hour before we set course. In this half hour the whole squadron must climb to fifteen thousand feet, then set course over Elsham for Sheringham, the rendezvous. A second plane breaks through. Passing it we read its identification.

"K Kitty — Berry's kite."

A third and a fourth plane rise from below us. Beautifully they bank and climb. Ted's voice reaches me, metallic on the intercom. "There's a small break in the cloud. I can see the Humber and Reade's Island. Now it's closing over."

Against the roar of climbing revs our voices sound distant and unreal, as though, instead of sitting close together, we were separated by many miles in the outer emptiness. Out of the east night is rising, majestic and overwhelmingly lonely. Jupiter hangs pale above us. We are England's no longer, but creatures of the void. About the edges of our consciousness lap waves from our other life, memories of places and persons and spoken words. Even as I glance out at the chill host of stars, I see with another eye the faces of those very far away, further away in time and spirit than the stars themselves.

"Can you see anything more?"

"Nothing but cloud."

In the background of the intercom the note of base beam is guiding us on our climb. We remain on it to 15,000 feet, the height of setting course.

"How long to go?"

"Five minutes."

"Thanks."

I fasten my blackout curtain and turn up the anglepoise lamp. The outer scene becomes something unreal; the real world is this glaring chart with its bare outline of coasts and rivers. The Gee indicates that we are approaching Elsham, not the Elsham of the mess and the barracks, but an Elsham that is a spot of ink on the chart before me.

"Set course on 135 degrees magnetic in one minute."

"OK. Set 135 on that compass, please, Doug. Check the deviation."

A following wind is waiting to join strength with our engines in hurling us into the conflict ahead, as though they not we were masters. While I listen for the words "Setting course", as a sprinter listens for the starter's gun, my mind reaches out to tenuous links with the life we have left behind — an Air Almanac, published at His Majesty's Stationery Office; my cap, at the back of the table; a tin of orange juice from some Californian orchard.

"Setting course, Navigator — one hundred and thirty-five magnetic."

B's leash is slipped and the game has begun. . . .

Those moments before setting course were moments of waiting. Then would come the avalanche of work at high speed, the dodging of coastal defences, the ceaseless watch for fighters, the sight of the target in its unbelievable ferocity.

I would try to tell myself then that this was a city, a place inhabited by beings such as ourselves, a place with the familiar sights of civilisation. But the thought would carry little conviction. A German city was always this, this hellish picture of flame, gunfire and searchlights, an unreal picture because we would not hear it or feel its breath. Sometimes, when the smoke rolled back and we saw streets and buildings, I felt startled. Perhaps if we had seen the white, upturned faces of people, as over England we sometimes did, our hearts would have rebelled. . .

Geoff is searching for a way out. I go back to the cabin, fasten the black curtain and turn up the lamp. Before me the hand of the DR compass is progressing jerkily about its dial as Geoff makes his turns. After a long time I hear his voice, ''We're through!''

I begin to chew a piece of gum that has lain dry in my mouth and turn again to the chart. With dreadful slowness we begin moving across its white expanse. Astern, the target still appears within reach of our hands. These first moments of the journey home are moments of reaction; suddenly we feel overwhelmingly tired and indifferent to our fate.

''What do I want now? What do I want? A check on the wind; yes, of course, a check on the wind.''

But I sit motionless at the table.

Graham has begun to doze. I prod him with my long rule. He opens his eyes, his expression slightly startled, and changes his plug from the receiver to the intercom.

''What's the matter?''

''You had fallen asleep.''

His brow contracts angrily. ''Like 'ell! I was listenin' out on base!''

"Oh, shut up you two!"

Graham changes plugs again, his eyes expressing injured virtue. Silence returns, except for the endless throbbing of the motors. Very deliberately Graham closes his eyes, but from time to time he lifts his hand to adjust his various dials and prove his wakefulness.

Hell, what does it matter, anyhow! For all the good I'm doing I might as well be asleep myself. I should take caffeine, but the tablets are in the bottom of my bag and the bag is under the table. Perhaps Joan is awake, visualising me doing something heroic. Instead I haven't willpower sufficient to stand up and shoot a star. Joan with her hair about her face, her uniform laid aside . . .

Nearly two hours have passed since we left the target. Now I can speak that comforting sentence, "We have crossed the enemy coast and are well out to sea." Everyone, I feel, has sighed deeply. The nose is down and the engines have taken on a note of contentment. Though danger has not yet passed, the tentacles of Europe have been loosened. We have set course for Mablethorpe, point of entry on the Lincolnshire coast. The cloud is breaking, sometimes revealing the face of the sea. Lights there flare up and fade; or flash urgently. Each night we see them and each night we wonder whether men are drifting there in rafts; or whether the enemy is trying to attract us low over waiting guns. The Gee is clarifying, making navigation easy and enjoyable.

"Three degrees east. ETA Mablethorpe 0025."

Our evasive action ceases. As our height is now less than ten thousand feet we unclip our oxygen masks and rub our faces, Geoff leaves the controls to Doug and comes back into the cabin. Clad as he is in his fur-lined jacket, his eyes narrowed against the lighting, his clothing exuding cold, he reminds me of a Wilson, or a Cherry-Garrard who has reached his base after a perilous journey. Although I have listened all night to his voice, I feel that we last met very long ago, when he and I were waiting together to face danger. Pulling off his gauntlets and the silk gloves beneath them, he clamps a pair of cold hands on my neck. I swing my elbow back. He smiles and prizes up the edge of my helmet with his thumb. Above the roar of the engines he shouts, "You're lucky in here! It's dark and lonely out there."

I shout back, "This is all very well for the rest of you! I have to cross the coast at the right place, or we'll — "

"All right! All right! I'm going now."

He presses behind me on his way aft, pushing my face on to the chart. He speaks to Graham for a time, then passes through the bulkhead door.

"Searchlights ahead. Looks like Hull."

"Thanks, Ted."

The beams appear relaxed and friendly, raised as though in languid welcome to the incoming crews. Geoff presses by again, coming forward. He passes out into the darkness and becomes a voice again. Graham asks the question he invariably asks, "'Oo wants cawfee?"

Coffee is wanted by everyone. As I work out an alteration of course for Mablethorpe, Graham puts three flasks on the chart.

"Pass two up for'ard an' keep one for you an' me."

"It's the same every night — you put bloody coffee right where I'm trying to work."

"I could find the way 'ome from 'ere myself!"

"Alter course to 302 magnetic. ETA 0128."

Always when I give this ETA for the English coast my tension is relieved and I know sweet satisfaction. Future danger does not exist. We have come through tonight; we have done what we set out to do; there are no men on earth better than these men beside me. I pour a flask of coffee and raise it to those in a family photograph before me. "Another over! I'll see you yet!"

"Two beacons ahead — M Mother K Kitty and S Sugar R Robert." I glance at the code list. "Northcoates and Manby."

"Ah yes, I can see the coast."

We are at five thousand feet with only twenty miles to go. A milky sea breaks on the coast below.

"If the Wingco had the sandra lights on we'd see the drome. No damned initiative, that's half his trouble."

"There's the glow from the Scunthorpe steel works, Geoff. Base should be over to port."

"Yes, OK, I see the beacon now. Shut up, everyone, I'll call control."

The R/T clicks. "Hello, Hazel control; B Beer. Over."

A girl's voice rises to us. "Hello B Beer, this is Hazel control. Pancake! Pancake! QFE one zero zero fife. Over."

Sometimes I think of this voice as a symbol of the sanity and beauty we leave behind. There is gladness in it and welcome — or do I imagine these things after listening for so long to the voices of six men?

The night becomes full of voices, each with its own accent and inflexion.

"Hello Hazel control; C Charlie. Over."

"Hello C Charlie, this is Hazel control. Hold two thousand. Call funnels. QFE one zero zero fife."

"Syd Cook. We've just beaten them in."

"Hello Hazel control; K Kitty. Over." The English voice of Ken Berry.

"Undercarriage!"

"Undercarriage!"

The wheels descend slowly.

"Flaps!"

"Flaps!"

"Hello Hazel control; L London. Over." The Canadian voice of Rolly Newitt.

"Start calling airspeeds, Navigator."

We are losing height rapidly, the engines throbbing in coarse pitch.

"130, 125, 125 — "

"Why the hell don't they change the runway. It's nearly cross wind!"

"120, 120, 115, 110 —"

The wheels screech. We bounce and settle.

"Dreadful landin', Hartley."

"Shut up!"

"B Beer, turn right at end of runway."

We trundle among the patterned lights till a man appears in the beam of our landing lights waving us to our dispersal.

"Switch off!"

The song of the engines ceases. I slip off my helmet and rub my ears. Without the use of intercom I can hear Doug checking the petrol gauges. Geoff is impatient to be gone.

"Come on, Navigator, let's get out of this damned thing! You're always bloody well last."

"So would you be if you had all this stuff."

"All right! All right! I'll carry your sextant for you. Not that I can see the sense in your taking the thing — you never use it."

Frank comes forward, his face pained. " 'Shag' an' me want t' get t' bed! Shoove the navigator's bag over, I'll carry it out."

We scramble down the dim length of the fuselage to the open door. Oscar is there and Stanley, Bill Burchell and "Misery", the men of our ground crew. Beyond them and all about them is darkness, still and very fresh. A bus with dimmed lights drives round the perimeter track to our dispersal. Peggy, who always drives us, jumps out and takes some of the equipment from our hands.

"Good trip?"

"Very good."

Geoff puts an arm round her shoulder.

"Thought you were off duty tonight?"

"Well, I was — sort of —"

"Worries about us," says Graham, "that's 'er trouble."

We scramble into the bus and drive on to K Kitty. The shadowy figures of Berry's crew climb amongst us.

"Good trip, Ken?"

"Oh, it's you, Geoff." The voice is laconic and tired. "Not bad on the whole. They hit us a few times — bomb aimer's got a splinter in the corner of his eye. How do you feel, Hop?"

"Quite OK, really."

We talk half contentedly, half wearily, only the glowing cigarette ends marking our places. When we reach the buildings it happens that I go into the crew room alone. Five hours ago we stood here waiting and the room still seems to hold our suppressed excitement, as though every piece of furniture and every diagram on the walls had absorbed something of our mood. The crew list for the night's operation is still in its place on the notice board, rustling in the draught from the open doors. Harry Wright comes in behind me, humming dolefully. We exchange a glance which says, "So, we've done it again," more clearly that words could have said it. Then Harry remarks, "Young Morris isn't in."

"Hell!"

We walk out together to the locker room, listening to the few planes still overhead. The crew are waiting impatiently.

"Come on, let's get interrogation over."

We walk out into the darkness again, our shoulders

free of harness and Mae Wests. There are now no clouds in the sky and no planes. Someone asks if Morris is back.

"Not yet."

"Christ!"

Our footfalls and voices echo along the corridor of the ops block. The ops room itself is filling with air crew, each man holding a cup of coffee and each talking light-heartedly. All are obviously weary, but release of tension has lent them a heightened gaiety. Overhead are the fluorescent lights, chill, dispassionate and shadowless. Two WAAFS are serving coffee.

"Milk and sugar?"

"Thank you."

"Good trip?"

"Wizard."

Our eyes have been seeking for Morris's crew ever since we came in, but none of them are to be seen. Moving among the crews are the doctors, the padres, the group captain and the wing commander, men who never seem to sleep . . .

Interrogation is over. We are in the mess, sitting to bacon and eggs. There is fantasy in the conversation. We speak of the target, then of someone's shoes that need repairing, then of the plane that blew up near the coast. And we are thinking that Morris and all his crew are probably dead. Watching normal life flow about us, I marvel that our bodies continue apparently unaffected by the other half of our lives. We get hungry, we get sleepy; we see and hear and smell and touch everyday things as we have always done; but with the realisation that suddenly we might never know these things again as we know them now.

Geoff and I go out together. In the enveloping darkness we stand and listen. There is no sound whatever. Something about the night overwhelms the senses. It holds a secret; it knows the fate of the missing crew, but it says nothing.

"There's no hope now. If they had landed away the ops people would have known."

We walk along the road, wheeling our bikes; past the cottage that was once an isolated farm; through the white gate; past the cabbage field and the football ground.

"He was too young."

"A bloody shame; a bloody shame."

We turn then into our room.

NANCY WAKE

An Australian with the Maquis

During the early years of the war Nancy Wake, an Australian married to a Frenchman, led a dangerous life in France as a courier for the French Resistance, until forced to flee across the Pyrenees to the safety of England. Here, she underwent training with the Special Operations Executive, an organisation formed in 1940 to work with the Resistance Forces in German-occupied Europe. Her return to France in 1944 as an SOE agent is described in the following passage from her autobiography, The White Mouse.

29 February 1944

AS the Liberator bomber circled over the dropping zone in France I could see lights flashing and huge bonfires burning. I hoped the field was manned by the Resistance and not by German ambushers. Huddled in the belly of the bomber, airsick and vomiting, I was hardly Hollywood's idea of a glamorous spy. I probably looked grotesque.

Over civilian clothes, silk-stockinged and high-heeled, I wore overalls, carried revolvers in the pockets, and topped the lot with a bulky camel-haired coat, webbing harness, parachute and tin hat. Even more incongruous was the matronly handbag, full of cash and secret instructions for D-day. My ankles were bandaged for support when I hit the ground.

But I'd spent years in France working as an escape courier. I'd walked out across the Pyrenees and joined the Special Operations Executive in England, and I was desperate to return to France and continue working against Hitler. Neither airsickness nor looking like a clumsily wrapped parcel was going to deter me.

The reception field in operation that night was too small for the arrival of two agents. My co-saboteur, Hubert, jumped first. By the time I landed, my parachute had drifted over to the adjacent field, and I landed in a thick hedge. My parachute was tangled in a tree.

Everything around me was dark and silent. I couldn't see any lights or fires. I quickly detached myself from my parachute, removed the bandages from my ankles, took off my overalls and ran away to crouch behind some bushes.

Then I heard Hubert's voice in the distance and someone else said, "Here's the parachute." I ran towards them and forced myself through a hedge to find myself face to face with a good-looking young Frenchman. Being typically French he proceeded to make some very gallant remarks: "I hope all trees in France bear such beautiful fruit this year." I took this with a grain of salt. After all, I had lived in France for ten years, and was married to a Frenchman.

However, he scored the first point. He refused to let me bury my parachute, which I'd been trained emphatically to do without fail. Once he had retrieved it he folded it up very neatly and put it under his arm. (Much later, sleeping in the forest, I was grateful for those nylon sheets.)

The Frenchman's name was Henri Tardivat and we were destined to become lifelong friends.

Relieved that we'd landed safely, Hubert and I were whisked off almost immediately to a little village where we were to stay at the home of some friendly Resistance people until our contact arrived.

Two mornings later my hostess invited me for a stroll around the village. It was a beautiful sunny day so I accepted. Hubert had not recovered from the strain of the previous forty-eight hours and he declined the invitation to accompany us. I was relieved he stayed behind, as it soon became apparent the whole village knew about the parachutage from beginning to end. However, they had only expected one agent and when a second one turned up, and a woman into the bargain, it was more than our hosts could stand. Hence the stroll!

Having lived in France since before the beginning of the war, I understood how these incidents could occur during the Occupation. Security-conscious Hubert would have been horrified to see me standing in the village square, shaking hands with the entire population. Nevertheless my old "brain box" was already thinking of ways and means to find a safe house as soon as formalities would allow.

The point was that during the Occupation the majority of people (unless of course they supported the Germans) got such a thrill when something good for the cause happened they would simply let their exuberance overcome their sense of security. I did not mention my unofficial reception to Hubert at the time as I did not want to depress him any further. Our arrival and the fanfare which followed had been the direct opposite to any of the exercises included in our training programme in England. Hubert was also having language trouble, as his otherwise excellent French was too academically pure for easy conversation with these country people. Secretly I sympathised with him but I also believed we should not overlook the fact that we were strangers here and that our own reactions in the first vital days would be repeated by word of mouth, and our behaviour quickly summed up by the French people we were hoping to work closely with.

It was easier for me. I had witnessed the Occupation from its inception. Furthermore, I had lived in the country so long I could think like them and feel instinctively how they would react to certain situations. In a nutshell, I was French, except by birth.

*　*　*

Hubert and I were parachuted into France near Mont-luçon, and were taken to the nearby village of Cosne-d'Allier, where I did my meet-the-people in the village square.

I did not meet the farmer on whose property we had landed. Had the Germans made any enquiries regarding the activity so close to his farmhouse on the night in question, he wanted to be able to say he had gone to bed early and had not heard any strange noises.

Although we would have been happier and felt safer away from Cosne-d'Allier, we were waiting for someone called Hector to contact us, as he was our only link to Gaspard, the leader of the Maquis d'Auvergne. This was the group we were to work with, but we had to be taken to them by an intermediary.

By now I had given Hubert a watered-down version of my social debut in the village and he was even more anxious to find another place to live. We discussed the pros and cons fully and agreed we would wait another day, but miraculously Hector arrived the next morning. Trouble in his own area had been the cause of his delay.. . .

We were greatly relieved to see him in spite of the fact

that he did not have the information or addresses we required, but as he promised to send them with his courier in two days' time we were both happy to think our troubles were over.

Our happiness was short-lived as the courier did not arrive. And we did not see Hector again until after the war. He was arrested, survived Buchenwald and now lives on the outskirts of Paris. Sadly we had to face the cold truth. For the time being we were up the proverbial creek without a paddle. Hubert and I both decided we would have to forget all about security and confide to a certain extent in our host Jean and his wife. This done, he thought he might be able to find Laurent's hideout. Laurent was one of the leaders of a local Maquis group, and he would be able to take us to Gaspard, who was in charge of all the separate groups of the Maquis in the area.

We started out early in the morning in Jean's *gazogène* (a charcoal-fuelled car). He seemed to know all the secondary roads extremely well and assured us there was not much danger of running into the Germans. We looked at each other in silence as we had been briefed in London only to travel by bicycle or train, or better still on foot. Hubert was white in the face; as for me, once again I decided I was going to play it by ear.

Jean drove from one contact to another until, when it was late evening, we found Laurent. I was always grateful to Jean and his wife for delivering us into the safe hands of Laurent, who was a tall, handsome man. When I knew him better we became great friends. I respected him, too, because he was a man who knew no fear. He conducted us to an old chateau near Saint-Flour in the Cantal and went to inform Gaspard of our arrival.

The purpose of our mission was to meet Gaspard, who was believed to have three to four thousand men hiding in the departments of the Allier, Puy-de-Dôme, Haute Loire and Cantal. We were to make our own assessment not only of the leader Gaspard, but also of the manner in which his considerable army had been formed and was now being operated and controlled. If we felt reasonably sure that he and his Maquis would be an asset to the Allies when and after they landed on D-day, then the French Section of SOE, commanded by Colonel Buckmaster in England, would assist them with finance and arms.

Laurent had been gone for days before Gaspard arrived at the chateau and our meeting was not a happy one. He maintained he had no knowledge of Hector and had therefore not been expecting any assistance from SOE. He did not inform us that he was hoping for the support of an Inter-Allied team, a fact that London, for reasons of their own, had failed to mention in our briefings.

If Hubert and I had possessed all the cards in the pack we would not have wasted the time we did when we first landed. It was also unfortunate that, owing to the arrest of Hector, we had not received the detailed local information promised to us in London. The fact that our wireless operator chose to spend some time with a friend before joining us did not diminish our problems.

Hubert and I had the good fortune to overhear the group discussing us while they were sitting in the big kitchen where they congregated all the time. They seemed sure we had some money and they were plotting to relieve me of it and get rid of me at the same time. At a later period when Gaspard and I had more respect for each other he assured me the men had been joking. That could be true, but when I am stranded in an old, empty chateau, many kilometres from civilisation, surrounded by a gang of unshaven, disreputable-looking men, I tend to be cautious and take things seriously.

Without any radio contact with London we were not in an enviable position, so when Gaspard suggested he would send us to Claudes-Aigues in the Cantal, where a man called Henri Fournier was in charge of the local Maquis, we readily agreed.

In retrospect I can guess why Gaspard adopted the attitude he did. He was banking on the support of the Inter-Allied group but in the event it did not materialise he did not want to antagonise us irreparably. We were of no use to him without a radio and the money, which we said (quite untruthfully) we did not possess. He would kill two birds with one stone. He would dispatch us to a man he disliked who would have us on his hands if we failed to become functional. When many years had passed, after reading information that was gradually coming to light, I concluded that Gaspard had been under the misapprehension that an elaborate military scheme involving a French airborne force being dropped in the Massif Central area on D-day would become operational. It did not materialise, probably another case of the left hand not letting the right hand know what it was doing.

In normal times Henri Fournier was an executive in hotel management. He detested the Germans and he and his wife had come to live in Chaudes-Aigues for the duration of the Occupation. He was puzzled by our arrival but when we explained the situation I think the mystery was clarified because, when we became friends, he admitted to me in confidence that he heartily disliked Gaspard.

Fournier arranged accommodation for us in a funny little hotel high up in the hills, in a village called Lieutades. It was freezing cold, both inside the hotel and outside, and there was little to eat. We had absolutely nothing to do and we were both beginning to worry as our radio operator, Denis Rake, was long overdue.

Denis (or Denden, as he was called) had been one of our

instructors at SOE school . . . Even in those days when homosexuality was illegal he had never concealed the fact that he was queer. Indeed it was always the first thing he mentioned, especially to women, who often found him too attractive for his liking. We were both fond of him but knew he could be completely unreliable.

Denden arrived by car just as we were beginning to give up hope. He found me sitting on the wall of the local cemetery and wanted to know if I was picking a suitable grave! He realised that his late arrival had caused us needless anxiety and in true Denden fashion he told us a cock-and-bull story which neither of us believed. However, a radio operator is an important person in the field, and we were not going to give him a reason to leave us and go straight back to his lover, which was exactly where he had been. On landing in France by Lysander he had met the man he had been having an affair with several weeks before in London, and they had decided to have a last fling.

Nevertheless, we were absolutely delighted to see him for now we could put our plans into action. While waiting for Denden we had decided that if he did arrive we would help Fournier first of all. We had been impressed by what we had seen of his group. We respected him and knew that he had spent a lot of his savings on the Resistance. We packed our bags and left for Chaudes-Aigues.

Fournier was overwhelmed with joy when told that we would shortly be in radio contact with London and that his group would be the first to receive our report. He and Hubert were busy making out the lists of weapons and explosives they hoped would be sent from England, and Denden and I were busy coding the messages to be transmitted. . . .

The plateaux on top of the mountains which surround Chaudes-Aigues were ideal for airdrops. Fournier and his group had surveyed the whole area and were of the opinion that we could receive, unpack and distribute the contents of the containers on the field and return to our homes without any interference. As soon as London had received our messages and we were all organised we received airdrops on six consecutive nights. It continued to be a roaring success until later on when Gaspard arrived with his men and was followed almost immediately by the Germans.

We manned the fields from ten at night until four in the morning, unless the planes arrived beforehand. We would unpack the containers immediately. The weapons had to be cleaned and all the protective grease removed before we handed them over to the leaders of the individual groups. Every available man assisted. Nevertheless, sometimes it would be noon before we finished and after lunch before we could snatch a few hours' sleep. It was a strenuous time for everyone; we were kept on the go continuously, but it was also rewarding to witness the enthusiasm of Fournier and his Maquis.

Every now and then Hubert, Denis and I would receive parcels from London which would arrive in a special container. Words cannot describe the thrill it gave me to open mine, stamped all over with "Personal for Hélène". Here we were, in the middle of a war, high up in the mountains of Central France, yet because of the thoughtfulness of SOE Headquarters we felt close to London.

My parcel always contained personal items unobtainable in France during the Occupation, plus supplies of Lizzie Arden's products, Brooke Bond tea, chocolates or confectionery. Without fail there'd be a note and a small gift from Claire Wolfe, the only girl I'd been friendly with at headquarters. We remained staunch friends, and when she died at her home on the Isle of Man in 1984 I was grief-stricken. . . .

I was thankful that Hubert and I had arranged the tasks we would perform to our mutual satisfaction. He would deal with all matters of a military nature and meet Gaspard whenever necessary and possible. I would be in charge of finance and its distribution to the group leaders. I would visit the groups, assess the merit of their demands and arrange for their airdrops, which we would both attend if possible. The tables had turned. After being regarded as a bloody nuisance by Gaspard when I first arrived, I now carried a lot of weight. *I* was the one who decided which groups were to get arms and money.

Part 6
The Home Front

Tunnelling through the night, the trains pass
in a splendour of power, with a sound like thunder
shaking the orchards, waking
the young from a dream, scattering like glass
the old men's sleep; laying
a black trail over the still bloom of the orchards.
The trains go north with guns.

Strange primitive piece of flesh, the heart laid quiet
hearing their cry pierce through its thin-walled cave
recalls the forgotten tiger
and leaps awake in its old panic riot;
and how shall mind be sober,
since blood's red thread still binds us fast in history
Tiger, you walk through all our past and future,
troubling the children's sleep; laying
a reeking trail across our dream of orchards.

Racing on iron errands, the trains go by,
and over the white acres of our orchards
hurl their wild summoning cry, their animal cry . . .
the trains go north with guns.

Judith Wright
"The Trains"

PAT STUDDY-CLIFT

Down to Earth

The role of Australian women in running the farms and rural properties during the war is commemorated in these extracts from Pat Studdy-Clift's personal narrative, Only Our Gloves On. *The Joan referred to in the final paragraph was the author's sister, who had been serving in the Australian Women's Army Service.*

OF course, there was no room on the train! It was early winter of 1943, and I was standing on Sydney Central Station, with my mother, Grandmother Colwell, my five year old brother Tom and Lex, a young university student, trying to board a train back to Emerald Hill. There was a sense of urgency, crowds everywhere; uniforms from all the services, both Australian and American, and civilians rushing around. My goodness, how those American soldiers could embarrass you with their behaviour! They seemed to have too many hands, as far as women were concerned, not the least bit put off by disapproving glances. But we must not be too hard on them, they were making every minute count!

*   *   *

In the pre-dawn cold of a winter's morning, the train wheezed to a standstill at the small, deserted Emerald Hill Station. We stretched our constricted limbs, passed the luggage out the door to Lex, and climbed down onto the station in pitch darkness. The train blew its whistle and lumbered off into the night. "Here we are on the sunny side of the street," said Mum with a touch of sarcasm.

My mother, Jean, had a ton of spirit and could cope with anything. This ability to come to terms with life and enjoy it was a legacy from the past. She was a clergyman's daughter, and her family devoted their time to helping others with their problems.

On opening the waiting room door we found a lovely coal fire burning in the grate. We also found "Old Bill". Old Bill, who had been recruited by a neighbour to tide us over when our worthy manager had suddenly left, had a bad back and was a born pessimist. Mum asked him how he was.

"Me back's bad, there's a drought on, y'know, and what YOU think you can do up here, I don't know."

He had little or no confidence in the ability of either my mother or myself to run a property, and I must admit that he had good reason for his pessimism. He trudged out to load our luggage into the "double utility". This vehicle was the Studdys' trademark, a unique — well almost unique — utility built on a truck chassis. It was an International, fawn coloured, with a bull-nosed bonnet.

*   *   *

To this point my life had been carefree and loads of fun. School had ended at the end of 1942 and then it was Business College, combined with part time studies at the Conservatorium. I also joined the Women's Emergency

Signalling Corps, wearing a cheeky green uniform. After the training period, I became their youngest instructress on the part time basis. We helped the Air Force, Merchant Navy and American soldiers who just couldn't cope adequately with their Morse code, so essential in those years. We gave them special tuition and often solved their problems. The blackout in Sydney at that time made the walk to the tram an edgy experience, after the warm friendliness of Mrs Mac's Morse Code School.

One evening I arrived home at Fullerton Street to find a round table conference in progress. The family were discussing what to do, as the working manager of our farming and grazing property at Gunnedah, three hundred miles from Sydney, had departed suddenly, "shot through" as Dad put it. That left only old Jack Monaghan, the houseman, who did no outside work. There was no one to pump water for the stock or maintain fences. Every able-bodied man was engaged in war work, so we could not hire a replacement for the manager. To add to the worry, we were in the throes of a severe drought! It was finally decided that Mum, myself and four-and-a-half-year-old brother, Tom, would return to run Kareela to the best of our ability. We had been brought up not to duck away from a challenge and to pride ourselves on the ability to adapt to whatever circumstances Life presented. We were not deterred or downhearted at the prospect of all that hard work ahead of us. On the contrary, it was a happy and cheerful group of people who arrived back at the homestead in the early hours of the morning.

*   *   *

On our first morning home we were shocked to find so

many pressing demands crowding in on us. It was so sad to look outside — the garden was dead! Mum sighed, "This is the third time we will have to replant the garden." She and Mimi turned their attention to the household work, putting back the woman's touch. Old Jack had maintained a state of cleanliness in the house, but the poor old fellow was not cut out to be a housekeeper.

It was well that we remembered the lush green seasons for we found Kareela in the grip of unrelenting drought. Our recollections of earlier, good years helped sustain us as we came to terms with what now confronted us as we made our first inspections of Kareela.

Instead of a rural idyll we found a desolate landscape, swept by cold dry winds. The countryside was brown and bare. The farm dams, now pools of mud, were edged with the remains of dead stock and gaunt animals trapped in the mud waiting to die. Overhead, carrion birds circled and squarked in anticipation of the feast. . . .

Our return to Kareela was not only at a time of drought. On our minds too were the anxieties shared with all Australians of that period — concern over loved ones fighting overseas, a suppressed fear about the future, and wondering how to cope with the effects of shortages and rationing.

It was time to draw on one's own resources and try to be a cheerful comfort for each other. . . .

Lex and I rode out to assess the drought situation, checked the stock and the water and feed in the various paddocks. Our horses were reliable, and not too fractious for a medical student who had little riding experience.

We were home, but where were the home comforts? The electric light engine had stopped short, apparently never to go again! After six weeks of persistently ringing our overworked International dealer, asking for expert help, he finally came and the old engine was again chugg, chugg, chugging away. It was a battery storage system, only needing a weekly run to build up the batteries. We were able to put away the kerosene and Tilly lamps and once again turn on a switch! Ah, progress!

The next real problem was the septic tank. There is a little germ that lives in the tank and makes the whole thing gee, but if no one uses the system, then the little germ dies and nothing works! We put up a hessian shelter outside . . . two trestles either end, supporting two planks of wood, a gap in the middle, with a kerosene tin under the gap. Certainly not an ideal situation for a bare bottom, with the cold winter wind roaring around, to say the least!

The worst job I have ever done was to clean out the septic tank! The cement lid was lifted off and we pumped the contents into four open forty-four gallon drums on the back of our old Bedford truck. Lex and I transported the drums up the paddock out of the "sense of smell" zone, then we tipped them off. There was one serious problem to the trip; the glass window in the back of the Bedford cabin was nonexistent, the road was very rough, and I think we overfilled the drums. We spent our time ducking away from those smelly splashes that kept coming through our open window! Lex said, "This is worse than doing bed pans at the hospital." It is still a vivid memory!

*   *   *

After Lex and Grandmother Mimi returned to Sydney, Mum, Old Jack, myself and young Tom were established as the staff of Kareela. We were soon faced with more problems. Our firewood was running low. Normally, we would fell the dry trees then bring them home and start up the circular saw. This saw was run by the tractor, and we would saw the wood into the correct size for the wood stove — all very efficient!

Frankly, a sixteen-year-old girl was not capable of this exercise, so again the Bedford truck was taken by me up the paddock. Luckily, Dad had left some dead wood lying around. He believed it stopped soil wash and provided shelter for the sheep. Although untidy, it was ecologically beneficial. What a blessing! I was able to load the truck with dead wood and bring it home. Jack and I could then axe it up and we were in business again. At last, we were becoming organised.

We had been back on the land for six long weeks, and Mum and I realised that during that time we had not seen a man under sixty!

During the drought I used to ride daily around the stock. This was a dreary and depressing ride; some animals were usually bogged in the mud surrounding the dams as we had opened all the gates in a last resort to allow the stock to obtain any remaining feed.

I was unable to do the usual lopping of the wilga and whitewood trees for fodder, and we had run out of hay and molasses, so all that was left was to ride around and cut the throats of the sheep that lay helpless and dying on the ground. A razor sharp knife, carried in a pouch on my belt was an essential party of my equipment. Scavenger crows attacked the sheep. They were pitiful, the live sheep with their eyes picked out, maybe a half-eaten eye lying on their cheek. It was merciful to kill them.

*   *   *

August 1944. The Italians were coming!

The homestead was alive with activity as we prepared for the arrival of the prisoners of war. There was some degree of tension and excitement as we did not really know what to expect. It was rather comforting that Dad, although recuperating after being invalided out of the army, was on hand. How would we react to these captured enemies of Australia? How would they react to us?

We were fully aware that there was a certain amount of antagonism in some quarters to those who employed the Italian POWs. We personally did not think it was justified. Our need was desperate. We hoped that those folk who frowned on POWs on the farm would not condemn us for this step. We knew the risks but the seriousness of the situation outweighed other considerations.

But with Mum showing the way, preparation for the arrival of the POWs proceeded on the principle of tolerance and accepted standards of country hospitality.

Days were spent scrubbing and cleaning, and we provided such essentials as cutlery, crockery and linen. The POWs were to be housed in the old cottage near the house. This was a building in the traditional pioneering style, what I would call a "Ben Hall type house", with a hall straight down the middle, rooms on either side, a front veranda and a skillion back veranda with a laundry one end and a bathroom the other. Latticework gave privacy to the back veranda and at each end stood the ubiquitous galvanised water tanks . . .

Neither Carmo nor Peter could speak English to any extent, having only the odd word. We had obtained an English-Italian dictionary, and we often had to resort to our "little grey book" and point to the appropriate word. Thank heavens we always seemed to reach an understanding. Carmo was a cobbler by trade, so we bought a boot last with three different sized feet for him to do repairs for us.

The third man was Phillippe. He was a poet and a gentleman, and an academic. Fair of feature with deep blue eyes and light hair, he spoke English well, and would often quote Byron or some other English poet. . . .

The authorities who allocated our workers were singularly lacking in commonsense. We discovered that Peter and Carmo were Fascists and Phillippe was a Royalist! It was unwise to mix these two factions. On one occasion an argument arose and Carmo, of the quick temper, backed up by a rather reluctant Peter, began chasing Phillippe "at knife point" around the cottage! Phillippe decided that discretion was the better part of valour and locked himself in his room. The situation was smoothed over with some help from my father who was at home at the time.

When Peter was returned to Cowra, he was replaced with a carpenter named Mike. Swarthy and strong, Mike was also industrious and stable. All we had to do to keep him contented was to visit the cottage occasionally at night to listen while Mike played on his clarinet, tunes such as "Lili Marlene" and "Jealousy". We enjoyed our visits, as Mike was an excellent player. Before coming to us, Mike worked for a farmer named Rose, helping build the homestead. On the Roses' farm Mike worked with Vince, who was repatriated to Italy, but returned to settle in Gunnedah, where he now lives with his family.

Joan arrived home in late October 1944, and the two of us worked with the three prisoners. Many neighbours thought we took a grave risk but the men were always respectful. Only once did Phillippe try to kiss me. I was in the cottage making up a list of stores, needed by the men for their cooking. Out of the blue, Phillippe suddenly embraced me. It was a gesture on the spur of the moment. I believe he was carried away with thought of a sweetheart back in Italy or a great yearning for a feminine touch. There was a wet, smelly dishcloth within reach which I hastily put over Phillippe's face, and he got the message.

Poor man, he walked around with a very worried look for several days, anxious in case I reported him. As it was harmless and unplanned, nothing was said, and Phillippe stayed on, never again trying to embrace me.

DYMPHNA CUSACK and FLORENCE JAMES

Doing the Gentlemanly Thing

The novel Come in Spinner *by Dymphna Cusack and Florence James deals with the impact of the war on the lives of a group of girls, most of whom are employed in the Marie-Antoinette beauty salon of the fashionable Hotel South Pacific in Sydney. One of these girls is Deborah Forrest, whose husband Jack is away on active service with the AIF. Deborah's unhappy memories of the Depression years make her reluctant to contemplate a life of financial insecurity with her husband after the war and receptive to the attentions of the wealthy, self-centred, and middle-aged businessman Angus McFarland, who wants her to divorce Jack and marry him.*

DEB snapped off the ribbon from the florist's box irritably. Roses! They were glorious, deep velvety red ones on long stalks. But her room was already full of flowers and she had absolutely nothing to put them in. The basin was still crammed with wilted lilac and the vases she had got from the housemaid yesterday were full of carnations. Well, the roses would just have to stay in the basin overnight and she would take them down to the Salon in the morning. Really, her room was beginning to smell like a funeral. She threw the lilac into the wastepaper basket, fished out the slimy face washer she'd had to put round the plug to stop the water from leaking away, and dumped the roses into the basin. An envelope slipped to the floor from among the flowers. She picked it up with a sigh; she didn't feel she could take romance tonight. But this wasn't merely a card, it was too heavy.

She slit the envelope and took out Angus's card. A carved jade fob was clipped to it. *Perfection to Perfection* the card read. Oh God, she thought, more green! And nobody wore fobs now. It was probably priceless, but she wished that just once for a change he would ask her what kind of things she liked. But not Angus. His taste was perfect, and if she didn't like it then she'd just have to learn to. She would have to learn lots of things to keep up with Angus's standards, she thought with a sigh. Marriage to him wouldn't be all plain sailing.

The phone rang. It was Mrs Triggs from Suite 79, and she was hysterical. She had been trying to get a spot off her dinner frock and the cleaning fluid had ruined her nail lacquer. Would it be possible for Miss Forrest to come up and relacquer her nails? Miss Forrest was sorry but the Salon was closed and Miss Jeffries had the key. She slammed the receiver back. If Mrs Triggs didn't like it she could lump it. And that went for old Molesworth too. She was sick of being at everybody's beck and call. And anyway she had to get ready to meet Angus and that was more important than any SP guest who wanted private service.

She wondered what she would wear. It all depended on where Angus had decided to take her to dine. She hoped he'd have the sense to take her out of the city. What she'd like was a quiet dinner somewhere without an orchestra banging in her ears, and then a long restful drive afterwards. She would put on her blue frock. It was simple and cool.

She had a moment of misgiving when she took a last look at herself in the mirror. She usually dressed more formally for her dinner dates with Angus. Oh, bother formality, she thought, slamming the door behind her. Let him dress and dine to suit me for a change. I'm always trying to think a jump ahead of him, so that he'll be pleased with me. I've always done whatever he's arranged. It's stupid. I'll tell him I want to go for a run round the Harbour this evening. She found herself searching for just the right words, with just the right mixture of coquetry and insistence. "I adore you when you're stubborn," Angus always said when she reluctantly gave in to something he took for granted she would agree to . . . "That's little moue . . . fascinating!" "My God!" Jack would have said, "you're as obstinate as a mule!"

A pain shot through her temple as she stepped into the lift and she felt rebellious. What a strain life was going to be with Angus . . . always on the alert, always schooling yourself in case you might do or say the wrong thing. Still, she supposed you could get used to anything and in the long run it'd be worth it. Better than being a worn-out drudge like Nolly. She shuddered at the thought.

"I've booked for us at Prince's," Angus greeted her, and her hope of a cool, quiet evening was shattered in a flash of irritation. Bodies, she thought, more hot bodies. . . . I've been pummelling bodies all day in the Marie-Antoinette . . . I don't want to go dancing tonight.

"Oh," she murmured flatly, "that will be nice . . . though I wish you'd rung me and I'd have put on something more suitable. I thought we'd probably be running out to a beach on a night like this."

"You look perfect," Angus assured her.

"You don't think it's too hot for dancing?" she tried again.

"Not a bit of it. There's quite a cool change. I'll admit it was hot on the beach this afternoon, but a southerly has come up since then."

Half your luck, she thought, enviously, and said aloud: "How nice," congratulating herself on the agility with which she was learning the art of saying one thing while thinking another.

"You see, it really is quite cool," Angus insisted, as they stood on the hotel steps and felt the breeze that swept along Macquarie Street. "We'll walk down, shall we? It's only a step."

They turned into Martin Place. Taxis were setting down a laughing crowd at the lighted entrance of Down Under.

"I wonder the police don't do something about that place," Angus remarked. "They tell me it's practically a sly grog shop."

She felt a wave of irritation at his smugness. "None of the nightclubs ever seem to be short of liquor, from what I can see."

"True, but it's a very different matter with reputable places that are well conducted. Our liquor laws are so ridiculous they simply ask to be broken."

"I suppose that's what the people at Down Under think." She gave a little forced laugh to soften her words. Oh damn! she thought. I am behaving badly. And I haven't thanked him for the flowers or the jade.

"Your roses were lovely," she said, trying to infuse some enthusiasm into her voice.

"They reminded me of you."

"And that exquisite fob!" She hoped she sounded enthusiastic. "You really shouldn't, you know."

"Now just tell me why I shouldn't?"

She gave him a long smile for answer.

"Come along, tell me. I insist. You mightn't realise it, but I'm a very masterful man."

"You surprise me," she said feelingly, "I'd never have guessed it."

The banter went out of his voice, and he gripped her arm firmly. "Only three more days and I hope I shall have the right to give you everything I want to give you. I hoped you might wear that jade tonight. You've never worn anything of mine."

"I couldn't wear it with this colour," she explained lamely.

"No . . . no . . . I suppose not. It's rather a rare little piece I picked up in Peking. I had it made into a fob especially for you."

"Oh Angus, you do the sweetest things!" She put a hand on his arm in a moment of compunction.

They turned into Prince's and Henri hastened to meet them at the foot of the stairs. Coming out of the cool air the room seemed stuffy, and her head started to throb again before they had even sat down.

"How do you feel about grilled steak and mushrooms?" Angus inquired.

"I'd like something cold."

He pursed his lips: "Lobster mayonnaise . . ."

"That'd be delicious."

"I really think you should have a steak. You little girls don't eat enough, you know. I'm going to have one myself. I had lobster for lunch."

The waiter was desolated. The droop of his head, the curve of his shoulders, his outflung despairing hands all bespoke his desolation: "But M'sieur — Mr McFarland, sir . . . the steak. We have no steak."

Angus's brow clouded.

"It is not us that is to blame. You will not find steak in Sydney. We are the victims. It is the meat strike." The waiter hesitated while the full iniquity of the situation sank in.

"Monstrous. In wartime too. These fellows have no sense of responsibility." Angus picked up the double menu card and put it down again impatiently. He never put his glasses on in public. "Is there anything you can suggest that's fit to eat?"

The waiter was voluble. They compromised on turkey. A wonder bird, second only to the goose that laid the golden egg, if the waiter was to be believed; bred, reared, transported from the Middle-West for just such an occasion.

"I think you'd better have it too," Angus said, "there's nothing in a salad."

An excellent dinner restored his good humour in some degree but he still felt aggrieved. "If we don't take a firm hand with these strikers, we deserve all we get. Australia's going to rack and ruin. We're frightening away all foreign capital."

Deb, who was not fond of turkey, took up the theme out of pure contrariness. "But it's not only here that there are strikes, is it? The coal miners in England . . . America, and the steel strikes too."

"That's what makes it so dangerous, it's symptomatic. It's the typical irresponsibility of the fellow without any stake in the country."

Deb restrained a giggle. At first she had thought he meant s-t-e-a-k. She buried her twitching mouth in her table napkin.

"If we gaoled all the strikers we might really get somewhere."

"But who'd do the work then?"

He ignored her interruption. "A few prosperous years have gone to the workers' heads. They'll be brought to their senses when the war's over and there aren't enough jobs to go round."

The laughter drained out of Deb. "You don't mean there might be another depression?"

"The experiences of two wars have taught me that our only hope of restoring industrial efficiency is another depression."

"It's horrible."

"I agree with you entirely," Angus's voice was crisp. "But I am afraid there is no alternative."

"You can't realise what people suffered when you say a thing like that. The hopelessness — the misery."

"I realise it perfectly. But serious economists everywhere are agreed that all that is more than compensated for by the stimulus to prosperity a depression gives."

Angus smiled across at Deb. He felt better after his dinner and the steaming coffee restored his good humour.

"I think it's absolutely awful when you remember that half the men who are fighting in this war — in England and in America, as well as here — were on the dole for years because there was no money to do anything for them. . . " She broke off and stirred her coffee defiantly.

Angus smiled at her. How sweet she was when she was stubborn! "Go on. I like to hear you."

Deb felt her anger rising. Really, he was treating her like a child. "What I'd like to know is why, when there was no money then for anything useful, governments can find millions and billions of money to fight the war, and even before it's over they're talking about another depression."

"My dear little girl," Angus said with affectionate forbearance, "you can't treat matters like this sentimentally. Wars are inevitable and so are depressions."

"I don't believe it." Deb's voice was shaking.

"My dear Deborah, it's not a matter of belief, it's a matter of economic law that cannot be altered merely because a number of young men now fighting in the front line were once on the dole.''

Deb felt the sense of helplessness that always engulfed her when Angus launched into one of his long dissertations on economics and war. She felt that she was walking on the edge of a precipice and it terrified her. She just could not go through again what they had all suffered then — the insecurity, the poverty.

He leaned across and covered her hand with his. "Little one, you're too lovely to bother your pretty head about such dull things. Let us talk about you — and me.''

She ignored the tone in his voice. She was not going to be talked down. "Well, I think it would be awful if there was another depression after this war, and I wouldn't blame anyone for wanting to start a revolution if there was.''

He laughed fondly and turned her hand over, curling the fingers into the palm one by one, as though he was playing "this little pig went to market" with a child. "A twentieth-century Joan of Arc, eh? I should like to see you on a white horse riding up Macquarie Street to Parliament House. You'd look adorable.''

She withdrew her hand. "What would you do if it did come?''

"What came?''

"A revolution.''

He smiled patronisingly. "All that would be needed would be to tighten the purse-strings as they did in 1931 — and you'd see the revolution fizzle out in a few noisy speeches in the Domain. A general withdrawal of credit would paralyse the country and the rebels would soon come crawling back and be glad to take the dole.''

"That's awful.''

"But you'd have nothing to worry about, I assure you. Even if there was a revolution, we'd be quite safe. . . . I'd spirit you off to an impregnable castle and we'd live on our income and let the rebels stew in their own juice."

The orchestra was playing softly, the crooner began to sing:

The Southern stars are bright above . . .

"Our tune," Angus smiled across at her. "Shall we dance? I never want to spend any of my precious time with you on anything but loving you."

Deb rose reluctantly.

He drew her close and they danced without speaking. Words were unnecessary when her nearness worked magic in his nerves and blood.

She wished she had an aspirin. Her head was aching and her feet were sore and she hated the tune anyway. Every messenger boy in town was whistling it. Angus's words still echoed in her ears . . . They'd be safe, would they? Earthquake, war, revolution — yes, Angus would manage to be safe.

At last the orchestra stopped. Thank God she could sit down now, Deb thought. But Angus clapped with the rest of the crowd and smiled warmly down at her as the pianist went into the opening chords of the encore. He put his arm round her again. She smiled at him with her lips and her feet moved round the floor while her mind went back again. What would Angus think if she told him how the depression had affected them? A withdrawal of credit; a stimulus to prosperity! She'd like to know just how stimulating he'd find it to walk up to his bank one morning and find the door closed and a printed notice tacked up: PAYMENT SUSPENDED. He'd be most sympathetic of course, but he'd point out how wrong it was to generalise from her father's case. These were not personal things; no, they belonged to the vague impersonal world where high-sounding economic theories broke your pride and your heart.

Well, it had done something very personal to her — it had taught her a lesson she would never forget. If depressions were inevitable she was going to make quite certain that next time one occurred she was safe. She would never go through again what she and Jack and Nolly and Dad went through. Never. Dallas could talk about hardships building your character and all the rest of it, cementing partnerships, teaching you wisdom. Well, she was wise now as she had never been wise before, she knew that if you didn't look after number one nobody would do it for you.

The music throbbed away into silence. Angus released her and drew her hand through his arm possessively, leading her back to their table. She did not sit down, but stood looking up at him in appeal: "I'm awfully sorry, but I've got a frightful head. I'm afraid you'll simply have to take me home."

"My poor darling. Perhaps if you had a bromo-seltzer you'd feel better. I'll get the waiter to bring you one."

"I'm afraid it wouldn't do the least bit of good. When I get neuralgia like this I simply have to lie down."

Angus glanced at his watch. "It's very early," he pleaded. "You don't want to rob me of the rest of the evening, do you?"

"I'm sorry," she pressed her hand to her forehead, "I'm afraid if I stayed I'd be very poor company."

"Just to be with you is enough for me. I have an idea. I'll get them to ring through and have my car sent round and we'll go for a good long run by the sea and the fresh air will blow the cobwebs away."

Oh God, Deb thought, how silly men can be! If he'd taken me for a drive when I wanted to go I'd never have got this head. "All right," she conceded reluctantly and gathered up her bag and gloves.

But in the car, with the cool wind blowing on her face, the dark road sliding beneath them in the glare of the headlights, Angus's arm around her shoulders, some of the tension went out of her. She pushed back into the recesses of her mind the thoughts his casual words had stirred. What was the sense of thinking about them? Foolish to let old memories wound you, old grief waken. Her father's loss, his suffering — all that was so long ago. Unreal now, for her, just as the happiness of her early marriage was unreal. You couldn't let them decide your future. Perhaps it was true that you changed every seven years — became a different person. It was nearly seven years since Jack had left the Vineyard and come to town — the end of a cycle, the beginning of a new one.

Angus's arm tightened, drawing her closer to him. "Feeling better now?" he whispered, rubbing his chin against her temple.

"Much. It was the heat, I think, after such a stuffy day."

"My poor little darling."

The car turned away from the road and the white walls of South Head lighthouse glared for a moment before the lights were dimmed. Below them they could hear the sound of the surf thudding against the cliffs and a sea-mist swept across the windscreen.

"Poor little darling!" Angus repeated, drawing her closer. "We'll sit here for a little while till the wind blows your headache away and then I'll take you home so that you can get to bed early."

Deb sighed, snuggling against him. Sitting like this, with his lips against her cheek, made her feel safe. It was funny, she didn't feel so guilty about Jack now that she had found out that she didn't mind Angus touching her.

There was a lot of nonsense talked about this one-man business. Just because you were brought up that way there was no need to go on all your life. Not that she would ever have let Angus kiss her if he hadn't asked her to marry him. She wasn't cheap.

"You know, Deborah," he said, a stern note creeping into his voice, "this indecision isn't any better for you than it is for me." He squeezed her hand, his fingers roughly twisting her wedding ring.

She was silent. There did not seem to be anything she could say.

"I specially wanted to discuss something with you tonight — what I started to say to you on Sunday. You didn't misunderstand me when I said that I could get a flat for you when you left the South Pacific, did you?"

"Why — no — at least I don't think so."

Angus laughed. "What a little innocent you are! I was rather afraid . . ." he hesitated.

"Afraid of what?"

"Well, to be perfectly frank, that my talk of finding a flat and making a settlement might lead you to think that I wasn't really serious about marriage."

"Oh Angus!" Deb drew away from him.

"I couldn't have blamed you. After all, some men do those things."

She remembered the wardrobe saturated with Liz Destrange's perfume and pushed the thought away. She wasn't Liz.

"I'm pressing things now because — apart altogether from my own feelings and yours — all kinds of technicalities will be involved if you re-establish any relationship with your husband when he returns. I feel that if you could present him with an ultimatum — say you want a divorce — and then let me put the matter in my solicitor's hands."

An ultimatum! Why shouldn't she? Jack had presented her with an ultimatum. But at the thought of telling Jack she wanted a divorce, she had a feeling of panic. She could see him shoot out his jaw, his grey eyes narrowed. "What rot!" he would say, or: "What put that idea into your head?" the way he always overrode what she said when it didn't suit him. She gave in to him too easily, that was the trouble. The only thing she'd ever stuck out against him about was staying on at the South Pacific last time he was down on leave.

Angus was right, she must make everything plain from the beginning. If once she established a relationship with Jack again there would be more than technicalities. Jack was unpredictable, life with him was a series of mad leaps from one thing to another. Marriage with Angus would be peaceful, pleasant, civilised. With Jack — she pushed the thought away from her; it was too disturbing, even after all these years of marriage. Yes, there would be more than technicalities.

"All my suggestions, of course, are based on the assumption that your husband will naturally do the gentlemanly thing when you ask him for a divorce. But, till that is through and we can be married, I want you to believe me when I say that in no way do I desire our relationship to be altered except that I shall have the privilege of arranging for your welfare and taking you away from that wretched job. You realise that there will be gossip when this is known, Deborah, and I want no taint of scandal to mar our marriage." He switched on the dashboard lights, his face was set and frowning. "If you could make a decision before your husband's return . . ."

Deb listened to the silky purring of the engine. She could not think of any answer. She laid her hand on his as though to seek in his touch some solution of her own perplexity.

Part 7
The Prisoner of War
Experience

The clock on Changi's grey-walled tower
Went crazy overnight —
Its hands showed ten past two; its bell
Boomed in the evening light.

No ordinary range of chimes
By the bell that hour was rung,
But only after fifteen notes
Did silence grip its tongue.

Four years to the men in Changi Jail,
It rang "Lord, be my guide" —
To those enslaved a song of hope,
The knell of those who died.

Perhaps, like Lear, it snapped, insane
In one heartrending jangle,
And crazy weights like gallows men
Within its walls now dangle;

Or, maybe, learning that abroad
Peace by all bells was voiced,
It broke the laws of Time and Cog
And privately rejoiced.

Val Vallis
"The Ballad of Changi Chimes"

(The day after most of the Australians left Changi camp for home the prison clock, of its own accord, began irresponsibly chiming.)

RUSSELL BRADDON

Changi . . . the Phoney Captivity

Russell Braddon, a gunner in the Australian Eighth Division, was captured on his twenty-first birthday by the Japanese during the Malayan campaign and spent his first nine months as a POW under harsh working conditions at Pudu gaol in Kuala Lumpur. His transfer to Changi prison camp in Singapore brought trials of a different kind.

IF 1940 France was the phoney war, 1942 Changi was certainly the phoney captivity. To us who came from Pudu, it was unbelievable.

We arrived in our truckloads and were greeted with a certain official aloofness by a duty officer. This latter at once addressed us dispassionately upon our duties as prisoners of war and the need for discipline — subjects on which we were all of us infinitely better informed than he. He then lost interest in us and said: "All right, gentlemen, break off". So we broke off. Howls of rage. "Gentlemen", it appeared, meant only officers, of whom there were two in our midst: the remainder of us were emphatically *not*, he gave us to understand, gentlemen.

Gentlemen and scum alike, we Pudu-ites gazed at him with growing hostility and prepared not to like Changi. The man beside me, who in KL, by virtue of his ability to lead and the guts which had carried him from Parit Sulong to Yong Peng on a bullet-torn leg, had been one of our leaders, and who now — by virtue of his two pips — was one of the blessed few entitled to break off, stood his ground and said loudly: "Christ Almighty". That made us all laugh and when the duty officer tersely remarked: "All right, Mr McLeod, fall out", he did so to the accompaniment of amused comments from the rest of us of: "Ta-ta, Rod — see you in Australia", and "Oh, Mr McLeod, sir, your slip's showing". The duty officer was incensed at such frivolity and asked us what we thought this was. Harry replied, "Bush week", and the duty officer thereupon — having lost the initiative entirely — dismissed us.

Changi was phoney not because of the mass of men in it but because of the official attitude behind its administration. The Command determined to maintain full military discipline and establishments, regardless of circumstances or psychology, waiting upon the day when Malaya would be invaded by a British force. Accordingly, two principles seemed to guide every decision. One, to retain full divisional and regimental staffs pottering round achieving nothing useful at all in divisional and regimental offices: two, to preserve the Officers — Other Rank distinction by as many tactless and unnecessary orders as could be devised.

This latter was equally hard on both parties. It meant that officers could not freely mix with their friends who were ORs, nor ORs with officers. It meant that ORs were compelled to salute officers whom they had seen cowering in terror at the bottom of a slit trench as well as those who had done a good job. It meant that ORs were compulsorily stripped of clothing which (at their own discretion and on their own backs) they had carried from Singapore seventeen miles out to Changi, so that these garments might be distributed to officers who — though they did not work — must, it was deemed, at all times be well dressed. It meant that officers, far from waiting till their men ate and then eating the same food themselves, ate — under orders — in a separate mess and usually before the men. It meant that officers were allowed to keep poultry, ORs were not. It meant that there was fuel for an officers' club to cook light snacks, for the ORs there was not.

All of which casts no reflections upon the officers concerned any more than it did upon the men. They were under orders. Those orders were inspired by a sincere conviction at top level that it was absolutely necessary — in the cause of an imminent invasion, which, in fact, never came — to preserve the class distinction by privileges not based upon responsibility. It is no cause for complaint. But as a most relative factor in the life of those days, and one of the things most difficult then to comprehend, it must be recorded.

In the same way, to the naive Pudu-ite, Changi had other shocks. The docile acceptance of Tokyo time as the camp standard rather than the old British time to which we in KL had clung so tenaciously. The ceremonial parades at which we were handed from NCO to NCO and officer to officer until, hours later, we were dismissed — all so that the Japanese might know how many of us still languished in their custody. The rash of concert parties and theatres — dozens of them playing each night: everything from *Androcles and the Lion* to Army smoke-ohs. The drug selling ring which shamelessly traded M and B tablets from our own British hospital — tablets more priceless than diamonds — for bully beef from the

Malays and Chinese. A ring which could not publicly be
stamped out because, it was once rumoured, an MO was
one of its members (he left the keys of the drug store
where the stooges could pick them up) and because some
senior officers were also involved and to prosecute them
would be "bad for morale". For whose? we Pudu-ites
wondered.

Then there were the spivs of Changi — men with
courage and no scruples who went outside the wire each
night to collect tinned food from old Army dumps in the
rubber and then returned to sell their booty at black
market prices to their brethren back in camp. Every community has its villains — and Changi's preoccupation
with such laudable though impractical conceptions as
respect for officers and salutes thereto allowed its villains
a scope which to those of us who had lived the fraternal
life of KL was nauseating.

But if these follies and blacker sides of human nature
became obvious to us for the first time in Changi, so did
other things which were wholly delightful. For one thing,
we hardly ever saw the Japanese (and the ideal life is, of
course, one in which one *never* sees *any* Japanese). For
another, the common man of Changi greeted us with
overwhelming warmth. We had all been posted "Missing, Believed Killed" for nine months and though, upon
our return to the fold, we ruined many a model honour
roll upon which we had optimistically been inscribed as
"dead", we were, nevertheless, made to feel most
welcome.

Thus, all of us found ourselves equipped with a shirt
and a pair of shorts and boots. And Piddington, whom I
had last seen when I left him at Yong Peng at the beginning of the year, gave me a toothbrush and a pack of
Gibb's toothpaste — delightful gift after so long using a
finger and ground-up charcoal. The men of Changi were

solid gold right through, as men, on the whole, always are.

S.F. ARNEIL

To Coolies and Prisoners of War

The journey of "F" Force from Singapore to Thailand, which is the subject of S.F. Arneil's descriptive account, took place in April 1943.

EVERY war has had its prisoners and, for the captors, the problems that go with them. And in the normal course of events the captured do not expect to get much in the way of fair treatment, rather the reverse. They do not expect that a victorious army eager to crush the foe will bother to enlarge its administration to deal with them and a retreating army has not the time. In short, while sometimes a good thing to bolster up the morale of the home front, prisoners of war are a nuisance. The obvious thing to do is to put them out of the way and they are usually sent to where they can do no harm.

The journey of "F" Force, a party of seven thousand prisoners of war, from Singapore to the cholera-infested jungles of Thailand, a thousand miles away, exceeded by far what even the least reasonable man would be prepared to allow. For one thing, a journey of eight hundred miles through the tropics packed in airless, steel trucks, followed by a march of two hundred miles by jungle tracks beyond the limits of civilisation, left the prisoners so weak that less than half the unlucky force returned alive.

Blinding, suffocating heat enveloped the crawling trucks like a clinging veil, the panting engine pushed it aside; it reflected viciously from the sand until the sides of the airless trucks were dangerous to touch; the very landscape, capering and dancing in the shimmering waves screamed HEAT!

Within the trucks the only sound was the clacking of the wheels. Twenty-seven sweating prisoners packed together in a steel box with no food, no water, no latrine arrangements, nothing but the consciousness of the continual heat. Each man sat, almost naked, on his gear and the perspiration soaked through packs and kitbags. It ran down their bodies in dirty streams, stung the eyes and filled the truck with a nauseating stench.

It was impossible to think clearly because all thought reverted to the temperature. The two narrow doorways were strictly rostered and each man took his turn for the dubious pleasure of lying or kneeling in the wet mass of bodies, head poked outside trying to catch a mouthful of air which, though hot, was fresh. No breeze penetrated the crush at the doors and those inside sat with heaving chests gasping for breath. It was possible, by sitting quietly, for each main to obtain sufficient air for his needs but any undue movement or exertion would start a choking and straining for an extra breath until bloodshot eyes almost popped from their sockets. Many in this plight fainted and had to be placed near the doorway before they were able to regain consciousness.

The nights were little better than the days. The breeze made by the movement of the train entered the doors and chilled the wet bodies of the prisoners. It was possible, by crushing eighteen men into half the truck, to allow the remaining nine to lie down for a time. Four hours of uneasy sleep were as much as any man could hope to gain during the night and for most of the time men sat or dozed in a half-stupor, occasionally lurching forward against the bodies of fellow sufferers only to be rudely awakened and forced upright again. It was too hot for bodies to touch during the day and the weight of one person leaning against another during the night was more than a weary man could support.

Meals were irregular and dreadful. A mug of plain rice and a pint of watery soup, dished from fly-covered buckets, were deemed quite sufficient for troops who were sitting down all day. Cunning excuses were made for the absence of rations; at Ipoh a pint of rice, almost sour, and a dried fish, four inches long, were classed as two meals. That meant a day and night without food.

In Thailand even the boon of shade was denied the troops. The first meal was eaten in the full blaze of the sun while uniformed natives, barefooted but gleaming with brass badges and peaked caps, lounged in easy chairs on the cool station. Two-thirds of the prisoners were weak with acute diarrhoea and the Thais provided a small latrine about one-fiftieth of the size required. Men crawled under the trucks or simply lay between the lines, too dispirited to move.

When the train stopped thirty-six hours later for the second meal the one ray of hope was that the journey must shortly finish, and at six o'clock the following morning the troops tumbled off the train at Bam Pong.

Events moved so quickly and disastrously at Bam Pong that the whole system of administration used by the prisoners themselves was rendered useless. All records, stores, kitchen equipment and officers' trunks were piled outside the station. The party, carrying their gear, tramped two miles through the dusty streets to the camp. The dust rose in a choking cloud over the moving column and not a sound could be heard except the weary shuffle of feet on the road. Men with heavy packs and kitbags resting on their shoulders were too exhausted to raise eyes from the ground and nothing encouraged more than a passing glance. The town was negative in its attitude to the sufferers and natives watched the marching figures with neither sympathy nor hostility.

A dead tree, standing like a gaunt skeleton with arms pointing to the sky, brought derisive cheers and quick profanity from parched throats, for on every branch, clustered thickly together like bunches of rotten fruit, perched motionless cold-eyed vultures. Bald-headed, cruel-beaked and indescribably foul, they gazed unblinkingly at the staggering men. The omen was too strong for most of the men to ignore.

The camp was a group of atap-roofed shelters, built without walls and sloping to the ground from a centre pole eight feet high. The rubbish of previous trainloads of prisoners littered the area and the shallow drains were choked with rotting food. The stench of the open, crawling pits, passing as latrines, could be smelt fifty yards from the camp. Every leaf, twig, blade of grass or post in close proximity to them was covered with a revolting mantle of great swollen-bellied flies waiting patiently for the sun to dry their wings. Water for washing was drawn from a sixty-foot well by the native method of raising or depressing a lone bamboo pole, from one end of which was suspended a wooden bucket. The five feet of muddy water lying in the well was totally inadequate for six hundred filthy troops. Many men bathed in a bucket of water in which at least twenty had washed before them. One pint of boiled water for drinking was issued to each man.

Any thought of rest was dispelled as soon as the troops arrived at the camp. Hot and exhausted, within ten minutes they were marching back to the station to work for two hours carrying the cases of stores and officers' trunks to a central dump. It was a heavy task with no rests but after an hour of sweating toil a drum of fresh water was placed by the roadside and, pathetically grateful, the workers were allowed one mug of water. As each man stood, trembling with fatigue, to drink his issue of water, the full horror of the day seemed to centre in two things, the heat and the dirt. The miserable drop of muddy water with which some had tried to bathe after being unclean for six days and nights merely accentuated the grime rather than cleared it away. The filthy shirts and shorts of the men were wet, clinging rags and the dust and dirt, mingling with the perspiration streaming from their bodies, was so intolerable that some of the party in a mad effort to gain even temporary relief from their torment tore the shirts from their bodies and flung them away.

A surprise search threw the camp into a turmoil as almost every person tried desperately to rid himself of knives, compasses and souvenir weapons and to hide watches or valuables. The shouting of the NCOs mingled with the harsh commands of the captors; sticks were laid across the shoulders of the unfortunates who were unable to find gear in the press around the baggage heap. Ragged natives, hovering on the outskirts of the boiling mass, darted in and out grasping cast-off clothing, prohibited goods, old boots, even full kits. Hundreds of pounds' worth of precision instruments and what were previously considered to be essential goods were ruthlessly destroyed.

The search was over as quickly as it had begun and the party stood around, a little bewildered and at a loss what to expect next. The comparative quiet was ominous after the previous bedlam, but their fears gradually abated as a meal was served. The simple meal of rice and vegetable soup was just large enough to whet the appetite of the troops and the appearance of native women with huge baskets of eggs, tomatoes and bananas began a stampede.

Food was cheap and eggs, hardboiled, at seven cents, were too good to resist. Streams of panting children replenished the supplies and within fifteen minutes the whole party were sitting in little groups with piles of food before them. Eggs and bananas disappeared in thousands, men eating between six and ten eggs before starting on the small bananas which were consumed by the "hand", any number between eight and fifteen pieces of fruit making one "hand". It was a great feast and one man, rolling back on to the ground beside a heap of shells and peelings, expressed the feelings of many when he solemnly stated that it was the first time he had ever been able to try himself out on bananas. Results were more than satisfactory. The troops loosened their belts and relaxed; it was possible even to jeer at the vultures hovering over the camp, while in the hot sun the groups tried to sleep.

At 6 p.m. after a second meal of rice and soup the party assembled to hear the latest orders. They were staggeringly simple. Instead of a night's rest the party would move out that night on the first leg of an eighty-mile journey which would be covered in stages of ten to twelve miles. All baggage was to be carried, including medical panniers, stretchers and cooking gear; any person unable to complete a march would have to be abandoned or carried. The men were advised to travel light.

The troops digested the orders thoroughly. After six sleepless nights the prospect of a seventh was a bitter blow. However, it could and must be borne. Ten miles cf night marching did not sound too formidable provided the roads remained good and the rains kept off. Eighty miles was no more than a week's marching. The troops, who had once marched and fought a rearguard action for one hundred and forty miles, decided that the order to travel light was superfluous. The interpreter airily promised well-constructed camps and plenty of food at the end of the road. The party placed no reliance on the information at all and, prepared for the worst, hoped only for luck to fall their way.

Perhaps it was as well that they did not know that the promised eighty miles would stretch to one hundred and eighty; that there was to be not one march less than sixteen miles; that some of them would stagger into the final camps only to lie down and die of exhaustion.

In the black night the leaping flames of bamboo torches outlined the troops squatting in five lines on the road; each man carried besides his own gear at least one small carton of drugs. In addition there were buckets of rice for a midnight meal and the balance of the cooking gear to be distributed throughout the column. The men themselves were quiet; many fell asleep, sitting on the road, oblivious of the guttural screams of the captors who railed at the NCOs checking off the columns. A golf stick cruelly applied hastened the counting of the men and at 10.30 p.m. the troops marched into the night.

Within ten minutes every man knew exactly what he had to face. The pace set by the leading guard was reasonable but inexorable and with shoulders bent under the weight of heavy packs and kitbags the perspiration streamed from the bodies of the men and quickly saturated clothes and baggage. Where the loss of a yard meant so much extra effort to regain the line there was no time to adjust heavy loads to less painful positions and men even carried kitbags clasped in their arms until the first respite gave them the time to make adjustments.

Soft-padding natives appeared in the lines and when the bugle blew for the first halt the troops were feverishly selling as much gear as the natives would take. All the men realised that excess gear must be traded or thrown away and they accepted with alacrity the low prices offered. The natives, confident of their position, bought at prices that would have brought a blush to Shylock's cheek and bad money passed in the darkness more often than genuine. The sweating, cursing troops had no option but to lighten their loads and a great deal of baggage was thrown into the ditches beside the road.

Two hours' marching from Bam Pong the column stretched for a mile with men lurching along the road in various stages of exhaustion. Tired bodies almost screaming for rest were forced on and on until, in desperation, men staggering behind shouted blasphemously "For God's sake, HALT IN FRONT!" "Pass it on! HALT IN FRONT!" But the column halted once per hour and not before. Nothing could stop the march; it moved on, deathless, unceasing, and night after night the pitful entreaties to stop were passed up from the rear until the very words symbolised all the agony against which the troops had no redress.

At two o'clock the party stopped for a meal and rest. Every man was issued with a quart of boiled water from great earthenware containers and by the light of flaming torches ate his pint of plain rice and lay down to sleep. They slept in groups on the bare, damp ground, lying huddled together like lost children. Only the guards, prowling on the outskirts, and the regimental doctor, kneeling beside the stretchers on which lay two helpless malaria cases, remained awake.

Within two hours the march was resumed and by dawn the staggering column was too tired to lift its head. The medical panniers and cooking gear slung between poles passed slowly up and down the column. Those unfortunates who were unable to obtain relief from the heavy loads were beyond caring, they simply bent their backs a little more and trudged on. The road kept company with the railway line for a time. At least this much of the march could have been completed by rail in an hour. Realisation of this brought horrible curses from some, but most of the men said nothing and kept their eyes on the road.

The river saved the troops at the first halt. It ran past the open meadow, wide and swift-flowing and after four hours' sleep in the indifferent shade of a few trees the sun awoke the men and drove them into the water. Natives, gathered on the bank, were amazed and delighted at the spectacle of six hundred naked men yelling for joy as they scrubbed themselves, their clothes and each other until not a trace of the grime of a week's travel remained. It was a great cleansing and the men sat neck deep in the cool shade of the high tree-bordered banks until the native food vendors arrived.

The quantity of eggs, fruit, marmee and coffee consumed by the party shocked even the natives. Clean and refreshed, with plenty of time, the troops made a business of it and ate steadily all the afternoon, with no thought of the night's march before them.

When the shuffling, sweating column was counted the following morning most men had to be woken up to answer their names and the harassed young adjutant was almost in tears from fatigue by the time the last straggler was accounted for, two hours later. Not a soul paid the slightest attention to the proclamation read by the interpreter, and the now familiar first words "To coolies and prisoners of war" did not even raise the usual cynical smiles. The party was looking only for sleep. The announcement of a full night's rest brought audible sighs of relief. The interpreter was an understanding British officer; leading the parties to the rest area he quickly walked away.

The troops were shocked into wakefulness. Toiling wearily through the previous night the promise of a thirty-six hour halt had drawn them on as would an enchanting vision. In the worst places during the night men had struggled on just to be sure of sharing in the benefit of the rest. When they saw their resting place they stood speechless.

It was a stony half-acre, littered with refuse and in the early morning sun was already reflecting the heat. A few scrubby thornbushes struggled for a living in ground which was baked to a concrete hardness, but there was no other vegetation. With feelings too deep for words the party dispersed in groups to select the least filthy patches of ground on which to rest. A few crude shelters were erected by stretching blankets over the bushes, but the majority of the men lay down, heads pillowed on kitbags, covered their faces with cloths and slept.

By one o'clock the area was like a frying pan. The thornbushes were shimmering in the heat and the stench of the open latrines hung thickly over the camp. There was no shade. A hundred men clustered around a murderous looking native who hauled water from a deep well at ten cents per bucket.

With not even the consolation of a native market it had the aspect of a desert camp and rather than endure the heat most of the men marched two miles to the river to

wash their clothes and obtain temporary relief in its
waters. They gained a very dubious advantage; the
return march started the perspiration rolling once more
and a miscount by one of the guards kept the swimmers
on the hot parade ground for two hours.

The lack of shelter that night was not noticed by the
troops. The stony ground, after eight sleepless nights,
was a haven of rest and so dreamlessly did they sleep that
native bandits, moving quietly in the darkness, stole a
considerable quantity of gear, before arousing one
sleeper who awoke to find his blanket being lifted from
his body. A lively scuffle took place in the gloom and fists
and sticks were used to good advantage.

The troops were not sorry to see the end of the desert
camp. Hostile, waterless and filthy it was aptly named
and almost with relief they turned their faces to the
north. Four miles from the camp the party left the road
for good and plunged into the jungle.

The darkness of the rough track was a new and serious
problem. Where the tall trees met high overhead, even
the stars were obscured and the party travelled sight-
lessly through a complete absence of light. Heavily loaded, mis-steps resulted in bad falls, often for two or three
men together, and cuts and bruises were frequent. The
leading guard carrying the rifle walked briskly along by
the light of a torch. The column, carrying all its worldy
goods, groped blindly behind, unable to keep pace with
the front. The rear of the column, at the end of the first
hour, could not hear the bugle from the front and as the
march progressed the line lengthened to over two miles.
Men draped white towels over their backs and travelled
with one hand on the shoulder of a comrade. Later in the
journey the towels and pieces of white cloth were
discarded in favour of slabs of phosphorous-covered bark

which when rubbed on baggage left a slight glow quite useful as an indicator.

Where the column broke contact, which it did more and more frequently as the night wore on, there was a real danger of men losing the track altogether. Time and time again, a prisoner groping his way among the bushes would find himself twenty yards from the track with fifty men, hands on shoulders, cautiously following his lead. Interruptions of this nature meant a complete break of contact and many sections of the column travelled for miles in a torment of suspense fearing they were completely off the track, yet afraid to stop and risk being left miles behind.

For one two-hour stretch the column waded knee-deep in water. Many boots, already worn out before the march, fell to pieces. Men fell again and again in the water and entreaties to "halt in front" were shouted in vain.

By morning, the line resembled a retreating army. Friends travelled together in twos and threes, helping each other, carrying weaker men's gear and bolstering failing spirits with encouraging words. The strongest men floundered along under the weight of stretchers and medical gear. Unable to obtain relief from their burdens they refused to abandon them and finished the night march unutterably weary, with mud to the thighs from frequent falls, but triumphant. The last man to pass by the gaudy Buddhist temple at the camp was the regimental medical officer who plodded in carrying a sick man pickaback fashion.

The health of the party was deteriorating rapidly after this, the third march. Many men were suffering from acute dysentery and cut feet from worn and broken boots. The strongest of the party were finding each night the strain of carrying the sick too much. Accordingly an effort was made to leave as many men as possible at the camp. The troops spent the morning sleeping under a few trees and the afternoon sitting in the river. As usual no shelter was provided and as it was impossible to sleep in the blazing afternoon sun, a few hours' rest in the morning was as much as any man could expect.

The medical officer selected about fifty of the worst cases of dysentery and blistered feet to remain behind at the camp. The prospect looked a little brighter until half an hour before the start of the night's march when a guard, armed with a quick swinging stick, inspected the sick. He was prepared to allow only those men who were unable to remain on their feet to stay. During the immediate protest a bone in one man's hand was broken and the party were given no alternative but to march on as best they could.

The marches that followed were fantastic nightmares with only the most revolting sights or the most astounding incidents remaining in men's minds. Boots fell from tired feet, clothes and personal belongings were thrown away to lighten the loads; at the halfway halt each night men slept in the mud like exhausted animals. Everything faded into unimportance except the march. The troops had to keep moving, bodies screaming for rest were forced on night after night towards the consolation of the end of the road. Good camps had been promised and tired eyes lit up at the thought of food and sleep at the journey's end.

The staging camps passed by as in a dream. Temple Camp, with its temple sitting above the river, and the yellow robed priests drifting along with shaven skulls bowed in meditation. Big Bridge Camp, where mounds of steaming, plain rice, heaped on grass mats, were ladled to lines of troops as if they were starving stock. The Dutch Canteen Camp, where the golf stick swung more than usual. Bamboo Creek, a wretched, squalid patch where the men sheltered during the day in the bamboo breaks and washed in a miserable pool no bigger than a bath tub.

To the marchers, as they lurched from camp to camp, there seemed to be no end to the road. The sandflies came one night to add to their misery and remained ever after a nightlong menace to men's sanity. They bit into every exposed portion of skin without mercy and clustered on damp scalps until in desperation each man carried a smouldering bamboo brand which smoked them away.

At one camp the men were herded into a stockyard fifty yards square on the bare side of a hill and remained there all day. At another halt a Japanese with a passion for military discipline stood on a small mound and formed the troops up in eight lines, facing a corresponding number of meal points. Each time his martial arm descended the first eight men dashed forward to receive their rations and so on until the whole party was fed. It was all very regimental, but plain rice and a bucket of vegetable water to every fifty men left the troops so hungry that many dived in the river for mussels and boiling them ate the resultant leathery morsels with what was almost enjoyment.

To men who had been used to drinking strong tea four or five times a day the total absence of it was a hardship far greater than the scarcity of food. It had to be borne to be realised. Many men even boiled dried bamboo leaves in a vain effort to find a substitute for the drink which had previously been looked upon as a necessity.

One camp, perched on the top of a hill, departed from the usual routine and fed the prisoners well. Four meals of whale meat and vegetables were consumed by the hungry troops with delirious joy and they assured each other that they were approaching the district where good food was to be had in abundance. It was a short-lived hope, however; there was a lack of food in the next camp, as usual.

At Konkoidah the troops were beyond all the elementary stages of fatigue and shuffled into the camp with backs aching from the weight of packs, now shrunk to contain the barest necessities, and with eyes dulled from lack of sleep. The camp was even worse than most, with hundreds of Tamil labourers living in overcrowded huts under the most primitive conditions. The natives, having not the sketchiest knowledge of hygiene, and always suspicious of constructed latrines, answered the calls of nature wherever they happened to be. The resultant stench hung foully over the camp and any movement sent clouds of flies whirring into the air.

The medical officer was almost desperate; without cholera serum he felt the responsibility of hundreds of lives hanging heavily on his shoulders. The disease had struck suddenly at the previous camp and the memory of two men vomiting their lives away in a few hours turned the troops cold with fear. They lay in the blazing sun as far from the natives as possible, waiting for the night to fall and the march to be resumed. Nobody attempted to bathe or even wash in the cholera-infested river and the strongest men spent the day working over roaring fires like ash-covered demons to boil sufficient drinking water for their comrades.

Men carried out orders without complaint and on completion of the tasks lay down again to await the night. One party of unfortunates carried bags of rice over a mile, wordlessly, barefooted and almost too weary to lift their heads. Unnecessary words were a luxury only to be used by the stronger men.

Twenty horrible days from Bam Pong, in the hour after dawn, the vanguard of the column splashed across a shallow creek and halted on the side of a hill to obtain the first view of their future home.

It was the end of the road at last, the mecca for which men had marched two hundred miles with little food and rest, leaving sick and dying at every halt. Two tumbledown bamboo huts, roofless and with sagging walls, yawned open to the sky. Weeds and saplings flourished on the earth floors and the jungle, like an inevitable fate, crept hungrily up the very sides of the rotting structures. There was no sign of any recent habitation and only the splashing of the stragglers, crossing the stream, broke the silence.

A cloud passed over the sun and the first big drops of the rainy season fell among the column. A premonition of horror passed through the troops as they gazed at the roofless huts.

An interpreter appeared and began to read the proclamation: "To coolies and prisoners of war . . ."

JESSIE ELIZABETH SIMONS

Like Sisters of a Family

Jessie Elizabeth Simons, an Australian Army nursing sister, escaped from Singapore on the small ship Vyner Brooke *on 13 February 1942, but fell into Japanese hands when the vessel was sunk by Japanese bombs off the coast of Sumatra. In the following extract from* While History Passed, *Simons describes the trials and comradeship of life in the women's POW camp at Muntok on Banka Island during November 1944–March 1945.*

MUNTOK camp was new, and had big airy buildings surrounded by a thirty-five-foot bamboo fence. Inside the bamboo was a narrow path designed for the use of the patrolling Malayan guards, but separated from the camp proper by a barbed wire fence. The improved barracks gave a fillip to the hopes of the exponents of the repatriation theory. "See," they said, "the Nips are putting us in a show camp so that any neutral inspectors who come along to arrange things will be suitably impressed."

But it did not take us long to discover that appearances were false to the facts, that Muntok was as near hell as we were likely to get and come back. For instance, the only water supply inside the camp came from wells which were generally dry and, anyway, were only a few feet away from the lavatory pits; both wells and pits were mere unlined holes in the earth.

Determined protest secured us permission to use the heavy chunkels to dig a series of steps down a steep slope to a stream about a mile away. Sick and desperate women, moving more slowly each trip, crawled up and down this Jacob's Ladder bringing in the camp's main water supplies as we had carried irrigation water for the Japs at Palembang.

The boat carrying the hospital staff to Muntok was struck during the trip by a violent tropical storm which almost succeeded in wiping out the whole institution — staff, patients and equipment. Arriving wet and miserable, the staff set up hospital with sinking hearts under the crudest conditions yet, without beds, bedding or effective equipment. Only a few simple drugs in poor supply, and the devotion of the doctors and nurses redeemed the work from farcical burlesque.

Mavis and I were both in bad shape after the trip, but we were not worse than the majority. Our legs were badly swollen to the knees as a result of beri-beri and I was weak from an attack of dengue, having come straight from bed to board the boat, which no doubt accounts for the fogginess of the trip in my recollections. Malaria and beri-beri were by now so universal that little notice was taken of them. The very little quinine available was reserved for the worst malarial cases, and these patients were compelled to swallow the tablets in the presence of a member of the nursing staff. They might otherwise have yielded to the temptation to sell the quinine on the black market, where a regular price of one-and-a-half guilders was quickly established, although it rose later as high as seven-and-a-half guilders per tablet.

Naturally, the death rate soared to a new record, daily

248 Jessie Elizabeth Simons

broken. We had to dig graves, construct rough coffins and bury our own dead, often at the rate of three a day in our own circle of acquaintance. For mothers who had sacrificed from their own rations for the past two and a half years to give their children a better chance of coming through, Muntok camp was a grim, never-to-be-forgotten last stand against their children's starvation. Far too many of them fought a losing battle; one woman saw four of her five children die within a week from the accumulated effects of malnutrition. Total war!

Somehow there were always a few flowers for the funerals, pathetic little processions of a few friends paying respects to one who had "gone before" — a banal phrase that leapt to new life and meaning as the half-dead wondered whose turn would be next. We managed to keep the cemetery tidy with a wooden cross marking each grave. The crosses were made from material at hand when needed but, although there was no conformity about them otherwise, we tried to keep the same approximate size; each had burned into the wood with heated wire the name and other details, with the date of death. This work was very neatly done by the capable Norah Chambers.

Christmas of 1944 came and went as other days did. Not for us the newspaper reviews of the year's events, the contrast of "Now" with "One Year Ago". Germany and Italy were rapidly folding up; American forces were closing in for the final blows on battered Tokyo; President Roosevelt had been swept back by the tides of war and the world's respect to that White House in which he had become an institution; but no word of all this penetrated the bamboo fence that shut Muntok camp out of the world. We did make a tired effort to arrange a Christmas concert as in other years, but poignant memories joined with our depleted strength and numbers to make the effort abortive — we just could not be bothered.

Though we had all been pretty low at times, the AANS still numbered thirty-two, the original survivors of the landing in Sumatra, but early in February 1945 a new blow fell, the first death among the nurses — Sister W. Raymont, a South Australian. Attending the funeral in as full uniform as we were able to muster, we felt that we had reached an all time low despondency.

We began to realise what a Jap guard meant when he addressed us one blistering afternoon back in Palembang. I took notes at the time and I still have them: "I want pay attention to you," he said. "You all people have individualism; you are having the collective life now. Important conditions of the collective life have two things. They are comradeship and order. If you cannot be having them we shall not can say that you are the foremost nation. And we shall give you them compulsorily." Yes, we were getting order, comradeship and the collective life in Muntok, all right! It was a race, each for all and all for each, against weakness, sickness and starvation. When there had been more hope there was more wrangling and struggle for what was going, but in Muntok we were welded into a new solidarity by the relentless struggle for survival in which we were all engaged. Everyone was ill, but those who could still stagger took up the responsibilities of all, cooking, chopping wood, carrying water, painfully dying on our feet. Many unsuspected talents were uncovered by the demands of necessity; one of the daintiest of our nurses turned up trumps as a perfect maker of axe handles that stayed in place, despite the crude tools with which she had to work, a gift no doubt destined to be wasted in civilisation. The various camp jobs were divided amongst us according to our estimated strength and abilities.

Mavis and I took over as our camp responsibility the task of boiling water for the sick, after three women had been defeated by weakness and compelled to give up; two of them later died and the third came out of Sumatra on a stretcher. Since none of the water we had available could be trusted for purity, every drop for drinking purposes had to be boiled over an open fire, fed with green rubber-wood. The heat and smoke were incessant, and the job was a full-time one which occupied us from 7 a.m. till 8.30 p.m. with very little let up. Just for good measure we added to this chore cooking duties on behalf of the more-or-less-well internees who could still afford to pay. This was just a new angle on the eternal necessity of earning money to stave off starvation on the official rations.

For the sick we supplied unlimited quantities of boiled water (without charge, of course), and at one time we included in this service the dragging of the water from the depths of a ninety-foot well. For others the charge for boiling was ten cents per bottle, the customer supplying the water, but we were always ready to waive the charge for any who could not afford payment. Gradually our establishment grew in popularity and we began to fry rice cakes, to boil soup and cook other specialities at a small charge.

With all the cooking we undertook, Mavis and I found it necessary to become employers, obtaining the services of a Mrs Iris Frith, wife of a rubber planter in Malaya, at a wage of two guilders per week and an extra ration of rice. Her long and willing work made us daily ashamed of the small pittance, but it was the best we could manage. With this extra help we were able to assume some new responsibilities on behalf of the hospital patients. To induce them to eat we tried to deliver their meals, especially their private delicacies, piping hot and as decently cooked as the conditions permitted. During the "dinner-rush" we were kept moving at top speed to keep up this standard for the forty odd patients. I usually acted as "runner", first collecting from each patient the food and oil for frying, and then returning the cooked food, too often only fried rice, to its owner as rapidly as possible. One problem was remembering who was a rice cake and who a boiled soup (made of vegetable skins and a handful of rice), but only rarely did we have any confusion. In this way forty people were served at each meal, and many of them were tempted to eat the unappetising foods only because they were hot and freshly cooked.

The official allowance of cooked rice was one cup per person for each meal, and one could buy more on the black market at one-and-a-half guilders per cup. Occasionally a little fish or a few prawns would be added to the fare, enough to allow each internee a small ration rather less than once a fortnight. We developed a technique of cooking these delicacies slowly so that we could eat the bones and so waste nothing.

Mavis and I had no responsibility for cooking the official meals, a duty allotted to special squads; other similar squads had charge of sanitation, wood-chopping and water-carrying just as we had the duties relating to the hospital. The wood-choppers had no shelter for their hot work of trying to cut tough green wood with axes that were extremely blunt and liable to fly off the handles without warning. The cooking squad had no chimneys in their kitchen, but worked with makeshift appliances in a constant haze of acrid smoke. The *boeboe*, stock breakfast dish made with a little rice and a lot of water, was cooked in huge saucer-shaped iron *qualis* set in bricks like a copper. Each *quali* held ten buckets of water, and the gluey mess had to be stirred throughout the entire two hours required to cook it. This is typical of the difficulties of the kitchen staff who began the daily operations about 4 a.m., and were soon busy serving the whole camp with hot tea to start us off on the day.

The official meals served as welcome interludes in those days over the hospital fire. To the breakfast of *boeboe* at 8 a.m. we might be lucky enough to add sugar, coconut oil or chillies; for lunch (any time up to 3.30 for us) there was more rice with vegetables and very occasionally a little very salty fish; dinner, which we usually got around to about 8.30 p.m., was a variation of the same theme plus anything available on the black market. To us, this depended on finance; we were always very hard up. After dinner came the one bright spot in our day, a few minutes leisure and about half a bucket of hot water for a bath.

The black market was a strange affair in Muntok. On our arrival the Nips had threatened with bloodthirsty relish such dire penalties for anyone caught in black market dealings that only a very few hardy women took the risk until we discovered that the market was actually operated by the Nips themselves. The threats, I suppose, were just a spot of face-saving. Occasionally we got out from the camp enclosure to gather wood in the jungle to eke out the general camp supply or to feed the private fires on which many groups did their cooking of black market supplies. On these trips we raced like demons. We were only allowed on a certain area. After a few outings, the area presented an almost lawn-like appearance; everything that would burn had been removed. Always wood was extremely scarce.

In Singapore we heard an apocryphal tale about a mosquito who landed on an aerodrome but was not distinguished from a Spitfire until after someone had pumped ten gallons of aero spirit into him. The author of this tale must have met the Muntok mossies — after dark they came in to attack in furious mood, and it was not long before Mavis and I, as a result of providing them with a meal while working in the open after dark, were down with malaria. We carried on as best we could, though never fit or free from the recurrent attacks until after our release. As if this were not enough misfortune, we had a bad burning accident. While talking to a customer, I noticed that a pan of oil on the fire had caught alight and instinctively grabbed it. The fire ran up my arm and in the confusion I dropped the pan of oil over my own and Mavis' feet. Unfortunately she had the worst of it, and was in bed for two weeks. But this, by comparison with the plight of others, was a minor matter. Between February and April, our battered uniforms did their best to make a show of respect and hide the depths of our emotions at the funerals of three more of our girls.

"Rene" Singleton, 2/10th Australian General Hospital, a Victorian, will always be remembered for her dry humour. Emaciated almost beyond recognition save for her deep blue eyes, poor Rene was always hungry — on the day she died she kept asking for "more breakfast, please!"

Blanche Hempstead, 2/13th AGH, a Queenslander, was notorious for hard work; this assuredly hastened her end. She said she was sorry for the trouble her illness had caused and, when she realised death was inevitable, that she had taken so long to die.

Always frail Shirley Gardam, 2/4th Casualty Clearing Station, a fellow trainee of mine from the Launceston General Hospital, although very sick for some time, mercifully died quite quickly on April 4th, 1945. During the three years of imprisonment, she had received no letters. She did not know her mother had died in 1942. I later realised that she would never have stood up to the gruelling trip from Muntok to Loeboek Linggau which then was still ahead of us.

Mavis was now the only survivor of the 2/4th CCS, and her chance of coming through was very slim.

We buried four more Sisters in the next four months. Gladys Hughes, 2/13th AGH of Victoria, who belonged to New Zealand, was a popular girl — famous for new cooking ideas. Winnie May Davis of New South Wales, 2/10th AGH, one of our youngest Sisters, was a marvellous girl who gave herself for her friends. "Dot" Freeman, 2/10th AGH, another Victorian, was a sweet girl, with whom internment went very hard. She slipped out quietly one night early in August.

P. Mittelheuzer, "Mitts", 2/10th AGH, a Queenslander, died on August 20th. The only thing she wanted was to hear her people call her by her Christian name.

After living for over three years with each other, we were like sisters of a family. Of course we did not always see eye to eye, but what sisters do? I have many times heard people vowing they never wanted to set eyes on a certain person again, but when trouble came, they were usually the first to rally round.

And so we buried our friends and companions, and as we watched them die, and others grow weaker through dysentery, malaria, beri-beri and malnutrition, we said, "Those girls on the beach were lucky. I wonder what the plan is for the rest of us." This was indeed a very grim and heartbreaking time.

The Japanese interpretation of the Geneva Convention continued, and we often wished that scrap of paper had never been thought up. In Muntok we had no electric light, so when some Jap came across the terms "brightly lit" in the Convention, a new decree was added to our annoyances. Each hut was compelled to keep a kerosene lamp lit all night, but because of the Jap fears of fire, one person in each hut had always to be awake to attend to the light. We took hourly shifts at this duty, on which the

Jap patrols insisted that the guard must be not merely awake but on her feet and out from under any netting, to the mosquitoes' moaning delight. How often we cursed that "brightly lit" kerosene lamp, which was always hurriedly doused if an air raid siren wailed!

That mean-souled scoundrel, Siki, was still camp commandant, but Mrs Hinch, a YWCA representative, was in charge of British internal arrangements. Though middle-aged and not robust, Mrs Hinch upheld the best traditions, and did a great job despite odds very much against her in the struggle for better food and conditions. About the only result of her efforts was ill-treatment for herself, but this had no effect on her persistence. Siki was always difficult to deal with, and the only one who had any success against him was Mrs Muller, a Dutch-woman who could talk Japanese; she argued back very vigorously with the Nips, but even the concessions she extracted were few and slight.

The camp for men, not far away, was better provisioned than our own, judging by the goats, chickens and pigs which the men sent up when their camp was moved and they were prevented from taking the livestock. The chooks were taken over by the Japs, and that was all we ever saw of them. The goats were milked for the hospital patients, but they were not a huge success as milk-producers. There was a suspicion that the hospital milkmaid was not the first one on the scene. However, the Japs really loved those goats and, whenever an official appeared, they paraded the goats as evidence of good treatment. The only one of the men's animals the Japs gave us a chance to eat was a pig who died, presumably from exposure. We debated for a long time the advisability of adding him to our diet, but finally reckoned it better to die of slow starvation than swift poisoning. Occasionally the Nips brought us a wild pig, but it did not go far among seven hundred of us after the Nips had had their cut, even though we wasted nothing but the large bones; the smaller ones were baked and then pounded to be eaten by those who were calcium-conscious. We treated fish bones in the same way, but poultry bones, on the rare occasions we were able to try them, would only splinter. The best we could do was to pick them clean. On reflection it seems probable that we had not more than one pound of meat each during the whole three-and-a-half years of our internment.

I remember that we once asked a more than usually communicative Jap, "Have you ever been to Australia?" "Not yet," he replied confidently. Now we can appreciate that confidence as a good joke, but in the sweating heat as we stoked our fires at Muntok, or joined a silent procession to the cemetery, it looked to us as though even if he were wrong, victory would come too late for us.

RAY PARKIN

Morale

After the sinking of HMAS Perth, *Ray Parkin was held prisoner by the Japanese in various POW camps. In this passage from* Into the Smother *he describes a number of incidents that, in one way or another, bore on the subject of the morale of Australian prisoners during their period of captivity.*

LAST night the sergeants were paraded before the adjutant, a major. He strongly criticised the falling-off of morale. He commended the WOs and blamed the sergeants. We saw a little bit of red, because we think the WOs simply pass on the orders verbally and leave the dirty work to the sergeants, who live with the men. We think, too, that the officers have got out of touch with the men and can only wave the Manual of Military Law at them in an endeavour to intimidate. This only produces a violent reaction in the men, who become even more bloody-minded on seeing the officers vaunting privilege and neglecting responsibility. Often they seem more concerned with traditional niceties of the parade ground than in facing the vital situation of survival with the men: this is not to detract from some officers, who have, from their own pay, given food and money to some of the men. And the doctors are, in all things, impeccable.

But it does seem stupid to have this parade-ground stuff thrust on us as a "morale builder". These men are not disciplined, in the naval sense; but properly led they are as good as any men in the world. We are hoping that time will heal this breach, but at the moment it doesn't look like it. The men feel that, in facing this situation, the officers have half-a-head start on them and are using authority to their own advantage. I hear it said every day.

*   *   *

This afternoon Weary Dunlop came over. He is our camp CO, but primarily our doctor. He came over to ask me if he might read over the account I had written of the night the Germans declared war on Greece and blew up the Piraeus of Athens. He was there too. We talked for a couple of hours. At the outbreak of war he had abandon- ed the plan of his career, which he had been following for fourteen years, at the request of the commonwealth government who asked him if he were free. Being a man who never refuses a request for help, he gave up a great deal to join the AAMC. When the war is over he must slowly climb back in a catch-as-catch-can world and, I have no doubt, the government that so eagerly sought him will as eagerly forget him. He tells me that all his life he has been a scoffer; but he knows the conventions at which he has scoffed are the necessary weft and woof for the many, and he respects that. But I know he is a most kindly and gentle scoffer — except at the unrighteous. Here is a man who shoulders his own burdens so that they will not worry others, and then heedlessly piles on his own shoulders the worries of anybody who comes to him. He is a man the Japanese have already tortured several times; but about this he says nothing. I heard of one session they gave him. They put a thick pole behind his knees and then made him kneel, holding heavy stones so that the pole acted as a fulcrum to force the knee joints apart with the whole weight of his body (this is called the "knee-spread"). In addition, his bare knees were pressing into sharp gravel. For eight hours he was like this, and he did not hide from me the fact that it was painful; but, he said, the return of circulation was most embarrassing for, when he tried to stand at last in front of his torturers, he "stumbled like a silly fool".

The men would do anything for him and are proud to be with him. I am sure it is his presence which holds this body of men from moral decay in bitter circumstances which they can only meet with emotion rather than reason. He is a big man — some six feet four inches of him — and a most skilful surgeon: a simple, profoundly altruistic man, with a gentle, disarming smile. This selflessness, this smile, command more from the men than an army of officers each waving a Manual of Military Law. When we move, Weary always tries to carry all his surgical gear and books. He has to be bullied to part with any of them; and then, like as not, you will find him carrying something for somebody else.

He told me that, two nights ago, he and a major were sent for by the Japanese commanding officer in the English camp. They made their way over a very hazardous track in the dark, to find the Jap sitting up in bed with a mouth organ. They had to spend half the night sitting up listening in forced admiration to the murder of "Auld Lang Syne" and "Home Sweet Home".

*   *   *

The day dawned — the first day of April — shrouding the mountain with low cloud to the tops of the trees in the camp. It swirled and, for an instant, revealed the great peak above us — still with a veil about its waist. Austere and delicate, it might have been a Japanese picture.

It was certainly a Japanese picture that was etched into our minds that day. All Fools' Day! The top of the mountain and the tops of all mountains, and all hope, vanished for the day. The white obliterating cloud came right down to earth and wet us through as we waded on the hour's march through thick mud and patches of slush to our job on the railway. My aching stomach turned, in its turn, to water. The job was the same: one cubic metre, one man. The rain drenched us all day. The red earth stuck to our shovels and we had to scrape it off them into our baskets, as we cursed and sweated with ill temper. Many bare feet and falling bodies were sliced by the razor-sharp split bamboo and jagged stones buried in the muddy tracks.

Never, up till now, have I felt so hopeless. I think I must be the most dismal of the lot. Content to see us sacrifice our mosquito nets for scanty clothing, the Japs are even taking our tents now — one by one. The only thing we can be certain of having over our heads tonight is the continued threat of further deprivation.

At work we could only move at one-third of our normal pace. But we still had to finish our quota. We were hit with sticks, our faces were slapped, and we were kicked for nothing more than having fallen down with a sodden load of earth. The guards' tempers had gone with the weather.

Because I was sick on the job, Billy allowed me to *yasume* — but for no more than half an hour — and then I had to work through the dinner break. He said sick men didn't eat. All about were great piles of newly felled bamboo which were covering valuable earth.

Billy wanted to get at that earth; so he calmly told another miserable wretch and myself to burn the bamboo — the sodden, green bamboo. When we recovered and told Billy that it wouldn't burn, he screamed and bashed us half-unconscious. We scrabbled about, close to the ground, for something a little dry, under something, somewhere. We must have found it, I suppose, for at last we got a flame and built a fire that would have burnt the Devil himself. Cut and torn by thorns in the search, we staggered about feeding it, and got half-cooked. Then we stood away and shivered.

When at last in the gloom of drowning day we started for home, we climbed the big Hill on all fours. It seemed a miracle how the elephants had got down that day, but their bucket-like footprints made a stairway for us in parts. We arrived back smeared to the waist, and our arms to the shoulders, with the black road mud.

*   *   *

Weary's legs are bad — ulcers and beri-beri swelling. But he keeps going all day at the hospital. This affects all the fellows in the camp. They feel for him and worry about him. Many of them try to think of some ruse to keep him off his feet; none has been found.

Malnutrition troubles are attacking everywhere. Eggs have not been coming up, so we are beginning to feel the full weight of the inadequate Japanese rations. A few days ago a few came up, but only enough for two per man. There is no doubt in my mind that eggs will make all the difference to our chances of getting out of the jungle alive.

*   *   *

Tonight we had a stump concert with community singing. It is fine to hear men rise out of their dejection with "Pack up your troubles in your old kit bag" — when they have no "fag" nor "lucifer" to light it with. And to hear them sing without self-pity. Herb Smith sang "At the end of a dusty road". This was the song he sang the other night when we came in dead-beat. There was a grand yellow sunset riding on the back of a thunderstorm. There was the rumble of thunder; the first big drops began to splatter on the leaves of the trees above us. Bert was ploughing down to the showers, naked except for his torn boots. His voice came fine and clear with a volume which echoed under the tree canopy. "At the end of a dusty road!" And every man who heard the sheer spirit of this man's singing felt his own uplifted too. Never, I feel, will I hear a song like that anywhere in the world. It is a song that will keep singing to me all my life.

At night the blue smoke of fires makes cardboard cut-outs of the trees. But the sun, rising, draws the curtain of night *down* (not up) and lights the world. This impression is caused by the shadow of the mountain ridge which, as it cuts through the smoke, seems to descend slowly before the rising sun. The floor of the stage is twilight blue and the fires are gold, lighting up the greens and browns and reds of the forest. The curtain is down, and vanished into the earth as we stand on the work parade.

*   *   *

My feet are not too good these days because of the wet; and the ulcerous sores on my shins are troublesome. Bandages will not stay on because of the taper of my calf. However, I have been able to use the leaves of a ground vine, which are very thin. By licking them well and placing them over the sores they stick and keep the insects out. If they get torn off by the undergrowth, I can usually find more.

There is a lot to grumble about; a lot to be disappointed about; a lot to lose our tempers over; but there is also much to marvel at. For instance, the loyalty of a man's body — to watch a sore heal itself — to feel that pain is not so much a tragedy but a process. There is a fascination in trying to help it consciously, to try and break down any internal resistance to recovery by trying to quell devastating emotions like bad temper, hatred, fear, lust, envy.

Biographical Notes

S.F. Arneil (1918–   ), born Sydney, joined the AIF in 1940. Served in the 2/30th Battalion in Malaya. A POW after the fall of Singapore. Author of the personal narrative *One Man's War* (1980). His short narrative "To Coolies and Prisoners of War" was published in the volume *As You Were, 1948*. Awarded AO for his work in establishing credit unions in Australia during the 1960s.

Richard Beilby (1918–   ), born in Malaya of Australian parents and educated in Western Australia from 1929. Served with the AIF in the Middle East and New Guinea. Several occupations after the war, including novelist. Two of his novels deal with Australian soldiers escaping from invading German forces during 1941, *No Medals for Aphrodite* (1970) being set in Greece and *Gunner* (1977) in Crete.

Russell Braddon (1921–   ), born Sydney, educated at the University of Sydney. Joined the AIF and was captured by the Japanese in Malaya, becoming a POW at Pudu and Changi and on the Burma-Thailand railway. His personal narrative *The Naked Island* (1952) deals with his war experiences and *End of a Hate* (1958) with his life after the war. Resident of Britain after 1949. He has written several novels and biographies including *Cheshire, VC* (1954), *Nancy Wake* (1956), and *Joan Sutherland* (1962).

D.E. Charlwood (1915–   ), born Melbourne, worked on the land at Nareen (Vic.) for seven years before joining the RAAF in 1940. Flew with RAF Bomber Command in England during the war. Worked as an air-traffic controller in Australia, 1945–75. His personal narrative *No Moon Tonight* (1956) deals with his war experiences; later writings include the novel *All the Green Year* (1965) and two volumes of short stories.

Jon Cleary (1917–   ), born Sydney, left school at a relatively early age. Served in the AIF in the Middle East and New Guinea, 1940–45. Resident outside Australia for much of the postwar period. A prolific writer of scripts for television, radio and films. He has written many novels, including *You Can't See Round Corners* (1947), *The Climate of Courage* (1954), and *The High Commissioner* (1966), and two volumes of short stories, including the war stories *These Small Glories* (1946).

Peter Cowan (1914–   ), born Perth, educated at the University of WA. Served with the RAAF during 1943–45. Tutor in English at the University of WA and coeditor of *Westerly*. He has written several volumes of short stories, including *Drift* (1944), two novels, and a biography, and is editor of several volumes of short stories and West Australian writings.

Dymphna Cusack (1902–81), born Wyalong (NSW), and educated at the University of Sydney. A teacher, then a writer. She wrote twelve novels, including *Come in Spinner* (1951), written in collaboration with Florence James, *Southern Steel* (1953), and *The Half-Burnt Tree* (1969), and several plays, travel books, and children's books.

"David Forrest" (David Denholm) (1924–   ), born Maryborough (Qld). Served in the Australian militia in New Guinea during the war. A bank officer until 1964; later, an academic. He has written two novels, *The Last Blue Sea* (1959) and *The Hollow Woodheap* (1962), and is also author of short stories and articles on cultural and historical topics.

Lawson Glassop (1913–66), born Lawson (NSW). Journalist; joined the AIF in 1940; served in the Middle East, working on an army newspaper. Resumed career as journalist after the war. Has written three novels and a children's book. Glassop did not take part in the siege of Tobruk: his description of the siege in *We Were the Rats* (1944) is based on information gleaned from soldiers who were present and from other sources. The novel was banned as obscene in NSW in 1946 and a bowdlerised version was issued in 1961. His other two novels are *Lucky Palmer* (1949) and *The Rats in New Guinea* (1963).

Harry Gordon (1926–   ), a war correspondent in Korea, where he met Reg Saunders, who was serving as a captain commanding a company of the Third Battalion of the Royal Australian Regiment. His biography of Saunders, *The Embarrassing Australian* (1962), covers Saunders' early life, his service during the Second World War in the Middle East and New Guinea, his civilian life after that war, his service in Korea, and his later years. Gordon's other publications include *An Eyewitness History of Australia* (1976) and *Die Like the Carp* (1978), dealing with the breakout of Japanese prisoners from the POW camp at Cowra, NSW.

John Hetherington (1907–75), born near Melbourne. Journalist; war correspondent in Greece in 1941. Publications about the war include *Airborne Invasion* (1943), *The Australian Soldier* (1943), and the novel *The Winds are Still* (1947). Biographic studies of Sir Thomas Blamey (1954/1973), Melba (1967), Norman Lindsay (1961/1973) and others. Also wrote on architecture in Victoria. Autobiographic volume: *The Morning was Shining* (1971).

Florence James (1904–   ), born Gisborne (NZ), educated at the University of Sydney. Coauthor with Dymphna Cusack of the novel *Come in Spinner* (1951) and the children's book *Four Winds and a Family* (1947).

Eric Lambert (1918–66), born in England, educated in Sydney. Joined the AIF in 1940, serving in the Middle East, New Guinea and postwar Singapore. Seventeen novels, including *The Twenty Thousand Thieves* (1951), *The Veterans* (1954) and *Glory Thrown In* (1959). Also wrote short stories, a biographic study *MacDougal's Farm* (1965) concerned with Malcolm Dougal, who was a POW in Changi, and a biography of Oscar Wilde's parents *Mad with Much Heart* (1967). Joined the Communist Party in 1947. Resident abroad during his later life.

Ray Parkin (1910–   ), born Melbourne, served in the RAN during 1928–46. After the sinking of HMAS *Perth* he became a POW in Japanese hands. Three personal narratives describing his war experiences — *Out of the Smoke* (1960), *Into the Smother* (1963) and *The Sword and the Blossom* (1968).

Peter Ryan (1923–   ), born Melbourne, served with a special military force (Kanga Force) in New Guinea during 1942–43. After the war worked in public relations. Director of Melbourne University Press 1962–88. *Fear Drive My Feet* (1959) is his personal account of his war experiences. Also editor of the *Encyclopedia of Papua and New Guinea* (1972) and author of a biography of Judge Redmond Barry (1972).

Jessie Elizabeth Simons (1911–   ), served in Singapore as an Australian Army nursing sister. Escaped from Singapore in February 1942, but fell into Japanese hands after the sinking of the ship *Vyner Brooke* off the coast of Sumatra. The story of her experiences as a prisoner of war is given in her personal narrative *While History Passed* (1954), later published under the title *In Japanese Hands* (1985).

Kenneth Slessor (1901–71), born Orange (NSW), educated at Sydney Grammar School. Journalist. Australia's official war correspondent during 1940–44, serving in the Middle East and New Guinea. Resumed career in journalism after resigning this commission. Active in many areas relating to Australian literature as editor, committee-man, and literary critic. Several volumes of poetry, beginning with *Thief of the Moon* (1924) and ending with *Poems* (1957). Prose: *Bread and Wine* (1970), *War Diaries* (1985), and *War Despatches* (1987).

Pat Studdy-Clift (c.1927–   ), educated in Sydney, part-time student at the Sydney Conservatorium. Joined the Women's Emergency Signalling Corps in Sydney. Returned to help run the family property, "Kareela", near Gunnedah, NSW, in 1943. Continued farming with her sister Joan for five years after the war. After marriage engaged in sugar farming with her husband on the Tweed River until her retirement to Kingscliff on the far north coast of NSW. Author of *Only Our Gloves On* (1981), which deals with her life at "Kareela" during the war.

George Turner (1916–   ), born Melbourne, worked as a casual waiter during the Great Depression. Joined the AIF immediately after the declaration of war and served in the Middle East and New Guinea. Several novels, including *Young Man of Talent* (1959) and *The Cupboard under the Stairs* (1962). Also a well-known writer, and critic, of science fiction. Autobiography: *In the Heart or in the Head* (1984).

Nancy Wake (1912–   ), born Wellington (NZ), settled in Sydney at the age of two. Enrolled at a London college in 1932, specialising in journalism. Freelance journalist in Paris, visiting Vienna and Berlin where she witnessed Nazi persecution of Jews. In 1939 married French businessman Henri Fiocca of Marseilles who was killed during the war. After the fall of France undertook courier journeys for the French Resistance. Escaped the Gestapo by crossing the Pyrenees into Spain and thence to London, where she trained to become an agent in SOE (Special Operations Executive). Parachuted into France to work with a Maquis organisation, handling finance and air drops from England. After the war worked for various British government departments, with a three-year visit to Australia during 1948–51, during which she unsuccessfully stood for Federal parliament. Received several awards for work with the Resistance Movement. Autobiography: *The White Mouse* (1985).

Other UQP PAPERBACKS

Vietnam: A Reporter's War

Hugh Lunn

Assigned by Reuters to cover the Vietnam War, twenty-five year old Hugh Lunn left London with just ten pounds for expenses and a one-way ticket to Saigon. Arriving at the height of the war in 1967, the young Australian correspondent witnessed some of the most bloody and dramatic events, culminating in the 1968 Tet offensive, when the Viet Cong invaded Saigon.

Bombed, shot at, and lied to by the military, Hugh Lunn discovered that there was a war of words — and images — as well as bullets. This gripping memoir of his year in action won the *Age* Nonfiction Award in 1985.

The Soldiers' Story
The Battle at Xa Long Tan
Vietnam, 18 August 1966

Terry Burstall

D Company Six Battalion were honoured for their courage during the controversial Battle at Long Tan. Now the story of that battle is told from the viewpoint of the soldiers — a viewpoint at times in conflict with the official army version of events.

This detailed account of Australia's major Vietnam battle has been written by one of the participants, and his story reconstructs the action using secret documents as well as the recollections of many of the diggers.

The Battle at Long Tan was a critical episode in Australia's Vietnam involvement. As this account reveals, it was also a textbook nightmare in the history of jungle warfare.

The Barbarians
A Soldier's New Guinea Diary

Peter Pinney

Johnno's illicit diary was kept as a gesture of defiance towards the detested Lieutenant Zubric. In no sense a unit record, this very personal account of one man's clashes with enemies on both sides gives a dramatically different view of the Wau-Salamaua campaign and is destined to become a classic.